CRITICAL ACCLAIM FOR P

THE SEA AND THE SILENCE

'A book which will shorten any journey'
Éilís Ní Dhuibhne, *The Irish Times*

'*The Sea and the Silence* cannot come more highly recommended.
Once started, it must be finished, and once read, it must be re-read'
Susan E. Connolly, *Sunday Business Post*

'…Delightful and cleverly wrought. …as moving as it is skilfully
told'
Irish Daily Mail

'a terrific novel … moving and hugely entertaining'
Roddy Doyle, Booker Prize winner

'Peter Cunningham is a writer of great gifts'
Barry Unsworth, Booker Prize winner

TAPES OF THE RIVER DELTA

'Peter Cunningham writes beautifully; each character is expertly
defined'
Caroline Clark, *Literary Review*

'[Cunningham] has remarkable powers of description, and his
landscapes are breathtakingly visual, but he can also turn his hand
to smaller, domestic detail, and there is a wonderful twitch of dry
humour in his prose'
Stephanie Merritt, *Observer*

'It is a long time since I have been so delighted and entranced by a book
… for those who care about fiction, here is an unforgettable voice'
Madeleine Keane, *Sunday Independent*

'Clever … brilliantly conceived … Cunningham's descriptive writing is as superb as his characterisation'
Sue Leonard, *Irish Examiner*

CONSEQUENCES OF THE HEART

'Cunningham, a magician with words, has penned a vast panorama of a novel. His set-pieces trail a magnificence of grandeur, yet his prose can also glide effortlessly into the quivering recesses of the human heart'
Vincent Banville, *Melbourne Age*

'Simply breathtakingly brilliant'
Kevin Myers

'The intense passion of this book, like the nature of love it attempts to portray, is seductive, courageous and spellbinding'
Jim Clarke, *Sunday Independent,*

'A joy to read'
Arminta Wallace, *The Irish Times*

'Sparkling prose … great inventiveness … powerful images that reveal a rare talent for descriptive writing'
Mike Milotte, *Tribune*

THE TAOISEACH

'Nobody should call a book a work of genius on a first reading, but at its best this one approaches genius'
James Downey, *Irish Independent*

'A powerful narrative'
Daire Dolan, *Irish Post*

CAPITAL SINS

WAT... ...UNTY WITHDRAWN LIBRARIES

CAPITAL SINS

WATERFORD CITY AND COUNTY LIBRARIES WITHDRAWN

A novel

PETER CUNNINGHAM

WATERFORD
No. 418 52 53
CITY LIBRARY

NEW
ISLAND

CAPITAL SINS
First published 2010
by New Island
2 Brookside
Dundrum Road
Dublin 14

www.newisland.ie

Copyright © Peter Cunningham, 2010

The author has asserted his moral rights.

ISBN 978-1-84840-071-9

All rights reserved. The material in this publication is protected by copyright
law. Except as may be permitted by law, no part of the material may be
reproduced (including by storage in a retrieval system) or transmitted in any
form or by any means; adapted; rented or lent without the written
permission of the copyright owner.

British Library Cataloguing Data. A CIP catalogue record for this book is
available from the British Library.

Printed in the UK by CPI Mackays, Chatham ME5 8TD

New Island received financial assistance from
The Arts Council (An Comhairle Ealaíon), Dublin, Ireland

10 9 8 7 6 5 4 3 2 1

For dearest Carol, with love.

PART ONE

DUBLIN — Early Summer 2006

ONE

Sometimes on those Saturday mornings Albert wondered if he was ever going to be free. To soar beyond his worries and be truly happy, to wake up one Saturday morning and not have to think about the net-net, the bottom line. To be out; to finally escape. In the den, a recessed nook with leather couches and a wall-mounted 40-inch television set, above which hung an embroidered sampler which said 'The Den', he turned on Bloomberg. Everything was up, the natural direction. Wall Street had broken new ground the night before; all the major European indices were soaring; the Irish stock market was on a winning streak that looked as if it could never end. In every little Irish town four millionaires had come into being, one for each of the four fields at the crossroads on which rows of houses and shopping malls had been built. Money making money, debt and property, property and debt; a magic formula; cash spouting like oil geysers.

He attended breakfast briefings in the Four Seasons with men like himself: broad-chested former block layers and plumbers, chippies and plasterers who had made fortunes as if out of thin air; men who could scarcely believe their luck as they chewed black pudding and listened to analysts from London – cocky youngsters with actuarial degrees, but smart – tell them where the best returns lay. Private equity funds, hedge funds, contracts for difference. Twenty-six per cent per annum internal rate of return. So easy. They were a breed apart from ordinary people, from the PAYE workers they employed; they were the kings of the earth they spent so much time moving. *So easy*. The first generation of Irishmen to make money at home, to realise their true potential.

He stood at =89 on Ireland's Rich List. He hated the = part of the =89. What did they know, these people? The other half of the

1

=89 was only there because he owned land banks in remote parts of Ireland that had been grossly overvalued to arrive at his net worth. Cutaway bogs, reed ponds, marshlands and swamps masquerading as real estate on a par with Mayfair or Manhattan. Albert, on the other hand, by his own calculation, should have been 48 minimum, maybe even 46. Gobshites.

Possessions on one side of his balance sheet, worries on the other. Tens of sites, from single plots to prairies beside motorways yet to be built and half-completed housing projects spread across eleven counties. Apartments that he'd trousered away in numerous schemes, units in shopping centres, bits of pubs and hotels, houses he'd have had to look up the file to remember exactly where they were, a slice of a cinema, a sliver of a ballroom, ten per cent of a bowling alley. He owned one-third of a deep-sea trawler, a box in Old Trafford, a share in a private jet. Five Jack B. Yeatses, six Sean Scullys, a bronze sculpture by someone in Italy whose name he could never remember, just the price he'd paid for it. Locked in the vault of a bank with the paintings. Four serious cars; wines of sublime vintage. Blocks of season tickets for every kind of sport – he always gave them away to suppliers. A dozen racehorses in training.

And yet – and yet he wasn't free, because of the financial commitments with which all these *things* had been acquired. The tentacles of half a dozen banks reached deeply into the recesses of his wealth, their rubbery suckers clinging to the very trusses of his brain. Couldn't have done it without them, of course, the banks. He was their investment, their payoff boy; his true wealth existed only in the ever-expanding surplus of his underlying assets, the froth that this crazy new millennium was blowing into common bricks and mortar, transforming them into something beyond the fabulous, into magic baubles whose price could only rise.

* * *

He took out a home-kit blood-pressure device, wrapped the cuff around his arm, switched it on and felt his arm tighten. Every night he swallowed one tablet for his elevated cholesterol and another to let his pee out over his benignly enlarged prostate. That one was a real bitch. I'm here dying for a piss, Albert told his doctor in the Blackrock Clinic, but I can only dribble. He went straight to the chemist with the prescription and within twenty-four hours he was like Shergar, the proud sire of a joyful steaming yellow flood. But that night when he had sex, he came backwards. Frigging weird sensation.

At least he had not yet started medicating for blood pressure, unlike some. Not yet. Kept the results from these Saturday morning tests in a little book, a tidy column of numbers. His worst ever result was 200 over 150, but that was after a feed of brandy the night he thought he was going to lose the Mullingar contract. To Kevin, his father-in-law, pills were like coins to a slot machine. A big, cadaverous former garda sergeant, a natural political animal, now in the cabinet. How did he operate? Kept saying he was grand, grand, thanks. Albert's doctor had whispered from the side of his mouth that if the Minister for Infrastructure Development didn't die of a stroke before he was sixty, then modern medicine knew fuck all.

The machine let out its air noisily, like a punctured tyre, and Albert watched the numbers cascade. The diastolic was the one you had to watch out for, his doctor had told him, although what the diastolic was, or why it was important, Albert had long forgotten. The machine beeped and the numbers came up: 125 over 78. Mystified but relieved, he recorded the numbers and went to the kitchen.

Except for the chorus of birds that had been on the go for three hours, an easeful, well-heeled calm prevailed in that part of Foxrock, County Dublin. A house up the road from this one without a garden half as nice had made four-and-a-half million at auction. The neighbours – people who had lived in this part of County Dublin all their lives, and in some cases, judging by appearances, beyond – had in twelve years yet to invite the Barrs in, and had in turn ignored 'Medb-Marie Barr – At Home' invitations, and had complained through their solicitors about the behaviour of Albert and Medb-Marie's guests at barbecues. Envy was part of life in modern Ireland and every bush hid a bastard with a grievance. Albert put the kettle on the Aga and ambled across the hall to his office.

One hundred and twenty-five over seventy-eight wasn't bad at a time when he was being described in the tabloids as THE SH*T KING!, the man who had left six thousand people in Dublin's Goose Point during the May bank holiday weekend with sewage coming up through their floor tiles. His blood pressure showed he could hack it, despite everything. Time was, and not so long ago either, when he could bring up the ankle of his right foot and put it behind his neck – behind his frigging neck! Used to do it to impress the birds he'd chatted up in Searsons and brought back to his one-bed on Waterloo Road, made them think of all the possibilities that lay in the night ahead. Would you like to see the moon upside-down? The good old days. Now look at the state of him: greasy skin, inkwells beneath his eyes, and middle-aged – incontestably, irretrievably middle-aged.

Sitting behind his reproduction antique desk, he took a key from behind the picture of his two six-year-old girls – AMETHYST AND AMBER; THE TERRIBLE TWINS! – and unlocked the middle drawer. The small room, more token office than everyday working space, was festooned with photographs of perfectly good countryside at the moment of its being gouged open by earth-moving machines. Above the desk, next to a picture capturing the moment the first sod was turned on a ring-road someplace in the midlands, a large framed print showed Albert beside Medb-Marie as she led their horse into the winner's enclosure at Leopardstown the previous Christmas. Medb-Marie, in a mink whose hem fell to her ankles, with her rich burgundy hair, looked like a film star, whereas Albert, on the other side of the horse, looked like a tinker on his way to a wedding.

As the desk drawer slid out to him, Albert removed the package wrapped in tissues, placed it on the unstained blotter and exposed the four-pack of Viagra. Every time he did this he thought of the

Burj-Al-Arab in Dubai. Albert had woken up and taken a Viagra, having forgotten that Medb-Marie had arranged a dawn expedition in a jeep with balloon wheels. Enraged by his own stupidity, engorged with chemically induced lust, he had pleaded illness and stayed behind. Thirty minutes later a chocolate-skinned girl had appeared to tidy up the suite. Crisp white and green uniform against her long, bare legs. Lovely little backside. The testosterone had made Albert desperate as he followed her into the bathroom.

— Is there anything I can do for you, sir?

Desert people, canny traders, they lived by their wits. God alone knew what went on in those tents. He gave her three two-hundred-euro notes and she gave him a hand-job in the shower.

Albert popped a Viagra out onto the blotter and then applied himself to the tricky task of cutting the dome-shaped sky-blue pill in half with a paperknife. Bringing down the point of the knife on the centre of the capsule, Albert pressed. The Viagra burst into a mound of broken shell and powder.

— Fuck!

Dividing the heap in two with the knife and pushing one mound away to the side of the blotter, Albert leant in and sucked, snorted and licked up the remaining shell dust and powder. From a decanter on the desk he took a swig of water. Mouth clear, he dusted what was left of the drug into the wastepaper basket.

Before ever he became the SH*T KING! of the tabloids, he had been identified as one of a small group of self-made Irishmen christened 'Los Desperados' by a Sunday red-top. It had been at the start of the boom and half a dozen of them had gone to Stuttgart to watch Man U playing in the Champions League – except that they had travelled on three private jets. Nothing would ever have come of the trip if they hadn't broken a few tables in a restaurant in Stuttgart's red-light district and been arrested. LOS DESPERADOS! the paper screamed the following Sunday over a shadowy picture of the three emerging on ten-grand bail each the next morning. All for a few poxy tables! Several women were interviewed who claimed they'd been *under* the tables at the time, working professionally. Then the shot of the lads boarding their jets... LOS DESPERADOS! Medb-Marie hadn't spoken to him for a month.

Spouts of hissing water were leaping as Albert got back to the kitchen. At times like these he yearned for the old days, the simplicity of owning nothing. He was two when his mother died and had grown up an only child with his father, in a house whose back upstairs window overlooked the cemetery in Tramore. Albert now wondered what it would be like to be a child again, helping Daddy as he fitted new grips on clubs behind the pro shop in the golf course, getting his hands cut as he helped the old man search for a golf ball that some fool of a bank manager had shanked into gorse bushes. Hanging out down on the prom and wondering what a ride was like. Trying to get into the Saturday-night dance without paying, and aching to find out what it was that some fellows had that he lacked. He could hear the ocean if he cupped his hands to his ears; could feel, if he tried hard enough, the cleansing sea spray that would make him innocent again.

* * *

Irish bank shares, along with all the other companies listed on the Irish stock exchange, had broken new ground the day before. It was phenomenal. A tiny island economy streaking heavenwards like a rocket. The price action was enough to put aside Albert's problems for the morning, to tip the balance sheet in his favour for a day or so, a profit of half a million, cash, if he took the profit.

He clicked open the inbox on his laptop and half a dozen brokers' recommendations popped into view.

> *While we always seek to keep an open mind, yesterday's vigorous upside action in the S&P 500 has given us another strong buy signal with the daily momentum-based indicator crossing over its signal line.*

We believe that this bull market has entered a powerful new phase where rich rewards await those prepared to 'ride out' the inevitable corrections and hang in for the long haul.

Albert's purchase for €350 million of the old Goose Point Brewery with 99 per cent financing, cross-collateralised on all his other assets, plus his personal guarantee, was just one of many similar transactions arranged by Irish banks that year alone. Goose Point would be a big project when it was finally realised: two thousand apartments, three hotels, a retail village, four office blocks, a miniature golf course, a micro-brewery and a zoo, all seven minutes from central Dublin. It would be extraordinary; it would be Albert's masterpiece.

Albert switched off the television and poured tea. His architects, at the time a preliminary survey of the old brewery site had been completed, had come back and observed that the original brewery – not the one that Albert was buying and would pummel to dust, but the one before that – had itself probably been constructed on top of much older foundations, about whose age the architects would not speculate.

— We could be talking Methuselah here, one partner in the architectural firm, a faggot, had said. — There could be heritage issues.

Albert, who had once drunk a Methuselah at his stag party in Munich, had reluctantly commissioned a heritage expert to sniff around to see if there might be any issues in Goose Point that he needed to smother. She was a tiresome woman with a doctorate and a West Brit accent, who rode a bicycle. A cliché incarnate. She scraped and toothbrushed, X-rayed and researched for nearly six months, despite Albert's increasing impatience, and went home after every meeting and regaled her family over bottles of Tunisian wine about the ghastly little man who had employed her. Finally, when Albert threatened to withhold her fee, she concluded in writing, albeit grudgingly, that whereas there could be significant evidence of Ireland's deep heritage beneath the brewery, there also might not be. This was changed, on Albert's insistence, to a statement saying that no such evidence could be proven to exist.

The banks had backed Albert. Twelve months later and the gigantic excavations which were needed to put five levels of parking beneath the retail complex had led to ancient underground tidal buttresses being removed, and this in turn had caused the Irish Sea to leak into the site. The Goose Point Residents' Association had turned out, a thousand strong, to object to further work with, at their fore, no less a person than the bitch – the filthy treacherous bitch! – who had prepared Albert's archaeological report for a fee of twenty grand, and who now claimed that her original fears had been realised. She accused Albert of bullying and coercion. GOOSE POINT SAYS STOP! had grown into a political movement. Albert had flown in sea-wall engineers from Holland and they had advised that nothing less than a series of massive interlocking concrete piles was necessary to save the project. Another €50 million, and Albert needed to reapply for planning permission in order to sink the piles. There had been over four hundred objections, but with Kevin's help the new permission had come through. Now, just when all looked well, interest rates were going up.

Albert sighed. That's why he lived in a five-million-plus house, had a dozen racehorses in training, owned a share in a private jet. All he wanted, in the end, was the best of everything for the twins. He wanted them eventually to go to school in England, but fucking Kevin made it known through Medb-Marie that if it got out it might affect his re-election chances.

* * *

Outside the two-storey picture window behind the stairs, doves tumbled in sunlight through the insect-laden air. Albert climbed slowly, the folds of his kimono sliding off his thick, hairy thighs. Medb-Marie: first seen, never to be forgotten. He and his then building partner were completing their first big project, three houses in a Dublin suburb, and she drove in one Saturday morning with her father to look it over. Tyre kickers, just out for the day; Dublin was full of them on weekends, Albert thought. She opened the door of the car. Tight, ribbed jeans and a white shirt.

— Jesus Christ, will you look at that arse, whispered Albert's partner as Medb-Marie emerged into view.

She never bought the house, of course, but Albert called her up the following week and within a month they were engaged. Never refused her anything in a dozen years, which he justified on the basis that she had a lot to put up with – his drinking, his gambling, the unexplainable nights in Munich and London with the lads. He was building an empire, for the love of God! But she liked the lifestyle all right – the horses, the jet, the Burj-Al-Arab, her 200-grand credit card that meant she could go into Tiffany's on Fifth Avenue and walk out with a gold necklace that cost more than ten years' wages for a builder's labourer. Albert adored her style, the way people feared her, her temper that made him tiptoe around her much of the time. She excited him! What could be better? She'd taught him the meaning of outrage! He loved the way an entire restaurant became silent when she walked in, imperious, the men drooling, the women cutting her to death with their envious little eyes. Jesus, she was gorgeous; every man's dream. Albert loved Medb-Marie dearly.

* * *

Until his rectal polyp.

The doctor would say that a rectal polyp was often as much the result of stress as of an over-rich lifestyle. Albert, on the bowl that Tuesday morning, having just mown through what they used to joke was 'the full Polish' – a full-on Irish fry cooked by Christiana, the Polish au pair; Albert, athwart the porcelain, was suddenly aware of something awry down there, out of sight, behind. A brief exploratory expedition with his fingers. Oh Jesus! Oh, Christ! Puddles of sticky blood! And the sudden excruciating pain! A nightmare from childhood in which a sailor shitting in a can is eaten by a giant crab he forgot he trapped down there flashed through Albert's mind. So much blood, although the doctor assured him later that no more than a teacup had been lost; yet in the bowl, on the bowl, it looked like he was haemorrhaging to death.

Medb-Marie was driving the children to school, so there and then, barely pausing to clean himself, still in his pyjamas and dressing-gown, Albert jumped into his speed-yellow Porsche 911 convertible, tore down the road towards Dublin and into the Blackrock Clinic. He drove right to the steps of the hospital – if he could have driven in, he would have. What was the point of ten-grand-a-year health cover unless you could be seen immediately as you bled to death?

First, the enforced sedation – the loss of control! – as they rummaged in his colon. Then the waiting for the result of the biopsy, one whole week, the thought of his probably cancerous tissue being tweezered and peered at by some lazy, indifferent technician in a lab someplace in Dublin, as if he or she – most likely a she, with a moustache and glasses; the type was well known – as if this bespectacled dyke, as she played with herself over the weekend, could give a damn whether or not Albert Barr was crawling with secondaries.

In the middle of this terrible week – no will, no specific provisions made; what exactly would the tax angle be? – Medb-Marie told him that she and the girls would probably move south. She meant, when he was dead. She meant, to the house in Inchigeela that Albert had built for her in place of the cabin in which her father had grown up. That's where she was headed.

He was astonished. She already had a strategy in place. Although Albert, like most men, had fantasised from time to time about playing the field with his old lady out of the way, he kept quiet about it; yet as he waited for his results, here she was actually informing him of her contingency plan.

A week already heavy with budding tragedy went off the deep end of grief. Albert withdrew into a cocoon of self-pity in which all

Medb-Marie's moves of more than a decade before could be seen in a new light. He'd never imagined that she had caught him out by becoming pregnant, but now he saw it differently. Her father, a widower, owned nothing apart from the Dublin semi-d he lived in and a government pension. Medb-Marie had worked as a relief-teacher of elocution in Dublin schools and all she had brought to their marriage was a twenty-horsepower Fiat. Albert had been blind to all that, he now realised. The rate at which she spent his money suddenly acquired new meaning. *His* money. The clever accumulation of years of hard work, rolled ever upwards, like the stock market, the hundred different tricks that cash-cash could do, the unnerving business of two separate settlements with the Revenue Commissioners, neither of them entirely truthful, the strain – the fucking awful nail-biting worry – of wondering where the next interest payment was going to come from, and all for what? To lie upstairs on his deathbed as downstairs his wife ate Pringles, watched *Eastenders* and planned her exit strategy?

He had moved into the guest bedroom and sent word through his secretary that he wanted a priest. Would this request appear hypocritical, since Albert had not been to Mass since the day he was married, he wondered? To hell with that; being a Catholic gave him entitlements, like building up bar credits in the golf club, and there came a time to cash them in. As he awaited the priest Albert began to pray, a recitation of simple prayers that soon led him to relive the up-to-then discarded days of his youth with feverish intensity. By recreating the streets and hinterland of Tramore and the thousands of hours he had spent on them, he felt that he could somehow be transported back to those happy days.

Unlike a boy who might have been raised amid the ameliorating influence of his mother's or sister's underwear drying at the stove, or the unseen but omniscient reality of menstrual blood that percolates a house of women, or the unavoidable, fleeting glimpses of breasts or pussy harvested by young lads with sisters, Albert had come into his adolescence with an almost complete ignorance of the female body or the facts of life.

Then, at fourteen, the year his father died, up in the back of the
pro shop under a stack of boxes where Billy, the pro, kept found
balls for cleaning and resale, young Albert one day found Billy's
copy of *Playboy*. The effect was immediate, dramatic and
unrelenting. Albert began a two-year cycle of masturbation that
contained within it simultaneously the delight of orgasm and the
agony of wanting almost immediately to come again. Those
tawny-haired, shining-breasted American girls who pouted every
month at Albert, who begged him to ride them, or failing that to
decant his sperm over their photographs, were as real to the
possibly dying Albert as they had been to Albert the teenager in
Tramore. It had taken two years to grasp that the kit sported by the
Playboy girls was walking up and down the prom in Tramore a
thousand times a day. Every day. Amazing, just tiny fractions of
millimetres of fabric separating Albert from heaven.

The pursuit of the real thing consumed him. Fending for
himself and beyond the control or censure of aunts or uncles, who
didn't care anyway about their horny orphaned nephew, his first
experience of the real thing had been with Agnes, his first cousin,
in the field behind Freddie Piper's Amusements. Thirty years later
as he lay dying and ignored by a coldly scheming wife, Albert was
racked by loneliness for the soft, loving, uncomplicated affection
of Agnes, a year older than him and no virgin, who for all that
summer had guided him into the secret niches of pleasure that a
woman keeps dear and who had told him that he would go far in
the world, but probably without her. He had wanted to marry
Agnes, but she had been removed by her parents to a convent in
Kilkenny at the end of a week of rampant hysteria. Albert had been
denounced as evil and the spectre of unnatural acts and
consanguinity had been thrown at him by Agnes's father, a
snivelling little greyhound walker, and by the moon-faced parish
priest, and by the garda sergeant, a big stupid bastard, who had
personally put Albert on the boat train and told him that if he ever
laid eyes on him again he'd break his neck.

In the long week of waiting for his biopsy result, Albert yearned for Agnes. In the lonely reaches of the night, he dwelled obsessively on an image of them together in a bed with white silk sheets, although the nearest they'd ever been to a bed together was the sofa in a disused caravan behind the Hydro. Agnes was still the sweet-smelling, bracken-haired girl with small firm breasts who held poor dying Albert to her warm little body and soothed his fears. Ah, Jesus, how proud she would have been of his achievements; how the greatest thrill in his life would have been to watch her walk up the fold-down steps into the jet.

He'd once bumped into a cousin at Croke Park during one of Waterford's doomed attempts at All Ireland glory, and this gormless countryman, whose tongue had been loosened by three hours of large bottles on the train up to Dublin, told Albert that Agnes had gone to Liverpool years before, and as far as he knew she had married a steeplejack. But how was she, Albert wanted to know? Was Agnes happy? His cousin made a lewd remark, the gist of which was that only one thing ever made Agnes happy and that Albert should know what it was. Albert felt like smacking this yokel one on the chin, right there, except Waterford at that moment let in their fifth goal and his attention was diverted.

Close on a dozen years of serial sex in London: sex, drinking and hard, hard work on the building sites. A number of those English women still made Albert yearn fondly for their presence beside him during that grim week, in a post-ride, non-sexual way; and that, Albert assumed, was love. As he waited and waited to hear if he was going to die, and if so, how soon – if he'd been a horse, he was told, the biopsy result would have taken 24 hours – Albert sought from the recesses of his memory the loving post-coital embraces of the women he now wished he had kept in touch with, some of them pretty, some plain, several married, a few old enough to be his mother. Balham and Fulham, Hampstead and Holborn, names that now made him twitch with old fondness. Home on the tube to Elephant & Castle, Highbury and Islington.

Landladies and their daughters and fellow lodgers, prim women who worked in local council offices as ledger clerks, who erupted into feral sex-crazed madwomen given half a chance. Time and again as he lay waiting, Albert had returned to the bedrock question that he admitted he had been avoiding for years: did he really love Medb-Marie?

* * *

The smells of night sheets and crumpled pillows, and of human flesh at its most inviting, beckoned him to the bedroom. Medb-Marie was lying turned away, the summer duvet fallen to reveal the bared small of her back. A shaft of sunlight through the crack of the open door picked out this pool of flesh and its golden, tactile hairs, like a spotlight picks out a rabbit. As Albert passed the cheval mirror he saw his own reflection and wondered why he had bothered with the Viagra in the first place.

He'd got the all-clear on the polyp, and they'd gone to Barcelona for a long weekend of celebration, leaving the kids with Christiana. Albert, still swooning with gratitude to a God he had briefly re-encountered; Medb-Marie, dazzlingly healthy and obviously rich; one night at dinner he gently confronted her. It was as much to sweep away his lingering reservations, for he nurtured a hope that she was so much in love with him that his illness had traumatised her. The things that get into the head of a dying man. Albert said, — I'm sorry I put you through these last couple of weeks.

He felt that contrition, even for his own impending death, was an unanswerable opening ploy.

— I don't really want to talk about it, Albert, she said with sudden stiffness, in the voice that had once been familiar to the elocution classes in Mount Anville. — Let's leave it, shall we?

You'd think she'd caught him playing with himself. He said, battling on, — I'm just sorry that you got such a shock, that's all, love. It must have been awful. For you.

When Medb-Marie closed her eyes, as she then did, briefly, her long natural-titian eyelashes splayed out like gilding. She said, — You can say that again.

— It made me think, Albert said.

— Me too.

A bolt went through Albert. As he had lain for a week in the arms of Agnes, of Doris, Dorcas, Fanny from Fulham, Mrs Thurmington from Elephant & Castle, with whom had Medb-Marie been internally consorting? A mutual recitation of past lovers had not been a feature of their marriage, but for sure there had been others before him; it would have been scary if a girl that good-looking had come to him intact.

— What did you think about? he asked warily.

Medb-Marie drew in nostril breath.

— I thought about how you had ignored your responsibilities to me and the children, she said. — God, you haven't even made a will!

— I hadn't planned on dying so soon, Albert retorted.

— Nobody plans on dying, Albert, she said tightly. — You think of no one but yourself.

Albert drank Rioja Gran Reserva deeply. Maybe he was living in a different universe, where the expected reaction of a wife to the looming death of her husband was concern and grief, and then the financial problems of succession, but in that order.

— You would have been taken care of, Medb-Marie, he said. — You're my wife.

— Oi know wha' Oi am, ducky, she said, switching to the cockney accent she used in arguments, when she was annoyed, a bad sign; something he assumed she'd picked up from *EastEnders*. — Listen, Albert, I nearly died of fright. I never felt more afraid. Do you think that's reasonable?

— I had a rectal polyp, Albert gasped. — How do you think I felt?

— What do I know about your business? Medb-Marie asked in a raised voice. — Sometimes when you're drunk, you tell me that if the tide turns we could be out on the street, that if interest rates keep going up we'll be fucked, to use your charming words. What do I know about your sordid deals, your…?

— Hold on! Hold it right there, Albert said. — You spend my money like it's your career, and you talk about *my* sordid deals?

— It's *our* money, Albert! she cried. — Or I thought it was!

— Medb-Marie, he said and leaned over to place his hand on her wrist, adorned with a silver and malachite bracelet that he had picked up that afternoon on the Ramblas for a grand. — I…

— Take your paws off me! she shouted.

The head waiter in the dining room of the Hotel Arts asked them to please keep their voices down.

— Get lost! Medb-Marie hollered at the man.

Outside, near the pool, when they had been asked to leave, over a couple of epic hours Medb-Marie secured herself an independent income. Albert was in awe of the steel in the mother of his children, wondering even as she laid out her stall – non-negotiable, luv, get my drift? – if he might not send her in to bat with the banks on his behalf next time round. But the instant Albert conceded all she sought, she fell sobbing into his arms and asked him to forgive her. Her scent, her skin, the accommodating shape of her warm body through her gold lamé dress. Albert experienced the exquisite sensation of his remorseful wife's tears on his throat – he was wearing an open-necked shirt – and although simultaneously recognising the disastrous effects of testosterone on his reasoning process, concluded that everything to which he had consented had been worth it. Medb-Marie told him, her soft lips to his ear, that she didn't deserve him, that his generosity was something she would never forget and that, as far as she was concerned, anything at all he wanted from her, all he had to do was ask. Albert phoned upstairs for a romantic bath to be prepared and they spent the next part of the night in candlelight, roses floating at their chins next to plastic glasses of champagne, legs wrapped around each other's waists.

It was, ironically, Kevin Steadman, then a junior minister in a key government department, who came up with the solution.

Wheedling, ever-dealing, conniving Kevin. I'm grand, grand, thanks, how are you? Good, good. Of course I can, to be sure I can. Grand. He had seized a 200-flat public housing complex in central Dublin and rammed it into private ownership. In a textbook piece of political corruption, a company owned by Medb-Marie was allocated 56 flats, paid for by Albert. Now Medb-Marie spoke of rent voids in the same way as leprosy, deplored immigrants from the Third World with their filthy cooking habits, and students who tore the plumbing out when they were drunk, and couples with small children who destroyed her walls up to a height of 24 inches. Her ideal tenants were childless professionals from England, or monogamous Irish gays. Both groups paid by standing order and when they vacated, the properties were always left gleaming.

* * *

Albert twitched back the duvet and slid in behind her. Medb-Marie's first reaction was to resent the intrusion and she turned further away from him, hunched her shoulders and let out an angry grunt; but Albert knew the routine and parted the strands of her shining russet hair with his nose to kiss the nape of her neck gently. He loved his power at this moment, his irresistible force. She groped back for him, like someone searching in the dark for the handle of a door. Albert licked Medb-Marie's ear. She began to turn towards him. Over the next ten to fifteen minutes, Albert's thoughts backed and veered around a number of subjects. As the sheets were kicked down and his wife's body came magnificently alive, Albert contemplated Medb-Marie's breasts; the hills of suspected archaeological significance on the new road to Gort that he had bulldozed at the dead of night before anyone copped on what was happening; the arse on the maid in Dubai; a pint of stout he drank the day before in a new hotel in Dublin in which he owned a 1.25 per cent shareholding; Agnes; Goose Point; the tall young Arab driver of the jeep in Dubai who Medb-Marie had

jokingly said she kind-of fancied; Medb-Marie's arse; the maid in
Dubai; the driver; his plan to bring the Porsche to the car wash in
Dalkey before half-nine if he wasn't going to have to queue; rising
interest rates; grilled back rashers.

Later, damp and happy, they lay side by side, Medb-Marie's
hands joined behind her head, a configuration that showed off her
breasts wonderfully and exposed the stippling of shaved hair
beneath her armpits.

— Albert?

— Hmm?

— Do you love me?

The texture of her skin alone sometimes made Albert delirious.

— Do you need to ask?

— Say, I love you.

— Does the silly little girl want her botty smacked?

— Please, Albert! I need to hear it from you!

— I. Love. You.

Out on the landing could be heard the hushed procedures
observed on Saturday mornings when Christiana got the twins up
and dressed and brought them downstairs for breakfast.
Medb-Marie propped herself up on one elbow.

— Nobody will ever take all this from us, will they? she asked.

— Nobody.

— Promise me, Albert.

— I told you, over my dead body, Albert said.

TWO

D read brought Lee out in a chill, wet slick. Couldn't keep doing this. His tongue was swollen, parched. His dead limbs. In the office they popped Solpadeine all day long, struggling over the line to file copy at half-past six or seven, then fled to the wine bar down the street where they started all over again. His headache made a mockery of the word, more an avalanche of pain every two seconds. Solpadeine was a joke; he needed a stent. What time was it? Many parts of his brain had died; he could imagine them – using the surviving parts – like dandruff, little white flecks of memory and intelligence, his sense of taste, of reason, the component parts of his ambition, his talent – his life, oh God – his libido, the parts of his brain that controlled his continence, so many intricate functions flaking off in a tank of booze. Murdering the real Lee. Leaving behind this devastated shell. The gawks. The jigs. Pure terror.

Eddie England, in the casino the night before, garrulous to the point of insanity, hour after hour talking about Hemingway, the muscularity of the great man's prose, the Spanish sun at noon, bullfighting, Cava, the smell of death. Eddie was a Chardonnay man. The madness in his eyes of slight talent rebuffed. Latched on to Lee whenever they drank, went on and on about the well-turned phrase, the Florida Keys, whiskey, sea fishing off Cuba, always things that Eddie knew nothing about. Eddie had a wife, unlike Lee. Someone to soothe him on a morning like this: there, I've ironed a nice fresh shirt for you, pet, it's hard for you, I know, only six more years in that dump and you're out. A little warm bunny; Lee had met her at the Christmas party; how in Christ's name she put up with Eddie no one knew.

Beneath: a toilet, shower and galley kitchen crammed into the rear half of the room; up here, a bed on an overhead platform, accessed by ladder. In the amputated space below, the bit with the window, he sat and read or listened to music on earphones (stipulated in his lease) or watched television and drank beer. The rent had just been hiked by ten per cent, but it was hard to find someplace that allowed a dog.

— Good boy, Des.

Born on the day of the JFK assassination, named not after the presidential assassin but after the river in Cork, where Mum had come from. Nonetheless, every time Lee's birthday came round his parents always remembered that day, not for Lee alone but for the events in Dallas, Texas.

— I'll never forget it, Mum said, it was in the late afternoon and I was in Herbert Park with Hilda Jackson, walking, I couldn't walk fast, of course, needless to say…

— You were gone full term, Dad said.

— … I was still as firm as the bonnet of a car, Mum said, full term or not.

A man came up the path towards them. Mum didn't know who he was from Adam, a civil servant, she thought, since he was off work so early, a tall chap with white hair that needed a cut; some people had lost respect entirely for their appearance, all that modern music and what have you. He let out a shout just as Hilda was giving me a recipe, for what, I can never remember now. Oh my God! this fellow roars. Oh, no! And Hilda and I both thought he was having a heart attack, but no, he'd been listening to a transistor radio, some programme, I suppose, and they'd interrupted it with the news from Dallas, and he told us. And there and then my waters went down my legs; your waters, Lee.

— Secret Service Agent Rufus Youngblood scrambled up on to the back of JFK's car, Dad said. — It was a Lincoln Continental.

Hilda sat me down and this man, I mean I'd never laid eyes on him before and never did again, he ran out shouting his head off up the road and got a taxi, bless him. Oh my goodness, I thought, I'm going to have it in the taxi.

— Jackie leaned back and caught Rufus by the hand, Dad told young Lee, and pulled him up.

They could talk of nothing else in the Coombe; all the radios were on, my ears were full of it as they rushed me down to delivery, was he dead, pray for his recovery, the Russians are coming, all the nurses were crying, hands to their faces, the governor of Texas is dead, a doctor said, a state of emergency has been declared, the nation holds its breath, the world.

— Her costume was covered in his blood, Dad said. — Poor thing didn't change until they got back to Washington DC.

Into all these lights, I was blinded, I didn't even have time to – Lee, close your ears – to take my skirt off, it had an elasticated waist, I never saw it again, like the civil servant; I still wonder what they did with it, and all I could do was push; missus, push, they kept telling me, and I was near death myself, I thought, push, girl, and you might have a chance, and I went grrrrrrrrrrrrrrrhhh! one last time, and the radio said he was pronounced dead at 1 p.m. Dallas time, and a young doctor said to me, it's a little boy, ma'am, and I said, his name is Lee.

— That was before they caught your man coming out of the cinema, Dad said. — Before he shot Police Officer J.D. Tippit.

— On the banks of my own lovely Lee, Mum said fondly.

The old happy days of his growing up, his parents' laughter, the smell of the upholstery of the new cars in Dad's showroom in Dublin's north city. What would the old folk think of their little Lee now, God rest them? Drinking cheap South American wine in unregulated casinos, broke, his health suffering – the paper had refused to make him permanent. You need a breakthrough story, Eddie said, something to wipe their eye; I know you can do it; believe me, I know a thing or two about talent, about the well-turned phrase. Have you ever read... ? Always blotted Eddie out at that stage, put him into the airlock and sent him out in a pod from the mother ship. Had never dared to discuss his ideas for a novel with Eddie, or to ask Eddie's advice about where his attempts had fallen down; God had not made enough hours. Lee's characters lived in places like Caracas, Venezuela. He had studied street maps and Google Earth, but somehow when he wrote about a beautiful rich girl who ran off with an apprentice cobbler to live with him in Petare (a slum district in Caracas, Venezuela), and then read what he had written, it came across as if he didn't believe it.

A tiny surviving memory cell flickered with the image of his lunge at the curtains the night before, coffee and sugar granules crunching beneath his bare feet. Downstairs the curtain rail listed like a sinking ship. In the twilight place of personal revulsion, sickness and inability to sleep, it was a comfort to think of women. The young women with the sharp heels and spiky little tits who worked up in marketing and who looked at him but never saw him. Months since he'd had sex with someone else. A sub-editor who had loved to drink, a big cavernous multi-loving woman, she had brought him home a couple of times, but the paper had let her go in the last round of cost-cutting.

When things went wrong after the old pair had died, Lee couldn't wait to get home from the garage to Tallulah. When he had a toothache or when his biggest customer left him or when the bank started returning cheques to his suppliers, he'd come back to the house on the seafront and allow his wife to kiss away his worries. When he met her first and started talking about books and writing, she used to snort with excitement and say she'd never heard books explained that way before. He had been in awe of her butterfly gowns and her eye shadow the colour of anaemic tangerine. Great sex, all day long, oh my big boy is so bold, oh look, oh gosh, you must be blessed with an inexhaustible supply of semen! Tallulah smoked Consulate non-stop in order to keep her weight steady at one hundred and twelve pounds, her body as trim as that of a girl of twelve, illegal but a turn-on, I'm yours, darling, I don't mind, she used to say, the lids of her huge baby eyes closing like jungle flowers.

As the garage started going down she became more distant, was often not at home when Lee got there, and only showed up much later with a vague explanation. On the day the receiver was appointed, the sky was blue as violets. He had expected to find her in the garden, painting her fingernails and drinking a white wine spritzer. But no; she had disappeared for good. Then sucked him dry over four years. At the court hearing, when she at last appeared with the solicitor she was shagging, she didn't even look at Lee.

* * *

At fifteen years of age, during the Easter holidays, working in the windowless stores of Dad's garage, an Austin dealership, keeping track on index cards of car parts handed out to the mechanics: young Lee. Floor-to-ceiling shelves divided into bins, each containing one part for an Austin car. Every so often a mechanic in filthy overalls would appear at the hatch, throw in an order chit and say, — Gissa fuse for a front left-hand fog lamp for an A-60 and be fuckin' quick about it, will ye?

Days were long in the garage stores. Mr Driver, the regular storekeeper, was drying out in St Pat's; he'd gone on the anti-freeze and nearly died. Some lunchtimes Betty from accounts brought back her sandwiches. Small and fat, she wore miniskirts. One lunchtime he realised with a start that she was standing behind him.

— Hey! he shouted in fright.

— What's the matter? Betty asked, and sat down, crossing her legs so that it seemed her torso sprang from a plinth of white flesh. — You afraid a me?

She peeled a banana and began to tease its revealed tip with her mouth. Inexplicably, Betty's short, fat, entwined legs and her lank, greasy, cardboard-coloured hair made Lee's heart glug like a sump valve. She did something funny with her eyes and said, — Did anyone ever tell you that you have a face like an angel?

— No.

— You like me, don't you?

— I don't know.

— I can tell when fellas like me. I can feel it. You like me, don't you?

— Yes.

— Shut the hatch and lock the door, she said with a gurgle in her throat.

When Lee came back she was unscrewing the bulbs from their brackets.

— Betty…

— Shut up.

— I can't see you.

— You don't need to.

Nearly thirty years later he still had no idea how she got her gear off so quickly; then she was at work on his. She whispered, — I bet you're hung like a donkey.

She laughed and had him in her hand. She said, — Jesus Christ, a fuckin' donkey!

— Oh… Betty…

— Hmmmmm, she said from down there.

Lee's legs nearly went from pleasure.

— Hey! Lee!

She was back up, panting.

— You ever done this before?

— No.

— In here, right?

He could feel her steering him. He croaked, — Isn't this the wrong way round?

— Do what your Aunty Betty says, she grunted and he got a mouthful of greasy head hair as she braced herself, one hand each on brake fluid and 5-mm jubilee clips.

— That's it. That's lovely. Oh, Jesus that's lovely. Oh Jesus, oh Jesus, let me die now, Betty moaned.

* * *

Although past noon, the features department of the *Sunday Trumpet* on the sixth floor was almost empty when he reached his cubicle. Blessed fresh air on the way into town, big life-sustaining gulps of it. The last Tuesday of the month was circulation results day. Eddie was always called up to the twelfth floor to see Dick Bell, the group managing editor, on the last Tuesday of the month.

No drink today, a pact. Lost track of how many pills he had swallowed, strained with all his might to think of an idea for a features piece. On his way in he'd seen the yellow-jacketed news vendors lining up to get their daily quota of *The Evening Eclipse*, the Valentine Newspaper group's post-meridian offering. Eddie sometimes drank with one of them, a black man with only one arm. To get the feel of the bush, you know, the colour of his tribe, I'm not talking about their skin, I'm referring to their cooking habits, cultural practices, art, their poetry, how they make love, the way they dress, work it up into a nicely turned piece about human endeavour, with pics, what do you think?

Stories were scarce in high summer. He thumbed through that morning's British tabloids, searching for a speck of worthwhile copy. English papers had a head-start at this time of year; they survived on vicar stories. **VICAR PAID FOR MY BOOB JOB; VICAR FONDLED ME IN TESCO; SODOMISED BY CAR-RALLY VICAR WITH VW GEARSTICK**. His own features on recent Sundays had described the mind of a man in Westmeath who ate pet goldfish; Cissy, the mother of triplets, who tried to sell them on the Internet; the bizarre social habits of Eskimos working on a north County Dublin potato farm. Two weeks before, Eddie, bereft of features, had run Lee's story about a fisherman who had gutted a mackerel and found a miraculous medal inside the fish.

The *Pat Kenny Show* was on somewhere and Lee could hear a discussion on property prices. Everyone on the show agreed that property prices would continue to rise, if not as spectacularly as before, at least modestly; and that if this was wrong, there would be at worst a soft landing. The support for the continuing upward price spiral in property was due to immigrants, Pat himself said. Rather than it being the immigrants who ought to be grateful to the Irish, it was the Irish who ought to be grateful to the immigrants, Pat said.

Eddie suddenly appeared. Shrunken, fifty-eight, caved-in face festooned with tiny scraps of toilet paper, his perambulation that of a man walking away from a motorway pile-up. Lee typed rapidly, random keys, a writer in full flow, uninterruptible. Eddie sat heavily, slumped, chin on his shirt button. Even if the circulation figures had held their own he would now be sitting here with Lee, sharing the latest stay of execution, going on about how when the going gets tough, the tough get going. Handed out free after football matches and big race meetings, the *Trumpet*'s weekly sales had for years been in freefall, yet the paper always put a brave face on the figures, ever seizing on the few nuggets of comfort thrown clear of the wreckage.

Abruptly Eddie wheeled and cast about, a terrified animal in an abattoir. Lee hunched over his keyboard; Eddie marched across the floor; Lee made as if finishing a sentence with a flourish.

— A minute of your valuable time, if you would.

The sharp fumes of twelve-hour-old alcohol, percolated through a defeated liver. Lee at least remembered Hemingway from the night before, but Eddie would not even know they had been drinking together.

— They can't monkey around with the numbers any more, not since those circulation watchdog bastards found 5,000 copies washed up beside the Pigeon House. Advertisers are vultures; they've already asked for a meeting to discuss rates.

Eddie was staring into space as he spoke, a man on his way to the chair.

— We take copy from a poor fool out covering the conflicts in Africa and the Middle East. He has survived carpet-bombing, kidnapping, roadside grenades and a plane that went down like a fireball in the desert.

Eddie flung his hands in the air in case Lee hadn't got 'fireball'.

— His copy comes in here and goes into the hands of hungover sub-editors who truncate and mutilate it, then it's passed up the

nt executives. Last week
sands of men, women
blical significance – was

epileptic.
relationships, fetishes,
: don't have readers any
are interested in brunch
n! Jewellery! What kind
he's composing music!
t fucking news! We need

a seal, carpet-bombed his
magination. Slowly Eddie
e world. Pat Kenny said,

heard a shot.
itar, Lee said.
forward and hissed,
. We're talking death row

his teeth, Lee said.
is hard drive had crashed.
ed one out and said in a
trembling

— I've just come from a meeting where this – this! – was given
as the example of why we've become the laughing stock of Ireland's
print media.

Tore open the paper and slammed it across the desk. Lee's
mackerel story.

— On the same day that we ran this… this ordure, the *Sunday
Times* went with a lesbian sex ring operating inside Leinster House,
the *Tribune* reproduced the credit-card details of a cabinet minister
dealing in underage porn, and the *Indo* had pictures of the

lunchtime bonking club used by traffic wardens. And what do we come up with? A dead fish!

— It wasn't just a dead fish, Eddie…

— It was a dead fish! Eddie yelled. — Is it any wonder the readers are turning away from us in fucking droves? They want tits, they want pussy and salacious gossip, not a close-up of a dead fish with the Infant of Prague stuck up its arse!

— It was a medal of Our Lady of Guatemala. And it was behind the fish's heart.

Eddie butted his head into the space between them, re-fouling the air, and snarled, — I've just come down from a meeting with Dick Bell where I was humiliated. You understand what I'm telling you? Humiliated. This paper is going down like 9/11, am I making sense? Vroooom – splat! No survivors – is the message getting through?

They both sat, Eddie's uneasy simile floating like asbestos dust. Eddie rubbed his face violently with one hand.

— The Chief himself has been on to Dick Bell and made the position very clear – we dip again in the next audit and two-thirds of the staff here are gone. Just like that, no further questions, end of story.

Eddie's eyes were dragged to the windows, to the warm open spaces of freedom, retirement and Chardonnay.

— I know we're pals, but this is business.

Unable to look at Lee, he leaned over and squeezed his arm.

— I'm sorry; it's nothing personal, you're a good writer, but you need to come up with something to write about.

* * *

Late afternoon sunlight dappled the parks between Rathmines and Rathgar. So peaceful in this residential area, so harmonious. Out on the main traffic arteries, malodorous refuse trucks and graffiti-smeared 40-foot containers crawled inches at a time in both directions; but in the hushed, solid Edwardian rows between Rathmines and Rathgar, serenity was the order of the day.

The air in the park was drowsy with the scent of shrubs and flowers that Lee had long vowed to learn the names of. He unleashed Des and the terrier ran ahead. Making a little empire in here, tree by tree, extending his fiefdom every time they came to visit.

Couples held hands as they strolled or perched on benches, looking into each other's eyes. Even in the playground section, whose brightly coloured gizmos glared through the foliage, the little kids played in twos. A couples thing, life, he realised with the dull thud of sobriety. Behind a new tree Des did his statutory growling and scraping the ground with his hind paws; then he re-emerged, a stick between his teeth, wagging.

Lee had worshipped the air Tallulah breathed – he'd never met such a beautiful girl. Although he hadn't seen her for years, it didn't stop him from thinking of her. Still called up the late-night request programme on lyric fm when he was pissed, alone, and asked for a piece to be dedicated to her. It had become quite a game – the lyric woman was intrigued by Tallulah's name and Lee wouldn't give his, not even his first name or initials. A secret love story, which, in a twisted way, was true.

> *Well, the week wouldn't be complete without a request for Tallulah – hi, Tallulah, wherever you are, you lucky girl, this is from the same someone as always who says he loves you very much but won't even tell us his name… Just for you, here is the New York Philharmonic accompanying José Carreras with Maria from* West Side Story. *Take it away, José…*

He rounded a bank of shrubs and saw Des sitting upright at a bench, paws to the fore, being fed bread crusts by an elderly man.

— Ah, Des! Will you come on out of that!

— He's lovely, he's lovely, said the older man. — Good boy, Des, attaboy! Do you know what? He's nearly a Christian, aye!

Lee smiled, proud parent. Despite the warm evening the old man wore a tweed coat with a quality herringbone, and a UCD scarf. He carefully folded the paper bag that the crusts had come in and Des returned to Lee's heel.

— Lovely evening, Lee said.

— It's good we have the time to enjoy it, aye. Nowadays no one seems to have time for anything.

— It's a funny old world, you're right there, Mr O, Lee said.

The old man looked up sharply. — How do you know my name?

— Everyone around here knows you, Mr O. I'm Lee Carew.

— You can never be too sure nowadays, said Mr O. — Had my gas meter robbed twice in the last month – in broad daylight. Called the guards; I might as well have called Duffy's circus. This country has lost its values, believe me – who did you say you are?

— Lee, Lee Carew. I'm a journalist. I write for *The Sunday Trumpet*? Lee Carew?

— I don't recall…

— I write features, Lee said. — Stories from real life with a slant?

— *The Sunday Trumpet*… Mr O shook his head. — I can't remember people's names any more. I can remember Des here, all right, but not people. Perhaps it's for the best.

— You don't have a dog? Lee asked.

— They won't let me! Mr O cried. — I had the most lovely little mutt called Pablo, but the building was sold to a group of investors from Iceland and the new management introduced a no-pets policy. Pablo had to be…

His mouth was quivering.

— …I told him it was his flu jab. He never felt a thing.

Disgust churned through Lee.

— Jesus, that's a dreadful story, Mr O! It makes my blood boil!

— It's the society we have constructed for ourselves, you understand, said Mr O. — Money has become our new god, decency is gone out the window. But we'll pay the price, some day, aye, mark my words.

— I'd love to be able to write about the bastards who did that to you, Lee muttered. — I'd love to show them up for what they are.

— Why don't you? Mr O enquired. — You said you were a journalist.

* * *

Rathmines, once a cosy village on the south side of Dublin, now a series of fast-food joints run by Indians, convenience stores operated by taciturn Chinese and a series of building sites in various stages of completion where the predominant language was Russian. Cranes had transformed the horizon into a pin-cushion. Lee turned on his mobile and retrieved a message from Eddie that had been left an hour previously.

— Hi, Lee, Eddie calling, I have an interview I want you to do ASAP.

Eddie's voice was upbeat, smooth, alcohol-enhanced and totally transformed from that of his recent hysteria.

— There's this new kid on the Dublin minor hurling team, name of Peader Petrowski. First generation Polish-Irish, parents came to Phibsboro from Krakow in the early 1990s. There's sure to be an angle on John Paul II; I think the dad knew Lech Walesa – he was the Solidarity trade union fellow? I'm thinking along the lines, 'John Paul II Family Friend is Dublin's Saviour'. A nicely turned piece concentrating on the human endeavour story, with pics? Call me.

With Des in close attendance he dodged through the traffic on Rathmines Road and wondered how long he could go on writing for the *Trumpet*, even if they didn't fire him. Eddie told Lee regularly of his own real ambition: to escape from Valentine Newspapers and write a novel, or as I sometimes call it, *the* novel, ah yes, it's all in here you know, every word, every phrase, superb characterisation. I've served a long apprenticeship, believe me, all I need is the time to get it out. Is that what awaited Lee down the road? Garrulous, drink-laden bullshit? All his dreams boiled into a headline such as, 'John Paul II Family Friend is Dublin's Saviour'?

Joe N. Lan's butcher's shop was up one lane and off another. Years ago the butcher was plain Joe Nolan, but when the O fell off his sign, everyone started calling him Joe N. Lan. Whenever Lee said Joe N. Lan to Des, the dog bounced up and down and barked with excitement because he knew he was going to get a bone. Joe N. Lan's was always busy, a good sign, mainly with women beyond child-bearing age waiting patiently to be served by Joe himself. Bluebottles that had escaped death from Joe's ultraviolet fly exterminator flitted between meat tray and hanging carcass. Des sat on the pavement outside since he knew that dogs weren't allowed in food shops; the waiting women, as they often did, remarked on how good he was.

— He's as good as a mortal, isn't he?

— I'd say he'd talk to you.

— He is a boy, is he, young fella?

— He is a boy, Lee said, pleased on Des's behalf.

The shop counter was wide enough for only two customers at a time. Joe, big and fleshy as one of the bullocks on hooks behind him, sawed, hacked, sliced and scooped meat on to plastic sheets which he then weighed before bundling into pages of old newspaper. Lee noticed with dismay that old *Sunday Trumpets* were stacked four-feet high behind the counter.

— Mr C, Joe said cheerfully when Lee's turn came. He nodded towards the sunlit door. — I see himself is in good form, as per usual.

Des wagged his tail and showed a flash of pink tongue. Lee said, — Two loin chops for me, Joe, please, and a couple of bones for Des, if that's all right.

— Do you know what I'm going to tell you? Joe said as he grasped a cleaver and unerringly whacked a section of pig. — My missus thinks you're a bleedin' genius. She reads you every week. She even keeps your articles.

Joe trimmed the chops with a thin, evil-looking knife.

— I mean, that story about the medal in the mackerel. Tell us, Mr C, was that true or were you having us on?

— It was completely true.

— I mean, could your man not just have put the medal inside the fish and then called you up? Joe asked.

— A good point, but I don't think so, Lee said. — He had only partially gutted the fish when he spotted something bright inside. There was no way from what I saw that he could have placed the medal inside the fish. The incision was too small and the medal was lodged behind the fish's heart. The heart had grown around the medal.

— I mean, it's incredible, isn't it? said Joe, lifting two large bones on to the counter and wrapping them in a tear of newsprint. — Our Lady of Guadeloupe, wasn't it?

— Of Guatemala, in fact, Lee said.

— Our Lady of Guatemala, Joe said wistfully as he handed Lee his parcel, then leaned over the counter so that they were suddenly intimate. — I mean, the fish had to have got the medal from someplace, right? So it probably ate it off the body of a drownded sailor, isn't that what it is?

— A Spanish sailor at that, more likely.

— You mean, that mackerel might have come up from Spain?

— It's quite possible.

— Jesus, the heart had grown around the medal, Joe said as his eyes went glassy and for a moment came to rest on Lee in an expression of uncomplicated adulation. Then he straightened up and said, — I think my missus is going to have that article framed. She says you're a bleedin' genius, Mr C, and you should see all the books she reads. A bleedin' genius, she says you are.

— Tell her she should write to the editor of my newspaper and tell him that, Lee said as he made his way out.

Joe N. Lan laughed loudly. He said, — I'm sure he knows that already. Good luck, Mr C.

THREE

The chairman liked to observe Inge from a distance. Three mornings a week at six-thirty, astride his exercise bicycle, he could view the German intern through the glass doors, cutting an arrow-straight path up and down the bank's basement swimming pool. Eight strokes each length, seven seconds. He relished the power in her broad shoulders, the tantalisingly brief flash of her rump as she executed the turn at the far end, her devouring strength in the butterfly. What he would have given to have her lie on him and gulp him down! Subsume him into her! Swallowed whole! Alone in his Ballsbridge penthouse, he fantasised most nights about her being there with him, perhaps as they worked late together on the flowcharts and projections of his latest takeover bid. He suggests champagne; ten minutes later, both of them naked, she has him in an arm lock. You're… choking… me! Or Inge asks the chairman to help her move house; she wrestles him up the stairs to the spare bedroom and rapes him. Not… so… hard! Most nights he went to sleep in her Teutonic embrace, his fevered mind crammed with images of her most private parts, which he imagined were tattooed with Nazi iconography.

Now he strained to see Inge surging from the pool, glistening, water running down the deep cleft formed by the long muscles of her back as she made her way out, tugging her rubber cap off. A large yellow wall sign with black letters said HUBBI on the top line and GYM on the next. HUBBI stood for Hibernian Universal Business Bank Ireland, and although GYM merely meant what it said, a joke had circulated for years among the bank's fifteen hundred employees that it meant Gimme Your Money.

Standing beneath the shower, post-tumescent, checking his Patek Philippe watch that could give the time on four continents at a depth of 39,000 feet, the chairman began to worry about the day ahead. First the meeting of the executive committee at seven-thirty, at which fresh orange juice would be served. Then at eight-fifteen, a review of the preliminary figures for the second quarter over coffee and croissants, followed at nine-thirty by a meeting with the bank's marketing and advertising people, plus a special PR firm from London, to discuss HUBBI's bid to sponsor the 2012 Olympics (bacon butties would be served). At eleven the chairman needed to be at the International Financial Services Centre in the offices of an industrial conglomerate, a HUBBI client on whose board he served, where their upcoming billion-euro rights issue, underwritten by HUBBI, was being signed off. Always a good four-course lunch at these meetings. The chairman patted his round, smooth stomach regretfully and stepped from the shower.

He had a three o'clock photo-call outside the bank with the ambassador of an African country whose name he worried he might not remember, whose new national parliament building HUBBI was sponsoring. At three-thirty he was opening the latest HUBBI branch in a Dublin suburb, then choppering directly to the Galway races where HUBBI was sponsoring the whole eight-race card. He had arranged for the writer of his approved biography to be on the helicopter with him; he could fill in details of his early life for the man on the internal headphones even as they had a picnic; time had always to be put to the best use. Home late tonight, supper in the Four Seasons, back in here tomorrow morning at six. Start all over again.

He knew that his work would never be finished – an overarching worry, an umbrella beneath which all his other worries huddled. He was never satisfied; which was, he knew, what drove him. The story of how HUBBI had come to be a major force in Irish banking had been dealt with in a dozen books, including three coffee-table books; a score of PhDs; a television documentary and countless newspaper and magazine articles, one of which had described the bank's ever-rising share price as 'the ascension into heaven'. The Nobel-Prize-contending Japanese economist Umi

Takahashi, speaking in 1999 at the Davos Forum, had explained HUBBI as 'the perfect creation of its chairman, that sad-faced Irish magician, Dr Eric Chester'.

The 'Dr' had been bestowed by a little-known university in the North of England, the same year that HUBBI donated fifty million to that university towards the construction of the HUBBI School of Banking. All a long way from the tiny, three-man and two-woman cubby-hole operation in central Dublin known as The Shirtmakers' Guild that he had joined as an accountant in the late 1970s. A quaint little place, a historical oddity left over from the Dublin guilds of the late seventeenth century, stranded in time like a bog fossil, an anachronism wrapped up in a time-warp and dropped through a black hole into twentieth-century Ireland. More specifically, the Guild had been located in three rooms over a former shirtmakers, by then an erotic lingerie shop, and was run by its chairman, Mr Thomas Buttonhook. Mr Buttonhook's daughter, Theresa, worked as her father's secretary. She was a tall girl with long red hair and had a certain way of looking at the new employee.

It was said to be the case that when Eric Chester became the junior financial officer at The Shirtmakers' Guild, Mr Buttonhook did not even realise that the outfit he ran was in possession of a banking licence.

* * *

The chairman's office on the ninth floor incorporated three large windows aligned with the compass points favoured by the sun, although that morning a cold mist still enveloped Dublin, so the blinds were drawn on two windows and the heating was on low. He was dressed in a bespoke double-breasted suit of dark green mohair from Louis Copeland, a white shirt with button-down collar and a HUBBI tie. He began to speed-read *The Irish Times*, starting with the business pages.

The chairman wore black-framed glasses with thick lenses. He was bald. He had celebrated his fiftieth birthday with the coming into being of the new millennium, a confluence of one man and his planet, as he had remarked ruefully at the time. In the year 2000 HUBBI had gone stratospheric: Ireland had not only caught up with the rest of the world, it had passed it out; now Ireland was passing itself out.

> *Even seasoned analysts confessed themselves 'bowled over' by the three-minute standing ovation accorded to HUBBI's chairman, Dr Chester, at the bank's recent AGM. A lady shareholder in the audience, a pensioner, told the meeting that she said 'a decade of the rosary every night' for Dr Chester.*

He put aside *The Irish Times* and picked up the *Financial Times*.

The expectations of the market were endless. HUBBI had reported sixty-five successive quarterly earnings increases; the bank's share price had become a national conversation piece as the market's appetite for all things HUBBI became insatiable.

In the pink paper he came to a photograph of himself, doleful, apprehensive, taken at the recent AGM, above a piece of in-depth analysis regarding HUBBI's upcoming quarterly results. HUBBI's slogan, 'If Your Money's In HUBBI, You're In The Money!' ran the full length of the podium behind the chairman in the photograph.

> *A progression, year on year, of 15 per cent, achieved since 1994, has become the normal expectation for this financial-sector favourite. We expect the trend to continue, with quarterly profits in the €200m–€220m range, and the interim dividend increasing to thirty-three cents. Recommendation: BUY/ACCUMULATE.*

He'd never said much as a child growing up in Nottingham, just watched, listened, worried and kept his eyes on the ground because people often dropped a coin. Began to loan cash to his classmates when he was eleven, a shilling here, two there, never recorded a transaction, kept all the details in his head. Told his borrowers that there was no rush, that they could pay him off at a penny a week. They thought he was mad. Borrowed more and brought along their friends. Years later most of them were still paying a penny a week when they sat their A-Levels, a return of three thousand per cent in some cases. Once they'd got into the habit of paying fat little Eric Chester his weekly penny, it just stuck.

* * *

At seven-twenty an Eastern European lady in a pinafore began to silently lay out glasses and a chilled jug of fresh orange juice at the adjoining board table. The chairman's ambition, apart from being subsumed into intern Inge, and turning HUBBI into an intercontinental financial behemoth, was to be slim. He had tried and failed. Paid a fortune to dieticians, spent one whole week in Budapest, sitting in a warm water pool, wearing a rubber suit, eating artichokes. Useless. He hated failing. When he was a tiny boy in the north of England his father, an immigrant from County Roscommon, had pinned a league table for each of the main areas of young Eric's life to the kitchen notice board: school, cricket team, stamp-collecting club, bible class. The week that Eric slipped simultaneously from first place in all four leagues, Pa Chester had gone around the house as if his son had died.

At exactly one minute to the half hour three men entered the chairman's office. The bank's head of markets, George Bailey, had come to HUBBI from Barclays in London and was known in the bank as Royal George, because he was a member of a sailing club of that name. He sat on the executive committee chaired by Chairman Chester, along with the head of treasury, Don Dunne, who had worked in New York for Goldman Sachs before being head-hunted by HUBBI and returning home at the birth of the Celtic Tiger. The fourth and final member of the executive committee was HUBBI's head of risk, Fagan O'Dowd, a small, somewhat threadbare, moon-faced individual in his mid-forties who had joined HUBBI a few years after the chairman and whose expression was ever one of pained uncertainty.

* * *

The chairman poured four glasses of orange juice, a daily ritual. He beamed around the table, then nodded to his head of treasury.

— Don?

— We've just a few items to get through this morning, Chairman, Don Dunne began. Tall and rangy, he specialised in strong eye contact. — Word came in overnight that Donald Trump is looking carefully at HUBBI to finance his subterranean hotel.

— I thought he might, the chairman smiled. Through the window on which the blinds had not been lowered he could see down to the floor below, to HUBBI's trading room, where the bank depositors' savings were already being skilfully invested by traders with masters degrees in stochastic calculus. — Next?

— We're pressing *TIME* magazine again to do a cover story on you and HUBBI, Dunne went on, drilling everyone around the table. — Our people in New York say it's now a real possibility.

— Well done, Don, the chairman said and he took a sip from his glass.

— Here's the list of our latest signed-off loan accounts over five million, Dunne said briskly as he handed around a sheet of paper. — As you can see, we're still ahead of budget.

Although carefully laid-down structures existed for loans and HUBBI's investment strategies, in reality it was HUBBI's chairman who made the big decisions.

— Competition in the domestic mortgage business has become intense, Dunne said, moving on, his eyes strafing his colleagues. — We have to fight for every loan we make. It's war out there; no one is taking prisoners; if you pause, you're dead.

The chairman knew that his head of treasury was not exaggerating. HUBBI was the most aggressive lender in the Irish property fairytale and was the first financial institution to have come up with the 200-year mortgage. This was the mortgage you never paid back – not unless medical science made some very big breakthroughs – and was based on the concept of lending not to people but to generations. A clause in HUBBI's mortgage agreements encouraged new house and apartment owners towards HUBBI Home Fittings Finance for their fit-outs and to HUBBI Auto Finance for their new cars, all of which came at mouth-wateringly low teaser rates.

— Otherwise it's steady as she goes, Don Dunne said with what looked like grim satisfaction. — Ahead of target, ahead of market. Win-win. Ever upwards. 'If You're In HUBBI…'

— '… You're In The Money'. Thank you, the chairman said and turned his gaze to his head of markets. — George?

Royal George, reassuringly large and avuncular with a booming voice, spent many long hours schmoozing with the investment officers of big financial institutions. Like the other members of the executive committee, he was on a six-figure salary and enjoyed an annual bonus the size of a grazing elephant. He said,

— It's all good news, Chairman, I'm very pleased to say. We have advance copy of a nice piece coming up in next week's *Economist*. Apparently it will say that if HUBBI's share price rises another euro, our 500-day moving average crosses a gold standard buy line, which means that forty euros a share is a ninety-eight per cent certainty.

— I am humbled, the chairman said.

— Demand for our shares from institutional investors is exceptional, Royal George said. — Everyone wants us.

Everyone included HUBBI's special customers – those who owed the bank more than fifty million – who could borrow from HUBBI to buy HUBBI shares at a margin of 1.75 per cent, floated off the base rate, interest to be set off against HUBBI dividends. These loans were non-recourse, which meant that they were backed solely by the value of HUBBI shares. Almost everyone was making money, including the chairman, who owned two-hundred-million-euro worth of the bank's stock, all purchased with loans from HUBBI.

— HUBBI has become Ireland's default investment, Royal George said.

— I really am truly humbled, the chairman said again.

Royal George shot the chairman an up-from-under look which signified that sometimes even the best news had to be leavened with a little bad.

— We continue to see small but persistent short positions being taken against us by hedge funds in London and Switzerland, he said with a pained expression. — They're losing heavily, but they continue to bet against HUBBI's share price.

— They have no moral centre, said the chairman sadly. — I just hate these people.

— Quite, Chairman, he said tightly. — I just had to let you know.

— I hope they burn in hell, the chairman observed and looked around the table. — Fagan?

— I've been looking at a fresh loan application from Albert Barr, said Fagan O'Dowd, head of risk.

The other members of the executive committee had in recent years come to regard the head of risk as a nuisance. They saw him as an anchor on the inexorable ascent of HUBBI, as someone forever pointing out the negative aspects of loan proposals; in other words, the risks. The fact that, alone on the executive committee, Fagan O'Dowd did not own shares in HUBBI said it all as far as his colleagues were concerned.

— The facts are as follows, Fagan began. — HUBBI beat off strong competition to advance Barr €350 million for the purchase of the old brewery site in Goose Point, Dublin, subject to planning permission, which worked out at €17.5 million an acre, which was deemed fair value for a property of this size less than two miles from Grafton Street. Planning permission was duly obtained and the purchase completed.

Royal George made little attempt to stifle a yawn. Fagan O'Dowd went on, — Although we financed 99 per cent of the Goose Point purchase price, which is mortgaged to HUBBI, we are also secured by a variety of other titles provided by Barr in respect of development land, apartments, shares in shopping centres, pubs, car parks and so on – many of which we share as security with at least five other banks. Our final loan-to-asset ratio is at 77 per cent. In addition we own five per cent of Barr's Goose Point development.

Don Dunne and the chairman locked eyes in a choreography of silent derision. Fagan was saying, — Demolition of the existing structures was put in hand together with groundworks, for which we advanced a further ten million. A week after the commencement of the ground works the site, which is adjacent to the Irish Sea, began to flood.

Outside in Dublin a church bell chimed. Don Dunne sighed.

— Barr came to us with a plan drawn up by Dutch engineers to address the flooding by installing buttresses on the site, Fagan continued. — Projected cost was fifty million, which we agreed to fund, but the actual cost was closer to a hundred. We extended our loan, bringing our total exposure to four hundred and sixty million. Albert Barr now says he requires a further twenty million to fund cash flow in the short term, to discharge a number of creditors who are pressing, to bring steel onto the site, and to pay off a local residents' group that is threatening to picket the place.

— What do you recommend? the chairman asked politely.

Fagan's eyebrows became for a moment like two small worms attempting to copulate.

— Our loan-to-asset ratio is too high, he said. — Unless Barr comes up with either more equity or more collateral, I recommend not increasing our exposure.

The chairman tried not to show his irritation. If he'd taken on board Fagan's advice these last ten years, HUBBI would still be funding supermarket inventories, he thought.

— Don? he enquired pleasantly of his head of treasury. — Do you agree with Fagan?

Don Dunne looked at Fagan contemptuously.

— Honestly, it's hard to see how we can lose money here, no matter what happens, he said with a dismissive laugh. — Barr is a very successful operator with top-rate political connections. Goose Point is an amazing site and the proposed development is unlike anything else that's been built in Dublin. There's probably not a piece of real estate like it in Ireland. It's gold dust. We must also remember that if we refuse him, Barr could probably re-finance the whole project with any one of our competitors. Although we're his biggest lender, we're not the only one. He's into every bank in town and they'd love to get more of his business. Of course we give him what he wants – maybe squeeze up his margin a little, but give him the money, please!

— When we looked at this first, before we lent him a penny, I pointed out that there were also archaeological issues to be dealt with, Fagan O'Dowd said doggedly. — They were never completely resolved.

— Oh, yes, the *archaeological* issues! Royal George bellowed and began to laugh. — If I recall correctly, Chairman, what Fagan is referring to is that one of our underwriters, in the course of his evaluation, came across an old newspaper article which claimed that the first prehistoric settlement in Dublin was in Goose Point on Barr's brewery site. We're talking five thousand years ago. To back up its claim, the article cited a text fragment found inside a wine jug that had been buried on a snipe bog in Monaghan. Hmmmm.

Don Dunne sniggered and the chairman had to bite his lip. He loved it when Fagan was crushed at these meetings.

— Despite the fact that no one else had even heard of such a claim, on Fagan's insistence we hired the best advice in Ireland at considerable cost, Royal George rolled on, and they concluded that no heritage risk issues existed. Now the project has full planning permission, so even if there were heritage issues, which there aren't, they don't matter. Fuck archaeology! Okay, Fagan? Happy now?

Fagan persisted: — We're too heavily exposed to Barr. If the property market should dip…

— That's not going to happen! Royal George boomed. — Why create a negative when one doesn't exist? Ever heard of the Celtic Tiger, Fagan? And even if the market were to dip, which it won't, we have full or partial mortgages on all Barr's other stuff. We're almost too well secured, for heaven's sake!

— We can never be too well secured, the chairman said by way of stern reprimand. — Never, ever.

— Thank you, Chairman, said Royal George, admonished. — I was just trying to point out…

— What does Barr own that we don't have a grip on? the chairman asked.

— Not much that I can find, said Fagan, head bowed. — His residence, which is worth five million at least, is already mortgaged to the Patriot's Building Society, which is not part of HUBBI.

— Not yet, the chairman said.

— Indeed, Chairman, said Don Dunne and the two men smiled.

Over a decade, HUBBI had hoovered up a clutch of tiny credit unions, building societies, loan-shark outfits, mortgage brokers, hire-purchase operators and lease specialists, and unleashed their cash-incentivised employees on the Irish public. It was well known in-house that the chairman now had his eye on the Patriot's Building Society. Fagan turned the page of his folder.

— There is something, however, that could be interesting, he said. — Barr's wife owns a couple of apartment buildings – Barr was able to get his hands on them when the government was privatising some public assets a few years ago. But as I say, they're not his; they belong to his wife.

— They'd be like cash, the chairman said as his watch chimed discretely, a pre-set signal that his next meeting was looming. He was also hungry. — Thank you, gentlemen. I'll set up a lunch.

FOUR

Although he hadn't yet got a headache, Albert knew that soon he would have. Was that normal, he wondered? To have a headache after just a few drinks the night before? Four pints on his way home from work with Kevin, his father-in-law, then a good-sized gin and tonic with Medb-Marie before dinner. They'd shared two bottles of Château Cheval Blanc at the table and afterwards, before he fell asleep in front of *Prime Time*, Albert had put away a snifter of brandy. Alcohol was a way of life in Ireland and he saw himself as no different to anyone else. He wondered if he should get an MRI scan. Finding some Nurofen Plus, he swallowed four tablets and drank a glass of water.

Kevin Steadman reckoned he had two years left in cabinet, if he was lucky. Grand, that meant another pension, grand. I'm grand thanks, how are you? Forty years getting his constituents houses and indoor toilets, planning permissions and rent allowances, getting their children jobs in the county council, or out of jail, or flats for their young ones who had babies when they were fourteen. I'm grand, I'm grand, you're lookin' well yourself. The Taoiseach didn't like him, had actually once said, Kevin, would you ever go and fuck yourself, in response to Kevin's attempt to be given Foreign Affairs. Kevin knew if he asked for Foreign Affairs he'd at least end up with something, but that if he just asked for, say, the Gaeltacht, he'd end up with feck all. Of course I remember you, how could I forget you? How is himself? He's a lucky man. No, you're grand, that's great, that's grand.

He'd told Albert over the pints the night before that the additional planning for Goose Point was a done deal. That it was grand. Albert valued Kevin for his faultless attention to his own betterment, a preoccupation that had served Albert well over a dozen years. And yet he had begun to see Kevin as a potential liability, trouble down the road as it became obvious that the minister's naked self-interest would one day bring him down. Kevin had no vision beyond the next corruptible project, whereas Albert looked forward to a day when he would not need to resort to bribery.

The offices of Barr None Enterprises were located in a two-storey detached red-brick on Shelbourne Road, an early acquisition to which Albert was superstitiously attached. Two accountants and three quantity surveyors worked in the building, and half a dozen bookkeepers who recorded the details from the clerks of works on various sites, as well as a team that dealt with an ever-moving river of paper.

Albert made himself read his post. Sheaves of payment certificates from subcontractors; fat wads of architects' plans secured by rubber bands in which shopping malls, flats, houses and multistorey car parks were seeing their first glimpse of earth light. Bank statements, interest-payment demands. Credit-card bills – he was sometimes afraid even to read them – investment proposals from banks, stockbrokers and shadowy halfway-house financial advisors, all of them after Albert's money, enticing him with tasty morsels that would tuck his cash away via a Luxembourg holding company for five or seven years and then give it back to him trebled.

We urge you, Mr Barr, to attend this presentation by the senior economist to the Icelandic government. It is, we respectfully submit, the opportunity of a lifetime.

A greeting card from a shop in Jermyn Street, London, where once, after an epic lunch, he'd bought a tie costing six hundred sterling; stacks of bills filed under 'miscellaneous': for the jet, for garden maintenance in Inchigeela, electricity, the phones, gas, car tax, the children's piano lessons. A solicitor's letter representing the Goose Point Residents' Association threatening high-court proceedings about non-payment of the May bank holiday sewerage settlement. A circular letter from a bishop in Botswana to whom Albert, in a fit of excessive piety, had once sent a grand and who subsequently had written almost weekly, as if Albert were his son.

He sometimes felt vaguely guilty about his wealth and had a hazy, inchoate ambition to set up a charitable foundation; or maybe it was too early for that, maybe he needed to be well out of the woods before that was a runner. He would need to get the tax angle clarified first, since charity began at home, and then there was the whole business of whether or not the money should be given anonymously. He liked the idea of people whispering knowingly about how, although he never spoke about it, Albert Barr gave more to charity than anyone. Charity was an obvious way for Medb-Marie to advance her social ambitions, but the one time she'd held a coffee morning for orphaned chimpanzees only three people, including Albert, had shown up.

In his office ensuite, he wanted to pee but couldn't. He clenched his teeth. Over the previous twenty-four hours he had taken three of the pills, but still his prostate was as ungiving as North Korea. Always the same when the pressure came on. His engineers were now talking about erecting further expensive tide barriers in Goose Point and when Albert began to lose the head with them, had referred him to the clauses in their contract that dealt with Acts of God. The residents' association was planning a march for the coming weekend and as many as three thousand people were expected to turn out. The banks, the banks. His every move picked over by little farts with the title of underwriters, every potential risk underpinned and buttressed by his assets. Would they come forward with the extra cash now needed for Goose Point? What would happen if they didn't?

The pressure, the pressure. It wasn't fair to ask one man to take so much pressure. Was a time when he'd duck out of a high-powered meeting into the gents for a quick resolving interlude of self-gratification, but the last time he'd tried, which was two weeks ago, he'd ended up with a blinding headache. All he sought now was a peaceful, happy place of rushing waters and gushing taps.

He gave up, flushed the unblemished toilet, went to the basin, stuck his chin at the mirror and straightened his tie. His image throbbed with wealth and well-being. No one would ever imagine, he thought bitterly, that this man in the mirror would right now give a grand for a good piss.

He wondered, a recently recurring thought, about an alternative way of life for himself, Medb-Marie and the twins. Maybe she'd been onto something when she revealed her plan to go south. What was it all about if, despite his money, he was bunged up like this every morning? He could surely squirrel away enough to buy his family and himself comfort for twenty years – more – educate the girls, they could go to university in Cork, get married. He had another hazy image: Amethyst and Amber as beautiful young women wearing Wellington boots and plaid jackets, leading in foals on the stud farms which Albert had bought for them when they married well-bred but penniless young, horsey men – amateur jockeys, perhaps, or assistant racehorse trainers.

Trouble was, everything was intertwined. Cross-guarantees on a dozen or more loans, he couldn't just write a cheque for ten million and disappear. It didn't work like that. Goose Point was the big one. When Goose Point began to flow, the waterfall of cash would wash away all his other debts and Albert would be free.

Despite these water-based analogies he reached his desk still wincing with discomfort. He hit the intercom.

— I'm going to lunch, he told his secretary.

* * *

Like other Dublin bank chiefs, the chairman employed a chauffeur; unlike others, he had deliberately shunned a limousine and chosen a Smart car. Savvy, the financial pages had chuckled; environmentally astute, the lifestyle pages had cheered. The chauffeur popped the little car out onto St Stephen's Green and they headed for the south part of the county in a haze of pollen and high-octane gasoline.

He never tired of looking for the new angle, realised when he was sixteen that nothing exceeded greed when it came to human frailty. An instinctive financial animal, he'd learned early on how cash was the lifeblood that everything depended on, how without it nothing was possible. And yet sometimes, even as he reached for the stars, even as he was fashioning HUBBI into a player on the world banking stage, he realised that little weasels like his head of risk had their worth.

The chauffeur threw the Smart car in and out of tiny traffic gaps and soon they were zipping along the coast road that led to Dún Laoghaire. He loved pitching the other three members of the executive committee into a snarling feud about a big loan and then watching what happened. Don Dunne and Royal George epitomised everything that was both good and bad about banking: vaunting ambition and unbridled avarice. He had made both men multi-millionaires. Fagan O'Dowd, on the other hand, was the chairman's daily reminder of the dangers associated with excessive caution. Fagan would never be really rich nor, by the look of him, truly happy. And yet no one that the chairman knew could focus more piercingly on the fundamentals of a tricky situation, or propose a more elegant solution.

As they drove south cranes reared into the County Dublin skyline, a goodly percentage of them funded by HUBBI. Each time the chairman saw a new crane, a warm feeling rushed beneath his ribcage; scaffolding churned his blood even faster. Sometimes when they were caught in the slipstream of a cement truck, he asked his driver not to pass it but rather to linger behind the gigantic machine on whose almost sexual rear orifice blobs of fresh concrete glistened like the mating wax of a praying mantis.

When he was eighteen he had discovered the profit inherent in grief. Observing how, on the death of his maternal grandmother, his normally thrifty mother threw financial caution to the wind and spent a hundred pounds on a hat, Eric Chester had applied this business model to the wider Nottingham community. Having sourced a cheap supply of badly printed St James bibles, his strategy was to read up the death notices for the far side of town, and then to appear on the doorstep of the deceased, bearing a bible in its presentation box.

— Is Mr Jones in?

A puckering of the lip, a sliding glassy tear. Eric knew that Mr Jones was at that moment laid out cold as mutton in the front upstairs bedroom.

— Who… wants him?

— It's just that he ordered this St James bible from us ten days ago, young Eric would chirpily say.

This statement produced an outright flood of tears in 98 per cent of cases. The late religious enthusiasm of the deceased, as perceived by his survivors, led to commercial blindness. Young Eric handed over the bible for a tenner and in the process made a 1,500-per-cent mark-up.

He blew it one day when he called to a house that he'd already struck six months before, but had forgotten. They called the police and only through Pa Chester's promise that his son would leave town was a charge of fraud not pressed. Eric Chester came to Dublin.

* * *

Sparkling midday sunshine illuminated the southern neck of Dublin Bay as yachts in small clutches dodged in and out of view. Briefly, the chairman thought of Inge, the intern, then sighed heavily and comforted himself with thoughts of what he had achieved in business.

For three centuries the shirtmakers of Dublin had put a percentage of their weekly earnings into the Shirtmakers Guild. The Guild had invested these monies with sacred care, and when its members could sew and cut no more, had provided them with pensions. Other guilds and trades, impressed by the steadfast nature of the Shirtmakers Guild, had, over several hundred years, also entrusted their savings to this impeccably honest company.

Within a year of joining the Guild, Eric Chester married Theresa Buttonhook. Now every March the chairman gave the annual Buttonhook lecture at Trinity, named in honour of his late father-in-law who had, malicious tongues insisted, died of fright when he learned that his son-in-law had loaned three times the bank's then share capital to a man who had, up to recently, mixed concrete for a living.

* * *

One of the unspoken rules at this level was that business was never discussed, except as an afterthought. And so, as a sallow-skinned individual in an apron to his ankles sprinted ahead to pull out chairs, and Albert ordered the special bottle of white wine that he knew the chairman appreciated and a double brandy and port for himself, the two men swapped yarns about golf and sailing – which in reality neither of them liked – and about how good a hurling team Kilkenny really was, and about the goal Beckham had scored the week before for Real Madrid. As they made their way through starters of, for Albert, prawn cocktail and, for the chairman, compote of prawns, mussels and crab, both Albert and his guest guffawed in high decibels about how much money Albert had won on his horse at Leopardstown the previous Christmas when the chairman had been a caller to his box, and how one bookie had offered his new Mercedes 220 in part-payment of Albert's winnings.

— I told you, I bet he didn't even own it! the chairman chortled. — I bet our car finance division did!

A mid-sized team that reminded Albert of the group that had surrounded him on the operating table in the Blackrock Clinic when he went in to have his bladder scoped served the main course. A wordless choreography climaxed in fake silver domes being snatched simultaneously from both plates to reveal shanks of herb-encrusted venison served on a bed of colcannon (the black sole was off). The two men became quieter as they discussed their personal charity projects. The chairman pledged to come to Medb-Marie's fundraiser, which would seek to protect Arctic seal cubs, although privately the chairman approved of seal-cub murder since HUBBI was financing at least two west-coast fish farms; and Albert promised ten grand there and then to the chairman's Save County Roscommon crusade, although privately Albert looked upon County Roscommon as beyond saving.

As a second glass the size of a chalice filled with brandy and port was placed before Albert, he felt at ease. He knew the routine: next up for discussion would be their children. He had written down the names of the chairman's children after the last meeting and had that morning memorised them; but now his mind was wiped clean of such memory. As the cheese was wheeled out on a chariot longer than a hospital trolley the chairman listened politely to the latest antics of Amethyst and Amber, the terrible twins, and about how Amethyst had perforated Amber's eardrum with a sweetcorn fork. The chairman outlined in some detail the academic achievements of his own children, whom he met under the terms of his visiting rights, including Siobhán, the youngest, who at five was already showing an interest in the Simplex crossword.

Just like a mating ritual being played out in a primal jungle, the chairman thought as he watched Albert use a neat little silver knife to load Stilton onto a biscuit. Neither of them could give a toss if each other's children drowned *en masse* in their private swimming pools, but such elaborate shows of false interest, like displays of peacock feathers, had been laid down over millennia when men met to talk about money.

— So tell me, what's the word on advance sales? the chairman enquired casually.

— Terrific, said Albert as he signalled for another bottle of the white and mopped his mouth. — Few dozen apartments gone already, two anchor tenants lined up for the shopping mall, and that's before we've even launched.

Albert's statement about the apartments and anchor tenants fell into the category of, if not outright lie, then borderline mendacity. Following the granting of initial planning permission in Goose Point the two thousand apartments had been 'released for sale', and since then booking deposits had been received on three of them. Another twenty-six 'expressions of firm interest' had been lodged with the auctioneers, which they hoped to arm-twist into legally enforceable contracts in the near future. But part of the problem was that when you announced you had two thousand apartments to sell, everyone assumed that there was no rush to buy one. Furthermore, although a meeting had been held with the property people in several supermarket chains, they hadn't yet even got around to discussing hello money.

— We were discussing your recent loan application the other day, the chairman said.

Albert felt a sudden shortness of breath. He said, — And?

— HUBBI's exposure to you is already considerable, Albert, the chairman said.

Albert noted the change in tone and wished he hadn't had the second brandy and port. He cursed his body for deserting him at key times, now felt his heart flutter, and wondered if he took a blood-pressure tablet would it be seen as a sign of weakness. He said, — This is going to be the most exciting development in Europe, Eric.

— I daresay, said the chairman. — I daresay.

— And? Albert asked as he broke out all over in an oily sweat.

— Loans of this size must be agreed collegially, the chairman said.

Albert, wondering what collegially meant, said, — We're building a city together, Eric; a city.

— I know; I'm in favour, the chairman said, smiling. — I enjoy doing business with you, Albert.

— Thank you, Albert said and dared to hope. — And you're in favour?

— That's what I said, said the chairman.

Albert had the sudden nostalgic urge to go on the bender of a lifetime.

— Thank you so much, Eric, he said.

— You're welcome, the chairman said.

— Let's have some proper Armagnac, Albert chortled.

Nearly there, the chairman thought, almost all grades taken and passed. He declined the offer of Armagnac – he made a mental note to inquire if Barr had ever received treatment for alcoholism – and switched the conversation to horse-racing, listening for ten minutes to Albert babbling about horses that the chairman had never heard of. When it was time to leave and Albert had paid the bill, they walked out shoulder to shoulder and into the Gents. Albert's brace of double prostate easers plus 50 per cent of three bottles of wine plus coffee and Armagnac had done wonders for his bladder. Side by side with the chairman of HUBBI, the flood of his uninhibited urine seemed to his suddenly exhausted mind like a symbol of the plenty flowing from this country they were building together.

— Just for the record, Albert, said the chairman.

— Eric?

— Just for the record, when I said back there, I'm in favour, what I meant was that *I'm* in favour of extending your loan, me personally, the chairman said as he copiously shook his discharged member. — But I'm only me, remember. My head of group risk, for example, is not in favour of lending you more money – not unless we acquire more collateral for your extra loan – just as a formality, of course.

Zephyrs coursed through Albert's head as he realised that his meeting with this fat little thief was not over. He tried to laugh it off and said,

— You're coming down with collateral, Eric! Come on!

The chairman, zipping up, said,

— Theoretically, yes, but you know these pen-pushers, Albert, they're never happy. 'Our collateral needs to be realisable, Goose Point is not realisable as things stand, blah blah de-blah.' They drive me fucking mad. What am I to do?

— I thought we had a deal back there, Albert said.

— We certainly have the makings of a deal, the chairman said.

— You said it was okay.

— I'm sorry, Albert, what I said was, I enjoy doing business with you, which I do. That's what I said.

— I need this money, Albert said.

— I know, the chairman said. — And I need to keep my people happy.

Albert said in a more wheedling voice,

— I've given you everything. You own the whole fucking thing.

Just the week before, his lawyers had brought him a stack of HUBBI loan documents thicker than a telephone directory, and it had taken him three hours to sign them.

— I have nothing more to give, he said.

— We're talking about a scenario that will never happen, the chairman replied, washing his hands thoroughly, suds gleaming on his smooth knuckles. — A completely doomsday scenario. Look, I'm on your side – I hate this kind of cautious shit, but sometimes I have to go along with it.

— There is nothing else, Albert repeated. — You've got the lot.

— Then we have a problem, said the chairman with sudden gravity, rinsing, reaching for the linen mini-towel. — I'm sorry, I didn't think this would happen. I thought we were there.

— You have everything! Albert cried. — What more do you want?

— We get your lovely wife's flats, Albert, the chairman said, you get your money.

FIVE

Eight forty-five next morning, strolling down a familiar road in Dublin's Ballsbridge, freshly shaved, Des on a lead at his heel, Lee felt good. Two vodkas on the way home from Rathmines the evening before, then the chops, fried, with takeaway chips and the three-quarters bottle of white wine that he had failed to find when he was drunk. Chilling in the toilet cistern. The craftiness of the serial imbiber.

He'd once lived in these wide, quiet leafy roads in a fine red-brick house on its own grounds. Dad had been apprenticed to a mechanic down in Skibbereen as a young man during the 1950s, when all anyone got out of rural Ireland was TB.

— I knew I had to get a trade, Dad used to tell Lee, my grandfather paid the mechanic to take me on and teach me. Lord above, can you imagine that now? Pulleys, levers and grease. Wrenches the size of hurleys.

— But you got your trade, Mum said with a knowing glance to Lee. — He got his trade.

— Borrowed a fiver from Granddad the day I got my papers, came to Dublin, oh Lord, what a difference. My first job was as a chauffeur, can you believe it?

— In those days a chauffeur had to know how to service a car, Mum said. — You weren't just a driver.

Mr de Breffni-White, dealt in art, la-de-da, lived in Dalkey, lovely house with sea views, owned a Rolls Royce Phantom IV, only eighteen ever made, imported it direct himself, it had once been owned by General Franco.

— A bachelor, Mum said. — Mr de Breffni-White.

Straight-8 engine, the only Rolls to have one, the chassis was handmade by a London coachbuilder. Sweet as a nut. Sailed down the country to Cork and Galway, to art exhibitions. Sligo, Donegal.

— Always had a gentleman with him, Mum said. — A young gentleman.

His assistants, they were, employees, learning the trade, students of art; he was a very generous man, Mr de Breffni-White, everyone adored him.

— He was very good to you.

I never said he wasn't.

— He gave you the money to buy your garage.

Worked for him for eight years, day and night, drove him across England, into France, spent two weeks in Normandy, it isn't all that long since the war, you know, Carew, he used to say. Put me up in the same hotels; once we even had dinner together. A fine draughtsman too on his own account, made a sketch or two of me, a good likeness actually.

— You were very good-looking; you still are.

Often wonder what became of him.

Mechanics from Dad's garage built a swing and erected it in the back garden, near the fenced-off lily pond. On summer days, young Lee sat on his swing and inhaled the scent of orange blossom. He searched for it now as he walked, but the morning was not yet warm enough to carry blossom scent. We'll always have our memories, Dad used to say.

Miss Gwendolyn Forbes met Lee in the basement of a substantial house, on whose gravel forecourt were often parked a silver top-of-the-range Lexus 4x4 and a racing-green BMW 3-series convertible. He both liked and disliked these Tuesday-morning sessions: he liked Gwen, her preferred name, who was softly spoken, pretty, considerate and quietly intelligent; but sometimes during their chats, advances were made into territory that Lee disliked and that left him wishing he had not come.

Gwen answered the door and bent down and patted Des's head.

— He's a great character, she said.

Des lay on a mat in the porch as Lee followed Gwen inside to a sitting room, where he sat in an armchair opposite Gwen. He cleared his throat.

— Ah, sorry about last week.

— No problem, it's up to you, Gwen said.

— I was, ah, busy.

Lee mumbled and coughed, took a drink from the glass of water that stood on the table beside his chair. Lying was very much not part of the deal here and Gwen had a way of showing her disappointment by means of a tiny smile. She was in her late thirties with wavy, straw-coloured hair tied back, and large grey eyes. She was on the small side and this morning was wearing a denim-blue skirt, a plain cream blouse and runners from whose upper rims peeped socklets, pink against her brown ankles. She asked,

— How are you – other than being busy?

— I'm, ah, the same.

— Tell me what that means.

— Same place, same job. I think they want to sack me.

— That's terrible.

— Our circulation figures are on a knife-edge.

— What can you do about it?

— I have to come up with something juicy.

— That's hardly a surprise; you work for a tabloid newspaper, Gwen said.

He knew almost nothing about her and had no idea how she could afford to live in a house such as this. He knew that she was well regarded in her field because he had once interviewed her for a piece in the *Trumpet*, and an assortment of doctors and other shrinks had spoken highly of her. Which was how they had met.

— I wish I didn't have to, he said.

— You have said before that your job with the *Trumpet* is a temporary position, Gwen said. — That your real ambition is to write a novel. What are you doing about that?

— Everyone who works for Valentine Newspapers is scared, Lee said. — The place runs on fear.

Gwen raised one eyebrow.

— Dolphin Valentine, the Chief, as he's called, just wants to make money, Lee said.

— I think I saw him on the cover of some book, Gwen said. — Was he naked, or am I imagining it?

— He was in swimming togs. He once won an Olympic gold medal for Ireland in the men's free-diving category.

— Mmm, interesting, Gwen said. — But you haven't told me how your novel is coming on.

He closed his eyes and said in a low voice,

— I'm blocked.

— We're all blocked to some extent, Gwen said. — But the unconscious is beavering away the whole time, working when we sleep, helping us along.

— If I lose my job I'll have to move to a cheaper flat, and most flats won't allow dogs.

Gwen re-crossed her ankles and rearranged her hands in her tidy lap. She said,

— Most of the great writers credit their unconscious as being their primary source of inspiration.

— Eddie – he's my editor – says that we could all lose our jobs. Including himself.

— What would you really like to write about?

— For the *Trumpet?*

— Whatever. Say the people in the *Trumpet* said, 'Lee, write whatever you like' – what would you write?

— That's the problem; I have no idea.

— Nothing inspires you? Not even love?

Lee's face must have shown what he was thinking, because Gwen then said very gently,

— You look so sad, Lee. You should try and find a way of writing about that sadness that we have spoken about here. About the love that you have lost. You've got to dig deep at times like these.

He relished the almost tender look that Gwen had floated his way, and although he realised that clients were in and out of here the whole time, when Gwen looked at him like that, he felt his case might be just a little bit special.

— I, ah, I didn't come here last week, he said, because, ah, you know, I didn't like, I didn't want to, what I mean is…

He knew that if he looked up he would see her unwavering grey eyes, and that he was now midway through a sentence that she would not help him to complete.

— … basically, the voice thing, you know, we were discussing the week before last, in my head, if you like, I didn't want to go back there, he said.

— You told me that one day you went for a walk on Sandymount Strand and heard a voice, she said.

— Over a year ago, yes.

— You told me that you didn't know if it was calling you or not, she said.

— That's right, yes.

— Nor could you hear what it said.

— Just a voice, calling something.

— Your dad was in the garage business, she said.

— Yes.

— When he died, he left the business to you.

— I fucked it up, I told you that. I pissed it away.

— You do remember, don't you, where you were on the day that your dad was killed in a car crash?

— Yes, on Sandymount Strand.

They were getting back to the place where they'd been two weeks ago, which made him regret having come here again, and yet he felt that something important was going on.

— He was delivering an Austin Princess Vanden Plas, a brand-new model, to a businessman in Wicklow, Lee said. — There was an oil spill. He skidded and hit a wall. They said he was killed instantly.

— That's what you told me before, yes, Gwen said.

Lee bit his lip as the old memory dominated. The big picture on the front page of the paper, you would have thought they'd have more respect, Mum said, and below it another, smaller picture of

Dad when he was young. He really was such a good-looking man, Mum said.

— Tell me about Uncle Dickie, your father's younger brother.

God, she forgot absolutely nothing, which was simultaneously gratifying and scary. Uncle Dickie had been a bachelor, quite tall and slim – the opposite of Dad – and wore white sports coats and pink flannel slacks and walked very upright. Uncle Dickie's face was red and his thinning orange-dyed hair was drawn straight back and curled at his neck. His father's brother had lived in a flat in Molesworth Street and worked in an antiques gallery. Lee feared him, although Uncle Dickie was always smiling. Lee could never understand why he feared Uncle Dickie, but he did, even now, when Uncle Dickie had been dead for years.

— We had been such a happy family, you know, Lee said.

— Had been? Gwen asked.

He hated when she pounced, as she just had. And yet if he delved into the doubt she had just seized upon, he wondered if he would be able to tell her accurately how he felt. Or if he was skipping something.

— I mean, happy until Dad was killed, he said.

— I see, said Gwen.

For if Lee strained hard enough, if he listened hard enough, he heard another note, something scary, slipping away from him even as he grasped it, even as he desperately tried to hold it and put a name on it.

— Gone, he said suddenly.

He could sense the tension between them as his heartbeat resounded in his ears.

— Something was lost, he said.

— Some ... thing?

— I don't know. Jesus, I mean, I lost Dad, I lost my business, I lost Tallulah, I'm about to lose my job, my flat, my dog...

He was in this yawning, dark, lost place, groping; he could feel the cold wet air of it. Without warning, he began to cry.

— It's okay, Lee, Gwen said gently and sat forward.

Lee grabbed a fistful of tissues.

— The voice, he sobbed.

— Can you hear it now? Gwen asked.

He nodded. He cried,

— It's saying… it's saying, *Come back!*

* * *

When the bus had been stuck in traffic for fifteen minutes, Des and Lee got off and at a furious pace walked the last half-mile to Phibsboro. A dense band of lead-saturated fug, a dirty grey stripe, hung across the mid-morning. The sessions with Gwen Forbes did weird things to his head – churned up old thoughts, more shadows than thoughts, that fluttered and teased in a remote part of his brain like dying moths. Yet he felt strangely relieved, as if his tears had swept away debris between him and the past.

He forged uphill and saw a woolly-headed man with a bulky shoulder bag at Kelly's Corner, leaning on a lamppost, drawing deeply on a cigarette, reading a paperback.

— Mick, sorry, Lee panted as he sprinted the last twenty yards.
— Buses, you know the story.

— No worries, Mick said. — Ah, will ye look at Des. How're ye, Des?

Mick the Pic, staff photographer for Valentine Newspapers, which worked him like a pack mule, who lived with his wife and God knows how many children in the middle of a housing warren in Lucan, was on personal terms with visiting heads of state, winners of the Nobel Prize, Olympians, astronauts, film stars on their third Oscar. That's nice, hold the pint just a little higher and to your right, Mr President, ah that's nice, could you stand a little closer to the Taoiseach, Your Majesty, ah, that's nice.

— D'you know what I'm going to tell you, Lee? I've been standing here for nearly half an hour, and out of the thirty-seven buses that passed me, twenty-eight of them were driven by blacks.

Mick went mildly pop-eyed, awaiting Lee's reaction.

— I mean, that's 85 per-fucking-cent blacks driving the buses; I worked it out. How in Jaysus' name could they know their way around Dublin?

— They live here, Lee said.

— Yeah, I suppose you're right, Mick said, I just never realised there were that fuckin' many of them.

They walked back down the street, looking for the number of the door. Lee said, — I heard Pat Kenny saying that they're the reason the economy is so strong.

— I'm not against them, like, you know what I mean? They're different to us, is all I'm saying.

— They're black.

— Yeah, but they're different. Did you ever see a black man drinkin' a pint?

— They smoke weed.

— Fair enough. At least they go to Mass and all, not like the Chinese, Mick said.

A tiny gate guarded a two-metre long, weed-choked path to the hall door of a terraced house. Mick rang the bell and said, — I sold my shares in the paper.

— I didn't know you had any.

— Not many, but I'm getting out when I can, you know what I mean? I'm going to put the money towards buying a flat in Latvia.

— Latvia?

— It's a country near Russia.

— I know where it is.

— Forty grand: sea views, four bedrooms, a balcony and exclusive access to a rooftop garden.

— What's Latvia like?

— A fillet steak, chips and a pint costs eighty cent.

— Jesus.

— It's a fantastic country.

— Will you use the flat much?

— I'm not going to use it, I'm going to fucking let it, Mick said as the door opened and a small, fat, hairless man in blue overalls stood looking at them.

— What?

— Mr Petrowski?

— Petrowski, sure.

— Lee Carew from the *Sunday Trumpet*; we spoke earlier, sorry I'm a bit late.

— You one hour late.

— Sorry, Mr Petrowski, how are you? This is Mick, our photographer.

— Okay, but no dog.

— Tie him to the railings, Mick said. — Good boy, Des; Jesus, he's a scream.

A gasp-inducing stench of fried onions clung to the short hallway. Mr Petrowski rolled ahead of them towards a tiny kitchen as Mick tapped Lee on the arm and handed him a large envelope.

— From Eddie.

A woman wearing a headscarf was standing on a box beside an ironing board, guiding an iron up and down a sports jersey. Small and round, like her husband. The footmen and grooms, maids and miners, servants of Napoleon's empire, and of the Hapsburgs. Various low-end sporting trophies cluttered the mantelpiece of the dark, tiny room. On one side of a television set showing cartoons on mute sat a girl, somewhere between thirteen and twenty, wearing a pair of earphones, the hem of her denim skirt up around her backside. Lee said hello to everyone and Mick said to Lee, — I have to be at Dublin Castle in twenty minutes. The Prime Minister of Canada is having a pint with the Taoiseach.

— Where's the star? Lee asked Mr Petrowski.

— Star?

— Where is Peader?

— Peader he go. You late.

— Where is he gone?

— Peader he train, the father said. — Come home later.

— How late will he be?

— Nine, ten, eleven, Petrowski said and spread his plump hands.

Shrewd, deep-brown eyes. Always calculating, measuring, working out how much it was worth.

— We need his picture for the paper, Lee said. — We need him here now.

— Sure, but you late.

Eddie's reaction when he learned what happened to his big story would probably kill him. The mother said, — I have picture of Peader.

She dismounted painfully and left the room, rocking from left to right like a Russian doll. As Lee tore open Eddie's envelope, the daughter crossed her legs and flamed a cigarette. Eddie had sent a full-colour head and shoulders of Pope John Paul II. Mick said, — There's no light in here. What's the garden like?

The father brought them out to a six-by-ten concrete yard where coal was piled in one corner and bulging black refuse sacks in the other. Mick squinted into his light meter and said, — Yeah, it's nice out here. I'll move the sacks if yous bring out chairs.

Lee returned to the kitchen as the father was putting on a blue dust coat and collecting a bunch of keys from the dresser. Lee said, — You're not leaving, are you, Mr Petrowski?

— Gotta go to work.

— Okay, sure, but can we just a get a shot of you first? Please? We've both come up here specially, you know? And you and I can talk while Mick shoots.

Petrowski looked at his watch, made a face, a calculation, then clicking his keys ambled back outside, where his wife had appeared holding a framed, low-resolution colour photograph of a shaven-headed youth with a hurling stick. She said, — Two years ago, but the same.

— No problem, lovely, Lee said.

— Nice, said Mick, already shooting.

The story would have to focus on the father angle, but that would be okay since he was the one who knew the Pope, which is what Eddie had said. The Petrowskis sat squinting into the sun as Mick sprang to different angles. Lee stepped back into the kitchen.

— Hi. Would you ever mind coming out for a minute and having your picture taken?

The daughter looked at him as if he had not spoken, her head bobbing gently to whatever music she was being pumped with. In the round made by her lips the tip of her tongue appeared and began to probe the exterior. Lee returned outside where Mick was squeezing off a thousand digital shots a minute.

— Hold on a second, Mick.

He took out Eddie's pic of the Pope and placed it so that Petrowski was holding it to his chest. He then positioned the son's framed picture on the mother's lap. Mick kept shooting.

— Yeah, that's nice, I like that.

— You must be very proud of your son, Lee said, his notebook open.

The Petrowskis looked at one another and Mick said, — Yeah, nice, just hold the Pope to your left, thanks, Mr Petrushki, that's lovely.

— Where you come from in Poland, Mr Petrowski? Lee asked, falling into dialect.

— Krakow, Petrowski said.

— When you come to Ireland?

— Ninety-one.

— What you do? What your job?

Petrowski looked at his watch and said, — Kill the fucking pigs.

A pause gripped the little group, a tiny interlude in which the staccato of Mick's camera ceased. Lee said, — What, ah, you mean?

— Kill, kill, Petrowski said impatiently. — The pigs. With a knife, I slit from here to here.

He stabbed at his throat and slashed an imaginary line from his chest to his groin. His wife turned her head and smiled at her husband as if he was one of the apostles. Mick resumed shooting.

— When you know your son was a gifted hurler? Lee asked. — I mean, when you realise that Peader good at hurling?

The Petrowskis exchanged glances. The mother said, — My father, grandfather, my brothers, futball, futball, futball.

— So there's a long history of athletic achievement in the family, good.

— Futball, futball.

Mr Petrowski said, — He mightn't even start Sunday.

— I thought he was on the team.

— On squad.

— That's okay, squad's okay. Tell me, when did you first meet Pope John Paul II? Was it when you were a child in Poland?

— Who?

— The Pope, the late Pope. What was the name of the last Pope, Mick? The one that died?

— John Paul the Second, Mick said.

— His Polish name. It doesn't matter.

Petrowski was looking at his watch again. Lee said, — You met the Pope.

— Him I never meet.

— Oh, I thought…

— Church? Pah! Religion? Pah! Viva Komunista! Komunista!

— But you know Lech Walesa.

— Walesa? cried the man and turned down his mouth and spat in the yard. — Fuck Walesa!

In the doorway the daughter appeared, a king-sized long-filter cigarette in the centre of her mouth. Cocking one hip so that her crotch material was visible, she spun the wheel of a lighter, brought it to the tip and looked straight at Lee through the flame. Blood surged. Yes. But careful, now, the father has a knife.

— Thanks folks, that was nice, have to run, said Mick, unscrewing lenses, unzipping, packing, zipping. — See you, Lee.

The kid reminded him of Betty in the garage stores all those years ago; things were that bad, and yet he'd heard it said that the first time was always the best and never forgotten.

SIX

Albert slipped the Porsche into first, jumped three places ahead in the traffic, then, narrowly avoiding a black family in bright anoraks as they negotiated a pedestrian crossing, squealed in a tight turn across blaring cars and into Foxrock. He was late. It was going on for eight; he had told Medb-Marie he would be home by seven. Normally it would not have mattered, but this evening was not normal. He stood at the last moment on the brakes and the car squatted at traffic lights like a steaming yellow cockroach. Albert's birthday.

Over the last ten days he had tried every trick he knew to lure HUBBI away from Medb-Marie's apartment buildings. His dozens of sites that lay scattered near motorways that Albert had cleared the earth for, those plots and scraps of title destined to become the land on which shopping malls and multi-storey car parks would be built, had all been revalued upwards on his instructions. Their new aggregate worth had almost doubled. HUBBI had been implacable. Albert had instructed his architects to embark on a desperate nationwide assault on the planning offices of city and county councils in an attempt to acquire planning permission for his sprawling land bank, wheat fields and forests, acres of tidy potato drills and cabbages that he had not previously intended to press into service for another decade. But in the meantime HUBBI had become impatient.

Albert accelerated away in a high-pitched whine of German engineering. Not so long ago he had been happy making a million a year shifting muck. And that part of the business was still booming, as the green hills of Ireland slowly gave way to machines owned by Albert and driven by men from countries Albert had never heard of, to whom he paid three euro an hour and housed in mobile homes parked on cutaway bog.

He needed access to the extra cash he thought he had been granted by HUBBI not just to pay his creditors, but to pay HUBBI a hefty interest payment on the main account that was falling due. Twice over the past few days he had tried to call Eric Chester, but had been unable to get through. Fat little robber was in there all right, greasing the wheels of his financial handcart. Albert had then tried to call one of the non-executive directors of HUBBI, a man whom Albert had last seen the previous Christmas in Leopardstown with his hand up the skirt of a Moldavian waitress; he had not returned Albert's call.

He slewed into the gravelled forecourt of his home, stones ricocheting on the Porsche's underbody. He had considered switching all the borrowing for the Goose Point project to another bank, but that would involve months of negotiations without an absolute guarantee of success. Time was against him. He had asked his solicitor to sneak a look at the title to the apartment buildings in order to see if Albert could somehow pledge the properties to HUBBI without Medb-Marie knowing. The solicitor, a man who had long ceased to be surprised by anything Albert asked him, confirmed that, even taking the most liberal view of the laws governing property in Ireland, Medb-Marie's consent would be needed in order to mortgage her flats to a third party. Albert slipped a heavy-duty prescription pill for indigestion under his tongue and got out of his car.

Normally he loved his birthday. His father had taken little Albert to the sea-front amusements on his birthday and they had gone up together in the swing-boats. Although Albert had always felt sick, he still remembered his childhood birthdays with affection. Medb-Marie tried every year to come up with a present that Albert could never have anticipated. Last year it had been the Porsche; the year before she'd given him a ten-year lease on the box in Leopardstown. Three years before it had been his wristwatch, which looked just like a chunky expensive wristwatch except for a little cylinder built in across the front of it. When the cylinder was ejected the watch sent signals to a satellite which in turn radioed Albert's GPS position to a firm in Switzerland, and they sent out a SWAT team to rescue him. He had never told Medb-Marie how he had ejected it one night in Paris when he'd been on the piss with Los Desperados and how he had had to pay a $25,000 fine on the q.t.

He tried to put aside the task that lay ahead of him that evening and to concentrate on his birthday. He was beginning to regret Goose Point, to regret that he had been egged on by banks like HUBBI. At the beginning when they were pitching for his business, every time he appeared in HUBBI he was received like a film star. Cursing Eric Chester, the European Central Bank, rising interest rates, the fickleness of fate, the absence of mercy in his life and the onset of a gigantic migraine, Albert let himself into his house and immediately noticed how quiet it was. Was this ominous? Where was his family? His birthday present? He began to sweat, a messy business.

— Hello! he called out. — Is there anybody here?

His voice bounced around the hall and back to him. Normally at this time, as the twins were being bathed by Christiana, Medb-Marie would be in the den watching a soap and eating Pringles.

— Hey! Albert shouted. — MEDB-MARIE!

The doors to the den were flung open. Albert jumped in fright. Medb-Marie, in a gold cocktail dress, looked like an apparition. Either side of her stood the twins in canary-yellow dressing gowns, and to one side, smiling hugely, sturdy, dependable Christiana. Medb-Marie and the girls stepped forward. Medb-Marie was holding out what looked like a thick catalogue with a white number disc stuck to it. The welcoming group began to sing 'Happy Birthday'.

* * *

Albert watched the waiter decant the vintage port and tried to gauge whether the time was right. He had rehearsed his pitch half a dozen times, shifting the emphasis from what it would mean should Goose Point run out of cash, to Medb-Marie's generosity, and back again. She was generous, but generous with his money. Of course technically it was their money, but it really was his fucking money since he had made it. She had just given him a present of a yearling racehorse which, he had learned, had cost a hundred grand. That was very generous indeed, but it was still his money.

He gave the port the nod and wondered if he should forget the whole project until the morning. She was out in the ladies' room, and had helped him drink two bottles of wine, and had given him a little sexy talk about how he was the most virile man she had ever met, and how he was improving with age. She was fucking wonderful when she was like that, enough to give Albert a military-grade hard-on. That in itself presented a new challenge: to get her consent on the apartments and a ride in the same night. Apartments first, he thought, as Medb-Marie crossed back through the restaurant, and Albert noted the heads that followed her, and how her dress and her hips made the muscles in his rectum contract.

— Wow, you look good, he said.

— Birthday boy, she pouted. — How's the birthday boy's port?

— Nice, Albert said.

Medb-Marie giggled.

— 'Nice'?

— It's not too bad at all.

— I'm sure it's not too bad at all, Albert, said Medb-Marie in the throaty, half-mocking tone she sometimes used to remind Albert that he was a plasterer while she held an honours Leaving Certificate and a diploma in elocution that she had acquired by correspondence course. She leaned across the table so that the valley between her tits was almost beneath his nose. — I'm sure it's bleedin' loverly, she whispered in her cockney accent.

— Not as loverly as you, he said gamely.

She was twiddling with the teaspoon beside her cup of single espresso, and looked up at him with her naughty-girl look. She said,

— You know what?

— Tell me.

— What I'd like for my birthday?

This was good, Albert thought, she wants something, and she's not ashamed to ask for it, even on a night like this.

— I'm all ears, he said. — Go for it.

— You'll think I'm crazy.

— I think you're beautiful.

— Yeah, but you'll think, Jesus, this bitch is really off the wall! Medb-Marie said with an explosion of pent-up self-obsession.

— My little girl? Never.

— Your big bold girl.

— My big bold girl who sometimes takes her knickers off in the car, he whispered.

— Once, she said, I nearly dislocated my back.

They laughed together and the waiter moved in to top up Albert's glass. It was a cosy spot in south central Dublin, and Albert had spent the first ten minutes of the evening doing a round of the other tables, glad-handing self-made men like himself, some of them the subject of government sleaze inquiries. Now that she wanted something, Albert felt a bit like a man with a big fish on the end of a line. He waited. She said, — I'd like a rainforest, Albert.

Albert didn't blink or even turn down the corners of his mouth.

— A rainforest, he repeated. — What for?

— I want to give something back, said Medb-Marie with sudden urgency that made Albert surge with lust. — We have so much; we own so many things, Albert. The world is overheating. I want to have my own rainforest that no one can touch or take off me. I want to climb up into the sky of the leaves, you know, and walk in the rain clouds.

— No problem, love, Albert said and thought: she's pissed. — Where had you in mind?

— You think I'm joking, she said.

— I don't, Albert said as he wondered what kind of timber rainforests were made of, and if they grew in countries that had double-taxation agreements with Ireland. — I think it's a lovely idea, honestly.

— You think I'm a stupid cow.

— If you want a rainforest, I'll get you one, Albert said. — Just tell me what to do.

— I was looking at the maps, said Medb-Marie. — Borneo, Brazil, they have them, but nobody speaks English. Then I saw Australia. Brilliant! I said. We could go there in the jet for holidays and build a house up in the rainforest like the one I saw in *Vogue*.

— I love it, Albert said. — I fucking love it.

— Do you really?

— Fantastic idea!

— You're not having me on?

— I'll make enquiries in the morning, he said.

— Jesus, she said in a long, slow gush of relish. — Whatever you want tonight, birthday boy, you got it.

Fighting back a projected image of his wife's head in his lap, Albert said, — You really mean that?

— Am I not always straight with you, Albert? she whispered.

Her mouth was partially open in a gesture of unrestrained wantonness, which under any other circumstances would have made Albert signal for the bill, abandon the port and get home as fast as possible; but which now, because of what he actually needed from her, was an unwelcome distraction. Albert mumbled, — There is one little thing you can do for me.

— They say the women who live in rainforests still have the skin of 14-year-old girls when they're seventy, Medb-Marie said. — Imagine! I'll stay like this forever, Albert – and all for you!

Albert grinned bravely and wondered again if he should just go for what was on offer and leave the apartments till the morning. He said, — I need to give the bank more collateral.

— Birthday boy, you can have anything, I told you, she said.

— They want the flats.

— I have *Vogue* at home, when we get back I'll show you the pictures, she said.

— Fantastic, he said and his heart thumped the way it had at Leopardstown when the horse had won. — You're a star.

— How many people do you know who own a rainforest? she asked and giggled. — Feck off out of my rainforest!

— You're walking on my rain, bugger off! Albert laughed, although the whole rainforest wheeze was beginning to do his head in. He helped himself to port and said, — It'll only be for a couple of months.

— Can we look at it tomorrow? Medb-Marie asked.

— Of course, Albert said hastily. — We'll go home now. I'll have the whole thing sorted by lunchtime.

Medb-Marie blinked. — I think it'll take more than a morning, Albert, she said. — Australia is a big place.

— I meant the collateral, Albert said with an enormous smile.

— Oh yes, no problem, whatever you want, birthday boy, she said. — What collateral?

Oh Jesus, Albert thought. Oh fuck. He said,

— Like I said, the, ah, bank want a loan of the apartments, darling.

— They can't have a loan of them, Albert, she said in a tone of fond remonstration. — People live there, sweetie.

Albert sank his teeth into his bottom lip. All his swamp instincts told him to back off, to play the rainforest card for all it was worth; and yet, she seemed to be in a place of ultimate pliability, and the bank was pushing. He muttered, — Fucking bank want it for comfort, for a month, maybe less, till we get sales going.

— Sales? she frowned.

— Yeah, down on the site, he mumbled. — You know banks.

Medb-Marie exhaled slowly, like the blood-pressure machine. She said, — I beg your pardon?

— It's completely fucking technical, Albert said.

A pause of two or three terrifying seconds, the kind of eerie time warp in which the universe was created. Medb-Marie's voice, small like a child's, floated across the table, — Please explain this technicality to me, Albert.

Certain words in their relationship were reliable code: just as high wispy clouds heralded a deteriorating weather system, the words 'please' and 'Albert' spoken by Medb-Marie in the same sentence bespoke trouble.

— I'd say four weeks max, Albert battled on. — A complete formality; they'll never exercise it, it's like an insurance policy. Win-win for everyone, actually. What I want to talk about is the rainforest.

Medb-Marie was staring at her husband. She said, — To hell with the rainforest.

— Ah, now, come on… began Albert.

— My apartments? Medb-Marie said. — My… my security? My *lifeline?*

— It's not me, it's the bank… Albert started to say.

— Of course it's you! Medb-Marie shouted. — Who else is it but you? Who's sitting there with a belly-full of drink and steak but you?

— Jesus, will you keep it down, Albert said.

— I… I don't think… I have never in my life been so *fucking* insulted! Medb-Marie yelled.

— Please, listen…

— I don't care who hears this, she gasped. — You have just… just come here, after the most lovely birthday party with your children… and a present that cost a hundred grand… and a dinner that I got a steak flown in from Texas for…

— Forget it, Albert said, forget it.

— And you have brought me here and buttered me up…

— Medb-Marie…

— Buttered me up for no other reason than to get my apartments? Oh, Jesus! To think I believed you when you said you thought the rainforest was a good idea! Oh my God! Oh, oh,

I've never been so betrayed. You horrible, twisted little rat, Albert.

Albert frantically scribbled the air to the head waiter, glugged down his port and stood up. Like a man travelling at the speed of light, he realised that he had now arrived into the dark galaxy of his wife's most evil disposition. Medb-Marie was heaving, on her feet. The white-gloved hands of a waiter trembled as he brought over her coat. She snatched it and walked out the door in queenly, unassailable strides. Albert, reflecting on the immensity of what he had thrown away, including a free run at sex as his crowning birthday present, flung money on the table and followed.

She was half way up the road by the time he caught up.

— Medb-Marie…

— Get away from me, you vermin!

— I want to talk to you! he cried.

— How can I ever trust you again? she spat. — Get away!

Albert, mist clouding his eyes, grabbed his wife's arm and shouted,
— I want to fucking talk to you!

She froze on the pavement, as if both her spiked heels had been set in concrete.

— Did you touch me? she gasped.

Albert stepped in close and pinned her to the railings of a garden. He snarled, — Where do you think all the fucking money comes from?

— You animal! Medb-Marie snarled. — I want the guards! Help!

— Shut up! he roared.

— You've done it now, Albert, she said between breaths. — Now you really 'ave done it!

— I want to talk to you.

— And I want a divorce, she hissed. — I should never have married you. You're common, a lout, uneducated. I want to leave you and bring up my children properly. My father was right.

— Your… *father?*

— He's a saint compared to you, Albert.

— He's a low-life scheming old cunt! Albert cried.

— Jesus, how dare you! I love my father!

— I wonder what he does nowadays when he's drunk without you to help him get his dick out to piss, you silly bitch!

Medb-Marie grinned crazily, like a madwoman enjoying the first few seconds of freefall over a cliff.

— You know *nothing*, Albert. *Nothing!*

Albert sensed a new projectile coming his way and felt his stomach somersault.

— You think I don't know what you got up to last year in Dubai? she asked with a twisted grin. — Don't you?

Plunging, Albert blustered, — Dubai? Got up to? What are you talking about?

— That little honey-arsed maid, said Medb-Marie softly. — I bet you think of her every time you're screwing me, am I right?

— What maid? asked Albert and his mouth hung open moronically.

— The one you paid six hundred to give you the hand job in the bathroom, remember? said Medb-Marie with appalling sweetness. — How could you forget?

Albert was so shocked by the precise nature of this information that all he could do was stammer,

— What... how... what...?

— Because, said Medb-Marie drawing herself up and towering over him, because every afternoon when you were off touting around the racecourse, she came up to the suite and blew me off for nothing! Yes, Albert! For nothing! So that's what I think of when you're fumbling around me like a gorilla in heat. Got it now? Got it?

Albert was assailed by so many conflicting emotions that he momentarily lost radar. News of his wife's lesbian affair with a black maid, which had just been presented as a *quid pro quo* for his own 90-second fling with the same person, opened up simultaneously horrific and wonderfully depraved vistas; side by side with these confused feelings, Albert was outraged to find that he was married to a dyke. He decided that pained dignity was his best immediate response. He said, — Medb-Marie, I have heard nothing you have just said. Nothing will be held against you; you have my word. For my part, I am truly sorry for anything I have done, or for my own shortcomings. Let's forgive each other and move on.

— Yes, I'm moving on, said Medb-Marie and shook herself. — I'm going home now, and if I find you in *my house*, I'm calling the guards. I hope that's clear?

She leaned in so close that he could see the ribs of her gums.

— At least I have my dignity, Albert. Goodbye.

She walked away, the shape of her receding rear-end causing Albert, even at that point, to twitch with abandoned lust. He leaned back against the sharp railings and called out in a plaintive voice, — It's my birthday!

SEVEN

At ten that evening Lee got a call from Eddie who said that an emergency had arisen and that he needed to meet Lee urgently.

— Can we leave it until tomorrow? asked Lee, who was trying to finish his Polish hurling article. — I'm still working on that piece you gave me.

— Listen, Mister Fucking Smart Arse, you think this is a joke? Lee could hear the familiar background sound of clinking glasses and pub talk. — We need to meet tonight.

An end-of-summer watery half-moon hung over Dublin. Lee walked up Leinster Road West, across Harold's Cross Road and entered the pub by the side door. A slight percentage chance – around one per cent – existed that Eddie had in fact something important to say, which left the overwhelming likelihood that the features editor had simply run out of drinking companions. On the other hand, Lee thought as he pushed his way through the busy pub, Eddie, a northsider, was a long way from home this late at night. Too far from home for Lee to take a chance.

He pushed past drinkers ordering double rounds to forestall the coming of the long night, and found Eddie, alone, sitting at a table on which stood half a dozen small empty wine bottles.

— How's it going, Eddie?

— Thank you for turning up, said Eddie drily.

He had arrived in a mental sector that he only seldom reached, Eddie knew, an achievement he had been attracted to since first reading about it thirty-five years ago: drinking himself sober. If only this was the sobriety of the crushing mornings, if only sobriety could be so utterly clear as this, so pellucid, so crisp and precise, with an edge, like good prose. He'd tried reading Joyce but found him too – what was the expression? – self-indulgent. All those pages without paragraph breaks – and anyway, what the fuck was going on? Always came back to the Master in the end, death at noon, bulls, dust, Sangria, the Florida Keys, fish scales glistening on the back of the great man's hands as his fingers swarmed over the Underwood typewriter.

— You're looking well, Lee lied as he put down a pint for himself and two further small white wines for Eddie. His boss was hollow-cheeked, pale, and his eyes constantly changed direction as they patrolled the frontiers of his paranoia.

— Oh, you know the old saying, Eddie said as he wrenched the tops from both bottles. — When the going gets tough…

He yearned for the cool command now at his fingertips to spill over into the everyday of his life. He understood that alcohol was a street in which everyone was affected at the same time, which is why drinking with teetotallers was a bore, they never knew the calm madness he was now immersed in, his ability to see beyond the confines of his present job, to experience the absolute certainty, for the moment, of where he was headed. He poured the bottles into a half-pint glass and gulped from it, like someone just in from a hayfield on a hot summer's day. Sitting back, the wine having hit the spot, he asked with a little swagger, — How's the piece coming?

— Good, good, Lee nodded. — It'll be nicely turned, Eddie, really tasty.

— I'm not surprised, Eddie said. — I mean, it was a nicely turned idea in the first place, don't you think? A nice angle – interesting, you know?

— I know; congratulations.

Eddie revolved his head to dispel accumulated stress and said, — I've always had a nose for a good story, if I may say so myself. Loved ferreting around, you know? Digging deep. And then taking time to turn out the nicely written piece.

— I heard you were second to none, Lee said, but I don't think I ever…

— You're too young to ever have read them, Eddie chuckled like a much-loved uncle. — Far too young! Or you may even have read them but didn't know I'd written them. 'The Fainting Fishermen of Farranfore'? 'Munching Maize in Mandalay'?

Lee made a brave show of trying to recollect.

— I still love that alliteration, Eddie said. — Rolls off the tongue, you know?

— It really does, Eddie; I love it.

— Wrote them a long time ago, of course, before I was promoted, Eddie said. — Before we went tabloid, in every sense. Back then there was money for quality, you know. I think I was given the job because my application letter showed I could write.

— That's interesting, Lee said. — Your job application.

— You see, I think my style was inspired very early on by the novels of Hemingway, Eddie said.

Back to where they had finished recently.

— Hemingway? Really?

— You know, often when I go home, I go up to the spare bedroom with a bottle or two of white wine and knock out a thousand, fifteen hundred words, Eddie said. — It's how he did it. I mean, have you read *For Whom The Bell Tolls*? Jesus, you can smell the whiskey!

Lee felt once again that he was entering a region of Eddie's psyche that was as dangerous as quicksand. Eddie said, — You're a literary man; you understand the torture of it all, eh? The glass of wine, the laptop with the empty screen, the scent of Cuban tobacco, the stench of fear in the bullring, the way fresh blood looks on the cape of a young toreador – you with me?

— Sure, Eddie, sure.

— I'm getting there, oh yes, two years I reckon, four tops, I'll be ready. No one will be prepared for my approach, for my honesty. The great man will be proud.

Lee nodded cautiously as the great man's personality shimmered, ghost-like. Eddie was stretching now, eking out the last hours of warm fantasy before re-immersing himself next day in the impossible task of sexing up the features pages of a testosterone-bankrupt newspaper. He reached across and gripped Lee's forearm.

— In the meantime I live vicariously, he whispered. — Write the piece and make me proud.

As time was called Eddie sprang to the bar and ordered a double round. He returned to the table clutching a brace of pints, with white wine bottles sprouting from his fingers.

— I have, even if I say so myself, always been one step ahead of the game, he said with a curl of his bottom lip as he concentrated on decanting the wine without spillage. — You see, I think we now have an exit strategy.

— We?

— You and me, son.

— Is this what you wanted to talk about? Lee asked.

Eddie nodded slowly, as if overcome by seriousness and wisdom. Lee let his pint slip down and waited for Eddie to elaborate, but all that happened was that Eddie's eyes seemed to become locked on some indeterminate object in the middle distance and for a moment it appeared that he might be asleep.

— Eddie?

— Sssh!

One finger to his lips, Eddie's eyes rolled left and right. Enemies everywhere, you'd think in a pub of labouring men you might be safe, *au contraire*, the cult of the informer never truly died here, Michael Collins played it to the hilt, little men in flat caps with the build of greyhounds, give them tuppence as soon as you'd look at them, miss nothing, loose lips etcetera, like Paris, 1944, the rue de Rivoli, the bar in the Ritz, heaven.

— Eddie?

Eddie looked up in sudden panic.

— What?

— They're closing.

— Christ!

Eddie focused on his watch, checked the almost empty bar again.

— You want me to call you a taxi? Lee asked.

Eddie upended his glass, swung over to the counter and ordered four small bottles of wine to go. A couple of tense minutes elapsed as Lee watched the barman explain with great patience to Eddie that all the small Chardonnay was gone, because Eddie had drunk it, and that he would have to settle for either Sauvignon Blanc or Pinot Grigio. Eddie, truculently, began to threaten an exclusive on the pub in which their short-ordering practices would be exposed; the barman looked appealingly in Lee's direction and Lee said, — Give him the Pinot Grigio, come on Eddie, we have to go.

Muttering, swearing, Eddie filled his pockets with the bottles and headed out into the night; he clipped the door jamb with his shoulder, stumbled, clutched at Lee, swore again and then strode on, all in one perilous movement.

— I'll call you a taxi, Lee said again.

— No taxi! Eddie shouted.

— You've got to go home, Eddie.

Eddie stopped and, breathing heavily, caught Lee's lapel in one hand, his eyes fighting to focus, tomorrow's offering to his electric razor already heavy on his chin.

— Iwantyoutomeetsomeone, Eddie said.

* * *

Kids with smoke streaming out from under their hoods stood on the corners like street traders in Marrakech. Eddie weaved a course by the closed gates of dark Mount Jerome cemetery, blathering about where he wanted his ashes scattered, off a cliff somewhere, Lee couldn't hear where, although he thought the Florida Keys were mentioned. The fuckers aren't going to get their hands on me, Eddie said, although who he was referring to was not explained. Lee linked Eddie into him with a show of fraternity, for if Eddie got killed or maimed by a bus then this whole evening had been wasted. Ever deeper into little streets they thrust with Eddie stopping twice for a piss, once at a flowerpot by a hall door where upstairs a man's head appeared and he shouted down,

— Fuck off outa here or I'll fucking brain yous!

Around a corner Eddie lurched, and up to a door where he pressed the intercom and said,

— Izz me.

There was a click and Eddie, who would have fallen in had Lee not caught him, made a drive for the stairs. A strong smell of cooking mixed with hash grew even stronger the higher they went. At the very top a door blocked the way. Eddie put his fingers to his lips, knocked, then as the door opened, turned around, his face a sudden ghostly white, and vomited down the stairs.

— Jesus Christ, Lee said as a black man appeared. — Sorry about this.

— It's nothing, we'll clean it up, the man said.

Eddie, on his knees, was spewing air and spittle. Lee followed the man into a rambling attic furnished with throws, beanbags and sticks of burning incense. Towards the back, snores poured out through an open door and Lee could see rows of sleeping figures. The man handed Lee a good pile of *Evening Eclipse*s and Lee went out and began to swab up Eddie's puke. Eddie was sitting to one side, gasping. The black man bundled the used newspapers into a refuse sack and then with a mop started to sluice down the stairs. Lee saw that his right arm ended at the elbow.

His name contained lots of Ns and Gs; nothing to worry about, Africa is in love with the consonant, my friend, he said when they sat down eventually. Eddie, in his underwear, a rug on his shoulders, sipped sweet tea. Nicknamed Delicato after a brand of ice cream in his home country because his mama said he was just as sweet. Might as well talk about the elephant in the room, my friend, smiling at his own erudition, holding up his stumpy right arm. The result of a machete that had been aimed for his head in a tribal dispute, so many generations and no resolution, he himself killed three men that day and severely maimed another eight. Shortly afterwards, tourniqueted and sutured, he boarded a bus for Addis, took another from there to Cairo, a journey of eleven days, a boat to Tbilisi and a train to Rotterdam. From there, by way of refrigerated container to Rosslare, Ireland, with eight others, six of whom froze to death en route; he unloaded in Longford, made his way to Dublin, here he is ever since. He left behind a wife, two children, girls, and a dog named Moonshine. He had been in Dublin for two years, turning up six days a week at noon outside Valentine Newspapers to be given his bulk allocation of *Evening Eclipse*s, which he then lugged out to the traffic lights at Kilmainham and sold to home-going motorists whose main interest was the small ads.

He handed Lee a plate and spooned out a meat-free stew of beans and sharply aromatic herbs. Eddie slept. Sitting on beanbags, Lee and Delicato ate sticky white rice with their fingers from little bowls. Although missing half of one arm, Delicato was a strikingly built, tall athletic man with gleaming coffee-bean skin and enormous eyes.

He had made certain observations during his time in the Irish newspaper business. Mondays and Tuesdays were slow days. People only started buying the evening paper on Wednesdays to read the ads for the weekends. For cars and flats, sure, but also men looking for women, men looking for men, women looking for men. Lonely people. Where he came from, who you live with was settled by your parents when you were born, but here it was settled by an ad in the *Eclipse*.

Delicato put down his empty plate and began to roll a long, fat spliff. Used his mouth and left hand to seal the joint, an action he performed with ease. Sucked down the smoke, leaned back and allowed his eyes to roll up into his head. Think of what the money he earns here means in the home country where a man works a week to earn a bag of maize. Think. It makes you cry if you think too much. A hundred brothers here, a thousand, all in the same position, their wives at home, their kids, waiting, waiting for the tiny remittances. He sits up here in this attic when it's cold and he sees his village in his head, his wife and girls, Moonshine.

Lee took the joint and drew deeply; not to have done so would have been to show disrespect.

Delicato thinks about the fire in their kitchen at home that never goes out, burning with the wood of a dead Acacia tree, and about his mother, hair like snow, and his father drinking beer outside behind the row of chickpeas. Every hundred *Eclipse*s sold means another week of food for them. Think of the loose riches that jangle around in the pockets of unthinking men in Dublin. Think!

— Sometimes the sorrow come down on me like a pure waterfall, pounding my head, taking me over. That's why I like my buddy here in my lungs.

The big spliff burned without hurry as, beyond Eddie's steady reverberations, Dublin settled down for the night.

The magnificent tragedy of Delicato's story inspired Lee in a way that was exciting and attainable. He was now asking Lee about where he wanted to go in life, about how Lee had, up to then, failed to fulfil his own ambitions. Lee was floating at speed into a cocoon of sweet sugar floss and a cosy-tongued life beyond the picket fence that would last forever. Delicato's words swarmed in little flocks, like butterflies. Time was bending.

— Last night I am in a canoe with Moonshine and we are going home. So peaceful. The water, the blue sky, the hot sun. I am happy, laughing. Moonshine is licking the back of my neck and for a joke I flick water at him with the paddle. I let the river current take us round the bend of the river. We come around and suddenly the river is gone, the water is gone, and all that is there is road, hard cold road like I sell the papers on. Oh, man.

Delicato's eyes slid like flies in amber into the very rims of his sockets. Lee blurted out,

— I want to write a novel about love. About…

He stopped, because all of a sudden the word he wanted had vanished, gone. Like gossamer, like… He sat, stoned, gazing on the toe of his shoe. He was convinced that he could hear the minute workings of Delicato's inner organs: heart, kidneys, intestines. His own brain was churning smoothly, like a tumble dryer. He cried out, — Life! I want to write about all the shitty things that come between a man and love. I want to scald the page with my words. People will gasp.

— That's good, that's good, Delicato said.

Lee took another pull and handed back the spliff. The dope had licked his legs into wet putty. Big lungs; he could once swim the whole length of a pool underwater. When? He said, — Trouble is, what story have I got to tell? I own nothing except a few dreams rattling around…

— You have your life. We both have.

— My life is empty. It began well, but it ended about five years ago.

— Write about that.

— My business went bust, my wife left me. She was a bitch.

— You got to get her out of your head.

— How?

— Write her out. Get it all out of your head and onto paper. I sit down to write and sometimes the whole of Africa spills out of me, Delicato said.

— That's fantastic.

— You wouldn't believe it. I can smell the dung of elephants, man.

— Jesus.

— You can do it, Lee. Tell your story.

— I have no story. Sometimes I think I am dead.

— Yeah, I know that feeling. The living dead. People look right through me. Like I is a ghost. Why do they do that?

— They're scared of us, of our potential.

— You think so?

— I'm certain of it. Which is why we waft through life, you and me. Two phantoms, Lee said.

Delicato frowned.

— Phantoms?

— Another word for ghosts. Imagine a white sheet with eyes.

Delicato stared at him open-mouthed for a second. He said, — Niggers' ghosts are black, man.

— Are you serious?

Delicato's shoulders began to go up and down as he started to laugh in high-pitched squeaks. He'd pulled Lee's trigger too, and soon both of them were shuddering away on the beanbags unable to stop, in Lee's case not even sure if it was all that funny, but it didn't matter, they were rolling. All of a sudden he sat up, cold and drained, the lower region of his ribcage aching. Eddie was standing over them, glowering.

— Where are my fucking clothes?

* * *

Wednesday was a busy day for the *Sunday Trumpet*'s features department. On Wednesdays the features section of the paper was sent electronically to a printing works in an outlying industrial gulag; the deadline was three o'clock on Wednesday afternoon. By noon every cubicle was occupied by hunched bodies doing last-minute spell-checks on gardening tips, medical diagnoses, lonely hearts letters – ninety-eight per cent of which were written in-house – chess moves, bridge hands and motoring notes. No one was sure who, if anyone, read these items.

Lee looked up from his keyboard and out the window over the north inner city. The weather had turned sharp and windy and the features department, which only a week before had been stiflingly hot, was now uncomfortably cool. This part of Dublin was never intended to be looked down on in the way which the Valentine building had made possible. In place of the neat rows of well-cultivated back gardens that one always assumed lay behind these prim northside houses, and that may even once have done so, now each rectangle was defaced by rusting car shells, discarded computer monitors, abandoned baths or piles of black refuse sacks stacked in rotting mountains and in many cases torn open by birds or rats.

The garage that Lee's father had built up from scratch into a thriving Austin dealership and then bequeathed to Lee was no more than half a mile from where Lee now sat. He wondered, even as someone whose ambition it had always been to write a novel, if he could ever have imagined the way his life had finally turned out.

He walked to the water cooler between the main door and a window. Looking down he could see the luminous yellow safety vests of the swarms of paper vendors. Delicato was down there somewhere. Lee shuddered. The hash had locked part of his thinking process away beyond his reach. He'd done his best with the hurling piece but he doubted Eddie would notice one way or another.

A cautious levity of spirit was palpable throughout the Valentine building. Valentine Newspapers had just announced its interim results: profits for the half year had held their own, although Lee had heard the *Trumpet*'s financial correspondent tell the man who updated the obituaries that the profit had been achieved only by the revaluation of the group's properties. Notwithstanding this detail, the Chief had received an annual remuneration package of fees, salary, share options and other emoluments amounting to €6.35 million. The *Daily Gael* was going big on its next day's front page with a photograph of the Chief perusing the results, smiling coyly, as if somewhat surprised to be so fortunate. Nothing in the story alluded to the circulation of the group's newspapers which, according to rival sources, was in evacuation mode. However, not even the word that a major two-page colour spread for geriatric furniture had just been pulled from next Sunday's *Trumpet* had failed to dampen spirits. At eleven-thirty, on his way upstairs to the editorial conference, Eddie had stopped by Lee's cubicle.

— Not interrupting some quality literary thoughts, am I?

Eddie hooked in a nearby chair and sat, heels out, hands behind his head, functioning. It was impossible to understand how he did it.

— Interesting evening, don't you think?

— Sure, Eddie, very interesting.

— I mean, he's not just a black man who sells newspapers, Eddie said. — He's an accomplished poet, as I'm sure I told you, and he also has ambitions to start his own newspaper.

— That I didn't know.

— I may have nodded off last night, Eddie said. — These fifteen-hour days. No, he's asked my advice on the editorial side, you know, strictly between us of course; mum's the word. He has the sales side tied up; oh yes, couple of dozen of his mates, if they only got fifty cents for selling each copy of their own paper, think how much more that would mean to them than the miserable percentage they earn from the people in here. This is going to be huge.

Lee had read about the creeping effects of alcoholic dementia, about how people appeared to be completely sane yet spoke utter gibberish.

— You're… going to work for *him?*

— I'll be a consultant, said Eddie blithely and got to his feet. — Fresh start, you know. Elevate the ordinary and all that. By the way, I look forward to your piece.

— It's slightly different to the way we planned it, Lee said.

— Let the writing carry it through, Eddie said with a confidence-boosting smile. — How do you think the Impressionists started? Hemingway adored van Gogh, you know? Adored him.

Lee spent the next hour trying to elevate the ordinary. It might not have been vintage Lee Carew, but it wasn't bad either, he thought. He was sure it passed what he now liked to think of as the Mrs Joe N. Lan test. He pressed the 'send' key on his computer and made his way out for an early lunch.

* * *

Working his teeth into a mixture of fish paste, margarine and white bread, Lee stood across the road from the Valentine building and thumbed through a discarded copy of that day's *Eclipse*. Sometimes an *Eclipse* story could be pumped up into a full-size feature for the *Sunday Trumpet*. That day's front page had gone big with the story of two Chinese chefs who fell out over the ownership of a wok and stabbed each other to death with boning knives. Page 3 had a picture of a pretty girl who, Lee knew for a fact, Mick the Pic was seeing on the side. Page 5 dealt with a gardener who slept with rabbits; page 7 led with a child of nine whose mother wanted him to run in the next general election. The editorial urged that the seats on Dublin buses be re-upholstered.

He threw the paper in a rubbish bin and walked the short distance to a nearby health-food shop. Des needed whale-oil tonic to keep his coat shining and Lee could buy it in here for a fraction of its cost in a high-street store. The turbaned gentleman behind the counter enquired as he handed over the bottle, — And how is the little fellow these days indeed?

— He's well, thank you.

— And you, sir, too?

— I am well also, thank you for asking.

As he pocketed the tonic and headed back to work, it put a spring in Lee's step to think that decent people who were concerned for the well-being of the likes of himself and Des existed beyond the clutches of Valentine Newspapers.

As soon as he reached the door to the features department he could see that in forty-five minutes everything had changed. Eddie was sitting, head thrown back, as if preparing to enter an orbit beyond stress. As Lee watched, Eddie rose from his desk and, pinching his eyes together with thumb and forefinger, stood there, face to heaven. This behaviour of Eddie's on Wednesdays coincided, it was generally accepted, with the arrival in Eddie's computer of a feature piece from another computer on the floor. Because the deadline was looming, Eddie knew there was little time for the piece he had just received to be rewritten. His dismay at what he had just read was, in microcosm, the dismay that over 150,000 readers would experience the following Sunday as they slogged through their *Trumpet*s.

Lee crept to his cubicle. He was pretty sure that he could not be the author of the offending piece – for one thing, he'd taken a lot of trouble to bring out the human interest in the story; for another, he'd filed the piece well over an hour ago and Eddie was now clearly reacting to something he'd only just read.

From the corner of his eye Lee saw Eddie leap like a wired-up torture victim, breathe heavily four or five times, then wheel around and walk straight for him. It was bad luck sitting where Lee did. Food, wine and travel were hidden at the other side of Eddie's partition and he never went near them.

— Lee.

Eddie was using a conciliatory tone. This was bad news, for it indicated a level of desperation.

— Eddie.

— Lee.

Eddie grabbed a chair, sat down heavily and did his pinching thing to the inner corners of his eyes. Sweat was running down one side of his face and continuing in a luminous track over his throat stubble and on downwards until it was swallowed by the collar of his shirt. Eddie said, — How are you?

— I'm good, Eddie, how are you?

— Oh, you know, when the going gets tough, the tough get going, Eddie said.

Lee sneaked a look over Eddie's head and saw some figures tiptoeing from the area. Eddie standing and pinching was one thing; Eddie actually sitting at someone else's cubicle at this time on a Wednesday afternoon was something else altogether. Eddie said, — I try to walk half a mile every day, you know?

— Really?

— My doctor, she's a woman, an attractive woman actually, she says that walking half a mile every day in the fresh air will help lower my stress levels, Eddie said.

— Makes sense.

— Problem is, on the days I don't get to walk the half a mile, and today looks like being such a day, I get even more stressed because I can't fucking walk half a mile in the fresh air.

The day's lost walk hovered for several seconds, until Eddie sighed deeply and said, — I've read your piece on the Petrowski family.

— Good, good.

— Mick's pic is really brilliant; I'm going big with it, Eddie said. — It's a great pic.

In every person, no matter how dire the situation, hope still flickers, even if remotely. Lee said, — Yes, it is a really great pic.

Eddie's whole face gathered itself in a superhuman effort to be calm. He said, — I want to talk to you about your copy, Lee.

— No problem.

— You remember the headline I had in mind? The suck-in factor that I based the whole idea for the piece on? Eddie asked.

— Yes. 'John Paul II Family Friend is Dublin's Saviour'. But…

— So you see, Eddie snapped but still managed to smile, so you see what I was trying to do, don't you?

— I…

— I wanted to put the Pope in goal for Dublin, Lee. Does that make sense to you? I'm not talking literally, of course, because we both know, everyone knows, that Pope John Paul II is dead, and even were he alive, hurling probably wouldn't be his game, Eddie said.

— Nor would he play for Dublin, Lee said, a wisecrack that he instantly regretted.

— What I'm trying to get across to you is a concept that newspapers use the whole time, Eddie said in a raised voice. — Advertisers too. It's the association of ideas. I wanted a kaleidoscope of ideas to surround Mick's brilliant pic so that our readers get this strong subliminal idea that the Dublin minor hurling team has the deceased pope playing for it as an extra man. Get it?

Lee had described these moments to Gwen Forbes and she had urged him to be strong, to calmly realise that it was he who was the sane one at such times. Eddie said, — You've sent me a story about a man who kills pigs for a living.

— Yes.

— The Dublin minor hurling team gets one line in paragraph sixteen, Eddie said.

— I rang the team this morning, Lee said. — The kid has been dropped from the squad.

— But he *was* on the team! Eddie cried.

— He never started one match, Lee replied. — I spoke with the team manager and he told me in so many words that Peader Petrowski is shit.

— That's why he needs the Pope on his side! Eddie shouted. — You think anyone wants to read a story about a day in the life of a communist Polish pig sticker? What kaleidoscope of ideas rush into the reader's head when they read your piece? Come on! Tell me!

— I don't know, Eddie. Pork? The Holocaust? I don't know.

— Oh Jesus, Eddie said and looked straight up at the bank of lights in the ceiling. — Oh sweet holy Jesus, son of God.

— And there is no connection between the Petrowskis and either the late Pope or Lech Walesa, Lee said.

— Listen, you, said Eddie and there was white stuff on his mouth as he rolled his chair nearer to Lee. — Here's the fucking story and you'll write it in the next fifteen minutes. Are we on message? There's this Polish family in Phibsboro called the Petrowskis. Lovely, warm, likeable people, we have a photograph to prove it. Look at them: they're deeply in love. They have a son, Peader, born in Ireland, the only person in the whole fucking country with the name Peader Petrowski. Peader plays hurling. He's no D.J. Carey, not yet, we accept that, but he's trying. He's training with the Dublin minor hurling team. His mother adores him – look at the way she's looking at his picture. His father is proud too – but how can he help his son get on the team? I'll tell you how. Every night he has a chat with his old buddy upstairs, John Paul II.

— Mr Petrowski is not religious, Eddie, Lee whispered.

— Then why is he holding onto a fucking photograph of the Pope? Eddie screamed.

— Because we gave it to him.

Eddie hyperventilated for a few seconds, then said, — He would not have taken an image of the Pope and been photographed holding it if he did not have some little bit of religion. Are you denying him the right to be slightly religious? I hope not. Now rewrite the story without using the word pig – *capiche?* And then…

Eddie suddenly looked defeated.

— … and then go downstairs, Lee. Human Resources want a word.

PART TWO

THREE MONTHS LATER—September 2006

EIGHT

On Upper Baggot Street, cruising past Searsons Pub, his hunting ground of former days, over the pedestrian crossing at Waterloo Road along whose leafy paths he had often stumbled home brimming with drink, Albert felt in the zone. The day was warm enough to have the roof down and U2 were belting out a song from *Achtung Baby*, an album that reminded him both of an affair he'd had with a formidable female bank manager and the fall of the Berlin Wall, events forever entwined in his cerebral cortex. The water-cooled, turbo-charged speed-yellow 911 throbbed at the lights at Baggot Street Bridge as a Mini driven by a young raven-haired woman pulled level and she looked across at him and smiled. He gave her his most raffish wink then, without missing a beat, as the lights turned green, left her fifty yards behind in less than three-point-eight seconds.

It was going to be okay. *It's going to be okay!* he roared out into Dublin 2 as he took the corner into Pembroke Street on the tilt and felt the pounding music and his blood become one. Medb-Marie had changed her tune, by Christ she had! She'd consented to the bank taking out a mortgage on the two blocks of apartments. The deal was done, the papers were signed. She was a proud woman and he'd just got her at the wrong moment, given her too much drink and then failed to spot the danger signs.

He was back in his house too – his house! – and although sleeping in the guest bedroom, he was sure that the old ground was re-forming so rapidly between them that he'd be right back in the nest by Saturday. She had never looked better either, a prize whose image he had manfully clung to through the long, lonely nights in the stable block. He turned right into Leeson Street.

At the same time, it was difficult to get everything right. The previous week, even then still out in the stables, he'd sent her a three-hundred-euro bouquet of white roses for her birthday.

Happy Birthday to the Most Beautiful Wife in the World.

Medb-Marie had sent out Christiana, the au pair, with instructions to the gardener to burn the flowers on the lawn.

But now he was back and he was well. His cardiovascular system felt as pure as a whale's, he was urinating without inhibition, he was eating properly and sleeping soundly, and that morning, although this was not something he could share with anyone, he had enjoyed a bowel movement of such epic size and duration that, five minutes after it had ended, he was still sitting on the bowl, glassy-eyed.

There had been a small problem. A week earlier at the most inland end of the Goose Point site, more sea water had appeared, twenty-four hours before concrete was due to be poured. More like a puddle than a flood, although it hadn't rained for a week, which is how it was spotted. It was nothing, really. In fact it was a good thing, yes, because imagine the problems if they'd poured concrete on top of seawater. The Dutchmen had flown in again – Albert had sent the jet for them – and were drawing up a report. Informally, however, they said that this now proved that the entire site was reclaimed land, and that further buttressing would be needed on the inland end. Not nearly as much as before, but still. Just a little more buttressing, *ja?*

Albert had immediately began to suffer double vision, chest pains, single incontinence and severe backache. He called his architect, who had drawn his attention to the problem in the first place. Albert hated architects, despised their namby-pamby farting around, their long hair, their precious attitude to what was just bricks and mortar. This one now informed him that further buttressing to stop the flooding would require further planning permission. Albert had had a fit. He let fly with a string of richly embellished insults and threatened legal action if the architect persisted in his view. The architect responded with his own surprisingly extensive repertoire of salty invective, cited his legal obligations under the new planning acts and threatened to go public unless Albert saw sense.

Albert, hysterical, called Kevin.

— This is a fucking disaster! he screamed. — This is your fucking retirement nest-egg that's going down here!

But Kevin, twice defeated in general elections, three times victorious, was used to presiding over disasters on a national scale. He calmed Albert down.

— It'll be grand, grand, the Minister for Infrastructure Development said. — I'll come around straight away.

Over a meeting with Albert and the architect, Kevin drew heart from the fact that the new buttresses would be only half the size of the ones at the sea end of the development, and that the new permission sought would simply reinforce the permissions already in place. It would take a month or two at the outside, Kevin soothed. It would all be grand.

* * *

From habit he parked on St Stephen's Green. More than twenty years before Albert had made the mistake of parking in the private car park of a bank for a meeting that had not gone well – and had returned to the basement to find that the bastards had seized his car. Those days were long gone, but Albert had never again used an indoor car park. Call it a luck thing, superstition, whatever – and today of all days, luck would be important.

Moreover, he had come to savour his walks through the Green, the ten-minute top-up to his facial tan when the weather permitted, the chance to see students on the benches with their hands down each other's pants, the opportunity to inhale the scents from the musky flowerbeds. Some days, like today, he had the urge to run around all the benches and lawns handing out fifty-euro notes to everyone he met: God, look at what that crazy, happy guy just gave me! Albert would skip lightly onwards, anonymously, a sort of Santa Claus, but dressed in a two-grand suit. No one would ever guess that this simple giver was a man on his way to the launch of a real-estate development that would make him a billionaire.

Albert nodded pleasantly to a pair of strolling nuns.

— Good morning, sisters!

Their pinched faces flowered into smiles and Albert took the next few paces on air. He'd even put aside his dislike of HUBBI for the moment. Did anyone on God's earth need to be told that bankers were cunts? The little fucker that presided over collateral, with whom Albert had been forced to sit down and negotiate on Medb-Marie's flats, had threatened to put the whole deal back to square one unless Medb-Marie signed over the deeds. It was shameful, all the more so since Albert hadn't seen it coming.

He shimmied across the bridge on the Green and took a left so that he could walk past the ducks. And yet HUBBI had agreed to roll up interest for twelve months, *plus* the Dutch engineering firm had given him an absolute assurance: building could commence in six weeks. Albert warbled at the floating ducks and they looked up at him shyly. With cash flowing again from HUBBI, creditors had stopped phoning, steel and concrete were being delivered on site, sandwiches were once more arriving.

Albert's chest filled with pride as he left the Green. The launch that evening would be the biggest, the most elaborate and by far the most exciting property event ever to have taken place in Dublin. Goose Point Wonderland was the new moniker that he'd okayed just twenty-four hours before. Sixty barges of Welsh sand would be brought in on finalisation to make a beach on site within the complex, a proper beach with a lifeguard on duty and no tide, unlike the wind-scalded strand at the other side of the road. For the launch he'd hired a dozen women from a model agency, crackers, to mingle in bikinis with the guests, emphasising what Albert liked to think of as the Dubai connection. And here was the really funny thing – he'd hired a dozen men and women from a theatrical agency to sleep in tents that he'd erected outside his company's sales office, but when he went down the morning before to check out that they were in place, he found upwards of a hundred people camping out there with them. Of their own accord! He'd sent word for the agency people to get lost since they were charging him time-and-a-half to arrange overnight camping – then he'd laughed himself sick. Success could be such a funny business.

The auctioneering firm appointed to sell the flats had proposed a three-for-two offer available for two weeks only; Albert had instructed them to go ahead, but with one proviso: the guideline price for each flat was to be raised by 15 per cent. He calculated that since his in-built profit was understated by 20 per cent anyway, when it came to actually building the flats he could save a further 15 per cent by skimping on such specifications as the depth of foundations, the quality of concrete and steel used in construction, the finishes to doors and floors and the calibre of fire-escapes. When he added in the fact that he hadn't the slightest intention in the world of completing the arboretum, children's playground, miniature zoo, sculpture garden and 'rose wilderness' that formed part of the planning permission and whose cost had gone into arriving at the asking price of the flats, he reckoned he could give away three-and-a-half fucking flats for the price of two and still come out with a healthy profit.

The porter at the Westbury greeted him by name and held the door. Albert was dressed in what Medb-Marie had once called his fuck-them-sideways ensemble: a very light charcoal double-breasted suit and a cream shirt with a full collar and luxurious French cuffs that Medb-Marie had had made up for him in Paris. The cufflinks, small, square, gold and discreet, were in fact miniature timepieces, each face of them revealing the time in a different part of the world. Albert's tie, a brilliant series of green and gold daubs, had been acquired by Medb-Marie from an Indian huckster in Abu Dhabi two years before. They'd gone to mark their wedding anniversary, for which Albert had presented Medb-Marie with a gold neck band that had set him back twenty-three grand wholesale.

He stood in the lobby and watched, glowing, as four men carried a giant sign up to the mezzanine. Against a background of gold, its green, dancing letters read:

GOOSE POINT WONDERLAND!

NINE

An old stone building was used to house four lawnmowers, including a twenty-horsepower, oil-pressurised Briggs & Stratton ride-on with automatic discharge box and a Suffolk Punch cylinder mower with a seventeen-inch blade that Lee's employer insisted he use to cut the croquet lawn. Not that he'd seen anyone playing croquet in the weeks he'd been working here. His employer came out every morning to have a look at what he had done the day before and to give him fresh instructions.

He took off his shirt and hung it on the door of the potting shed, a cosy place redolent of creosote, compost, ancient apples and grass cuttings. The day was warm and pleasant, a little jewel smuggled from summer into the end of September. If he'd been down in Valentine Newspapers he'd have been baked alive by now, dehydrated, hung over, anxious about a deadline, torturing his imagination for story ideas, dreading the appearance of Eddie, worrying about Des, the rent, money, drink. Seven weeks since he'd touched a drop. Clean. Woke up every morning feeling so well that he wanted to celebrate by having a drink, which was the sole problem associated with his new regime. He'd grown a beard to save money and lost his belly flab. Felt the way he had when he was eighteen, could see the tone on his muscles again. More time to think, too: of life, the past, the writing he wanted to do, which he would do soon for sure, and the love he might one day find.

He liked the work here, it was peaceful and easygoing, even when it rained. He'd been lucky. He'd seen the small ad in the *Eclipse* quite by chance. He'd phoned straight away then got a bus out to Foxrock and lied to her about his gardening experience. Not all lies, actually. He had cast his mind back to the days when he had lived in a house with a garden nearly this big, and had scuffled beds for Mum during one whole summer.

She had interviewed him in the walled garden between the raspberry canes and gooseberry bushes. She was dressed in a tank top that rode up over her trim stomach, tight white shorts and flip-flops. Even as he had spoofed about seedbeds and under-pruning, Lee found it hard to breathe when she was standing beside him; found it impossible to look at her in case she thought he was giving her the eye. He thought he recognised her, from where he didn't know. She was probably a film star or a singer or a model. Dublin was full of them.

— Can you?

— Sorry?

If he had been drooling she didn't seem to mind, for women who looked as good as this were used to men drooling.

— Hello? Earth to gardener. Can you start immediately by cutting the croquet lawn? she repeated sharply. — Use the cylinder mower.

— Tomorrow? Lee asked.

— Now, she said and began to walk away.

— I'm Lee, he called after her.

She had shrugged and kept going.

He had been afraid at the outset to ask her name, afraid to do anything that might upset the cash he needed. He paused at his work on a salad bed and wondered again if what had happened to him in Valentine Newspapers might not have been all for the best. The Polish au pair and the little girls here were friendly, and when the missus, as his employer was referred to, was absent, the au pair let him have a cup of tea. Lee had started to bring Des with him and the girls loved Des, especially when he did his begging trick, up on his hind legs. However, a few days after Lee started, your man who lived in the stables came by, glowering as usual, and saw Des.

— Who owns that fucking dog? he asked.

— I do, Lee replied and tried to smile.

— I saw it pissing up against the wheel of my car earlier. They're alloy wheels and the tyres cost more than you earn every month.

— I'm sorry.

— Yeah, so am I. D'you know how much acid there is in dog piss?

Hello, Lee wanted to say, car wheels are to dogs what telephones are to women: they can't resist the urge to communicate. And I'm sure that Des isn't the only dog to have used your garish wheels to broadcast his message to the world, and if you can give me one instance in history where a car wheel has had to be replaced because of a dog lifting its leg against it, then I'll take my hat off to you.

— I'm very, very sorry, Lee said, it won't happen again.

— It wouldn't fucking want to, the man said as he got into his Porsche and tore out the gateway.

Up to that moment Lee had thought your man was just a tenant to whom the missus had rented the stables, but in that brief encounter a sense of the proprietorial, not to mention the sinister, had come to the fore, and Lee began to discern the true outline of the household in whose garden he was employed.

He worked out some lettuce plants that were too close together and started a new row. A somnolent buzzing filled the afternoon, the glad sound of nature at work. He had wanted time off from the paper to write his novel and now he had it; however he had not yet succeeded in writing anything, since the old problem about what he would write, the problem that had been identified by Gwen Forbes, remained. He knew he should have called up Gwen and formally cancelled his sessions, but he had lacked the courage to do so. That would have meant telling her he had been fired, and for some reason he did not want her to know that. He missed their weekly encounters, and some nights as he went to sleep, he did so with an image of her slim brown ankles and the little pink collars of sock that sometimes adorned them.

Eddie England had called late at night on two occasions from a wine bar near Valentine Newspapers. Each time, Eddie had ranted on about the soullessness of the people he worked for, and about how the talents of the likes of himself and Lee were being smothered by Philistines. Another world. Sometimes Eddie appeared to have forgotten that Lee no longer worked for the *Trumpet* and went on about ideas he wanted to discuss: dogs in Somalia, the unusual vocabulary of some Norwegian budgerigars, work it up into a distinguished, well-written piece, with pics, make it stand out from the crowd, people will read it twice, talk about it, what do you think?

It was five o'clock when Lee put away the tools and rinsed his hands under the garden tap. The water was warm. He cupped it to his face and splashed his neck, shoulders and bare chest. He suddenly did not want to go back to Rathmines and spend the evening sitting in his cramped room, feeling guilty about not taking Des for a walk. Twenty-five minutes east of where he now stood was the long and wide foreshore of Sandymount, where as a boy his nanny had brought him to fly a kite. He realised that it had been ages since he'd walked beside the sea. When had he last had a swim? He couldn't remember.

— Come on, Des, he said as he closed the shed door and put his shirt on. Des clung to Lee's heel as he made his way out to the bus stop.

* * *

He had walked out nearly as far as the sea on Sandymount Strand before he remembered that this was where he had heard the voice in his head. The strand was a vast place at low tide; the houses back on the shoreline looked tiny and indistinct. *Come back!* Somehow, now that he was out here, he didn't feel nearly as bad about the voice as he had when he told Gwen about it, nor as sad.

Through the ozone-laden, heat-warped air that lay across the plain of wet sand, strolling couples held hands, or lone joggers jogged, or little family bunches squatted down around autumnal sandcastles. As he took his shirt and shoes off and waded into the warm tide, Des ran on ahead and a cloud of oystercatchers rose lazily, then landed fifty metres further on.

He whistled Des over and patted the terrier's head. He had felt all along that the voice calling 'Come back!' was his mother's, but he'd not told Gwen that. Nor had he told her, although he had wanted to, that he heard Mum's voice almost every day, and most clearly when he heard his own heartbeat.

He looked back to shore and wondered if it really was Mum's voice he had heard. Sometimes Mum seemed so real that he could swear she was in the room with him. On the other hand Mum, soft-spoken and gentle, had seldom raised her voice. Who else could it have been? His father, clearly, had to be a contender. The only person other than nannies, mechanics, tradesmen and gardeners who ever visited their house regularly was Uncle Dickie, Dad's brother. Every evening Uncle Dickie walked out of town to Lee's house in Ballsbridge. If Dad wasn't home yet, Mum made pink gins and she and Uncle Dickie sat in the conservatory where Lee could hear them chatting and laughing softly.

Lee walked south on the wide beach, the sun slanting as it made its way across the city. The image of his employer kept reappearing in his sex-parched mind, although Lee realised that the gulf between them was unbridgeable. Her name was Medb-Marie Barr and she was married to Albert Barr, a property developer, according to the gardener of the adjoining property, who had skived over to the fence the week before on the pretext of asking for a light. New money, said the neighbouring employee with a sniff of distaste. Prematurely old from weather and cigarettes, he told Lee that even from five doors down the Barrs could often be heard yelling at one another.

— They're not used to all this, you see, he said by way of explanation, adding, before he sloped away, I'd say she's some ride though.

That must be why Albert lived in the stables, Lee reckoned, they'd had a big row. Maybe he should write about it: a beautiful woman, living on her own in a multi-million-euro house in County Dublin's best postal district, rows with her husband, throws him out and falls in love with the gardener. This gardener is a handsome, muscular, bearded young man with a chaste girlfriend who works as a part-time counter assistant in Dunnes Stores. One day, on the pretext of helping him pick broad beans, the gardener's employer leans over as they are hidden from view by the gangly rows of verdure and sinks her tongue into his ear. The young gardener turns and stares at his employer; a moment later they are lying amid the beans, kissing passionately. The gardener yanks down the top of his employer's white T-shirt and one of her magnificent breasts suddenly presents itself, Cyclops-like, to his eager lips.

Lee closed his eyes and, rooted to the spot, inhaled ozone. The gardener and his beautiful employer make love on afternoons in the potting shed, lying on an ancient rubber Lilo. She cannot get enough of him; a mutual feeling. They are both young, fit and energetic: more than once, as rakes and shovels fall on their entwined, uncaring bodies, he wonders if she is double-jointed. The beautiful woman becomes obsessed with these encounters, during which she begs the fine-chested youth to perform acts on her which he has not even fantasised about during twelve months of courtship and dry rides with his Dunnes Stores sweetheart. But one afternoon on the sweat-soaked Lilo, as the gardener has achieved an almost unbelievable level of penetration and his employer is shouting her head off for him to keep going, the sound of the wheels of a Porsche 911 on the gravel shatter the afternoon.

— Lee? It is you, isn't it? Lee?

He swirled down from the delicious heights of his imagination into the cooling evening of Sandymount Strand. A small-sized woman wearing sunglasses, her hair tied up in a scarf and dressed in a sweat-stained T-shirt, shorts and jogging shoes was standing three feet from him. She repeated, — It's you, Lee, isn't it?

He narrowed his eyes. — Gwen? I, ah, I was miles away, Lee said. — What are you doing here?

— Running, of course, she said and smiled at him appreciatively. — You look well, Lee.

— So, ah, so do you, Gwen, he said and noted her customary ankle-socks and the healthy brownness of her supple knees.

— I like the beard.

— Thanks.

Des bounded up and sat on his tail, paws aloft for Gwen.

— Ah, he's lovely; I used to see him in my porch, Gwen said and stroked Des's ears. — When you used to come to our sessions.

He could hear no hint of recrimination for his abandoned sessions in her voice.

— Sorry, but they sacked me. I work as a gardener now.

— I'm really sorry too, Gwen said with a small, pained grimace. Then, — But maybe it's all for the best.

— You know, I was just thinking the same thing. I like the work; no one shouts at me. I've time to think.

— That's wonderful; I'm glad, Gwen said. She added, — You're enjoying life again; I can see that.

He felt that she was taking in his chest in a way that her husband who drove the Lexus would not approve of. He put on his shirt. Now his heart thudded to a different storyline, a story in which the hero, a gardener, is walking beside the sea and saves a pretty psychologist from drowning, drives her home in her car and invites her out to dinner the following week when her husband is on business in Paraguay. Gwen, still smiling, was saying, — Which way are you two going?

— Towards Merrion Gates, he said. — Towards home.

— Let's all walk this way, she said. — I'm parked near Irishtown; I'll drive you home.

As they walked, he could glance down every so often and see the very lickable peachy fuzz of her neck. To their right the red and white chimneys of the Pigeon House stood out vividly and through the lingering haze and wheeling seagulls the funnels of freighters slipping into Dublin Port could be seen. He flung a piece of driftwood for Des who scampered after it, yapping, then snatched it up with a growl and tossed it violently from side to side as if it were a rat.

— He's a character! Gwen said.

— Des, you remember Gwen, don't you?

Des made a throaty, friendly gurgle.

— I love dogs, Gwen said.

— Where's yours?

— I don't have one, not at the moment, she said. — My place is too small and there's a clause in my lease saying no dogs. Some day, though.

— Your lease? How do you mean, your lease?

— The lease on my flat in Rathfarnham, Gwen said.

— But you live in Herbert Park.

— I wish, Gwen said with a smile. — I just rent a room in the basement for my practice.

— And... the Lexus and the...

— The house belongs to old friends of my parents, Gwen said.

— I thought... I assumed...

— The only reason I'm telling you is because you're not my patient any more, she said and drew in sea air down to her toes. — Hey, Lee, don't you just love this space? Sometimes out here I think I can run and run forever.

For fifteen minutes they walked north, into a little breeze. He understood at last the absence of jewellery on her crucial finger, a matter that before he had put down to professional tact but which now he understood reflected her position. He suddenly realised that, unlike the dozens of other women whom he had dated and slept with, or tried to sleep with and failed, not to mention the one he had married, this woman knew almost everything there was to know about him – his fears and insecurities, his shitty dreams and his pathetic ambitions. And still she had suggested she drive him home.

— Lee?

— Sorry?

— Have you started your novel? Gwen asked.

— Sort of, he lied. — I'm tired and hungry when I finish every day. It's hard.

They had rounded a headland that would eventually bring them to the estuary behind Goose Point. A couple of kids stood on a wall, casting fishing lines into a narrow stream of water. He had been continuing to take in her contours for the last quarter of a mile; the outline of her bra strap across her back, the tiny race of golden hairs that plunged from the base of her neck down between her shoulder blades. A glow warmed his chest. He asked, — Do you like your work?

She looked sideways at him. Such an *elf*, thought Lee!

— It depends. Most of the time, yes, I suppose so. But sometimes I just get sick of being the dump for everyone else's problems. That's why I come out here, to leave everyone's problems behind and to think for myself.

— I never thought you'd have problems, he said.

— *That's* the problem. When everyone is dumping on you, they never think you're like them, a screwed-up person who has highs and lows, who's lonely, who's insecure, who's sometimes so fed up with life that she wishes she could just disappear to, I dunno, any place, someplace warm, someplace nobody knows you, where you can start all over again.

As Gwen spoke the most alluring blush filled her upper neck and cheeks, illuminating in its path tiny specks of golden sand that had settled there. The sudden need to protect her, with all the erotic paraphernalia that that entailed, surged in him. He wanted all at once to tell her in how much regard he had always held her, and how he often went to sleep thinking of her ankles. How would she react? He cleared his throat, but Gwen was walking up a sand dune and beckoning for him to follow. She said, — There's traffic over here, make sure Des doesn't run out.

As they breasted the hill an enormous billboard with pictures of houses and apartments blotted out the skyline. He said, — Gwen? Can I tell you something I've been meaning to say for a long time?

— The dog! Gwen cried. — Catch him! Oh God!

Des had sprinted down the path, across the snarlingly busy road and had darted beneath a gaudy wooden hoarding that ran in both directions to the limit of vision.

— Des! cried Lee and almost ran into a cement truck. — Des!

The hoarding was over two metres high, making it impossible to see what it concealed, although here and there, where the upright panels were not quite flush, Lee could squint in and discern enormous machines at work. Litter pooled the base of the hoarding and the air was suddenly thick with grime and dust. Difficult to imagine that less than a couple of minutes' walk away lay pure open spaces and peace.

— Des? Des! Come out here!

Gwen had crossed the road and was kneeling down, face to the ground, peering into the declivity through which Des had bolted. She stuck her wrist in and called, — Good boy, Des! Come to Gwen!

Despite the enormity of the crisis, Lee was overwhelmed by her concern, which although directed towards Des was equally, he felt, for him. He had to prevent himself from bending down and engulfing her kneeling, hooped figure in his embrace.

— What *is* this ghastly place? Gwen asked, getting to her feet. — How do you get *in?*

No ready answer seemed available. Standing back as near to the road as he could without getting smacked by a car or truck, Lee searched for an entrance. He could see the tips of cranes and a dense smog of builder's smut, but no way in. Sprawled for hundreds of yards in each direction were three-times-life-size depictions of tanned women wearing bikinis and sucking through straws from fruit-clogged highball glasses. Slogans in tall red letters shouted 'FROM ONLY €350,000!' and 'HOME AT LAST, HOME AT LAST, THANKS BE TO GOD I'M HOME AT LAST!'

Without warning, from somewhere deep within this unseen purgatory, came an explosion. The ground shook and as Lee watched, transfixed, a decent-sized mushroom cloud rose gracefully over Goose Point. Already polluted beyond any reasonable threshold of environmental acceptability, the air was now dense with muck particles, the feathers of incinerated seagulls and, insofar as Lee could make out, tiny shreds of brown terrier skin and hair.

— Oh Jesus, he said and began to weep. — Oh God, Des.

He felt an arm around his shoulders and fingers stroking his neck. No more than any man in the abyss of grief, Lee felt an overwhelming need to be comforted by an attractive woman. Gwen said, — Come on, Lee, I'm sure he's all right. Let's find a way into this godforsaken place.

She set out at a brisk pace, walking north along the fence, her pretty jaw set. There was a purpose to her that Lee clung to, since at that moment she was all that was preventing him from sliding into oblivion. After two hundred yards the footpath ended, but the hoarding turned at a right angle and suddenly, behind wire gates, the full extent of the enormous development was visible. Gwen made her way in the same determined fashion to a square cabin with wire grilles for windows. She hammered on the door, then opened it. A number of helmeted faces turned in her direction. She said, — I'd like to speak to whoever is in charge here, please.

The seated figures looked at each other, then the face of one of them broke into a broad grin and, gesturing crudely towards Gwen's diminutive figure, said something in a coarse, foreign language. The men bellowed with laughter. Gwen cried, — How dare you! Our dog has strayed in here to this appalling desecration. If we don't find him at once, we are calling the police!

One of the men got to his feet and shuffled out, bewildered. Lee, tingling from a collision of delight at Gwen's claiming joint ownership of Des, and despair from the knowledge that Des was now part of the Goose Point smog, made his way through the gate and stared into the massive excavations. Giant yellow machines crawled in every direction. Cranes swivelled. A shutter of constant noise blocked out any possibility of his voice, or Des's bark, being heard. He walked further and stood on the end of a cliff, below which a lake had formed. He stuck his fingers into his mouth and whistled. His whistle snapped back in the air, mocking him. It was as if in here, divided from the strand and sea by terraces of houses and ugly fencing, a malign new world existed. As he watched, a little fish rose from the lake, silver against the dim light, a flash of life in the midst of so much destruction. His eye was caught by movement beyond the lake and to the right. He stared. Trotting along the inside of the fence, shaking its head from side to side, was a small dog.

— Des? DES!

He scrambled down, down the steep incline of rock and shingle, unmindful of the shouts behind him or of the stinging cuts to his hands and to the backs of his legs. Along the side of the lake the ground crumbled treacherously and he had to claw his way to the end before he could straighten up and run on flat terrain. The dog had seen him and had halted by the fence.

— Des?

The animal's coat had been singed, the tip of its tail was no longer white and two enormous black rings circled its eyes.

— Des!

Des growled. The dog's jaws were clamped tight around a bundle of what looked like sticks with clods of earth on the ends of them.

— Good boy, Des, Lee said, good boy.

Des dropped the booty at Lee's feet. Silver glinted. Lee gathered the dog up and hugged him. Des growled his independence growl. Lee nudged what Des had found with his foot, then picked it up.

— Oh my goodness, look at you two!

Lee had not realised that Gwen was beside him. He turned and saw a line of men in helmets on the cliff, peering down at them. Gwen stroked Des's smutty ears. She said, — I'm going to bring you boys home.

* * *

Up to that evening he had not understood how truly devoid he had been of loving human contact. During his years in the *Trumpet*, in which his days had been spent trying to please Eddie and Dick Bell, the social side of his life consisted of drink-soaked evenings that often ended in the beds of matronly sub-editors or middle-aged married hacks whose husbands were doing the same thing in another part of town. All of them groping desperately for happiness, everyone fearing the next person up the line, hating what they did, for they had all started out with bright-eyed ambitions and a modicum of talent, but had watched themselves become transformed into bitter, cliché-ridden cynics.

He was nervous that he might have misinterpreted her enthusiasm, for a part of him still saw her the same way as a schoolboy sees his teacher. Was she simply concerned for him, he wondered initially, because she knew so much about him and feared, for example, that he might be going to top himself? That the dog-in-Goose-Point business might have tipped the scales of his sanity? Or maybe she had professional indemnity issues around him and feared that his untimely death might result in her premium being loaded. If any of such concerns were true Gwen gave no sign of it for, without being asked, when they arrived in his flat, as he washed Des she began to whip up omelettes with the kind of easy womanly competence that made him yearn for the lost years of childhood.

He wondered then if her obvious interest in him might simply be to get him coming back for therapy, for she had alluded more than once that she was finding the going tough in business; and yet she had also told him that she was glad he was no longer a client and that she hoped they could now be friends. Sitting side by side, plates on knees, Lee wondered if her physical closeness to him was inadvertent, caused perhaps by the fact that she was hungry and had not noticed that their limbs were touching. She was still in her jogging shorts and the minute but exquisite blonde hairs on her thighs caused a rush of consternation from Lee's groin to his ear lobes. Her ready laugh, in response to his remarks made more from nervousness than a wish to amuse, led him to suspect that she still saw him as a case study, which in turn made him speculate that she was writing him up for some journal and that this encounter was evolving under the heading of field work.

And yet as the evening wore on and he made tea, and she said to him, here, let me pour, Lee had to concede that if his only reaction to this pretty girl's freshness and keenness for his company was paranoia in its many manifestations, then he was indeed a sorry tosser. He observed the small yet firm bone of her wrist as she poured the tea, and then, as she placed down the pot, with his heart resounding, he reached across and placed his hand on hers.

Gwen looked at him sharply. She wasn't smiling. Lee withdrew his hand and stood up. He said, — I'm sorry.

— Lee, she said, sit down, please.

He did what she told him, even as he felt like a child about to be chastised. She looked so lovely.

— I… ah… I'm… he began.

Those were his last words, so to speak. Gwen was on him in a single fluid movement, her mouth on his, her hands caressing his head. As she straddled him, their mouths joined, she tugged up his T-shirt from the waist and over his head, breaking tongue contact for a moment, then tore off her own T-shirt, leaned back and unclipped her bra which she threw across the room, causing Des to perform a retrieve.

Lee, like a demented creature, sought out Gwen's breasts whose prominent nipples, ample size and overall firmness were in themselves a wonderful surprise, as Gwen struggled to unbuckle Lee, simultaneously kicking off her runners and making the dog howl at this sudden disruption to his domesticity. Lying on the couch, wriggling from his jeans like a frantic snake-charmer, Lee ripped down Gwen's running shorts and then snapped off her sling-shaped thong. Without warning the two-seater couch tipped over and Lee and Gwen's entwined bodies spilled onto the floor beside the yapping terrier.

— Fuck off, Des, Lee hissed.

Gwen was on top of him, hungrily, and now as Lee lay, gigantic and delirious, she kissed a track that began at his shoulders and descended by way of his nipples, chest and stomach until she held him in both hands and began to slowly suck the tip of his cock. As Lee gasped with pleasure, Gwen suddenly screamed with pain.

— Jesus! she shouted. — He just bit me!

— What?

— He bit my heel!

Lee pulled himself up into a kneeling position. He felt like a satyr. Des, crouching beneath the TV table, growled. The dog's bared teeth held her thong as he readied up for the next attack. Gwen, now sitting cross-legged, examined her foot on which a speck of blood had appeared. She said, — It's nothing.

— I'm sorry, Lee said. — He probably thought you were trying to eat me.

— He was right, Gwen said and leaned forward to kiss again. — Now, carry me up that ladder, please.

* * *

He angled the glinting, walnut-sized lump of muck on the end of the stick to the light as he held it under the kitchen tap and with his toothbrush began to clean off the multi-striped deposits of sand and soil. He could smell the tangy, salty smell of Goose Point sediment as layer by layer the compacted clay gave up its core. Putting aside the toothbrush and working his fingers into the nub, he felt a hard shape emerge. Moments later he was holding up yet another arrowhead with its stub of shaft. The head appeared to be made of silver. Lee placed it on the draining board alongside the other four similar arrowheads, some of them with longer shafts. Even to the untrained eye the twinkling crafts-manship was obvious. Silversmiths had engraved elaborate lines along the length of each arrowhead, and in one case, where the entire head was intact, the graceful symmetry of the design flowed delightfully, like a swift in flight. In one case, on the couple of inches of wood behind the head, he could discern the faint outline of engraved symbols. Des came over and began to sniff. Lee felt guilty about Des. The night before, when Lee had carried Gwen up the ladder to bed, Des had made such a rumpus that Lee had had to climb back down and lock him in the bathroom.

It was another warm, languorous, heavy-scented Saturday late-September noon. Church bells in Rathmines and Rathgar began the Angelus. A blanket of bliss engulfed him. Although Gwen had left at seven because she had a client at nine, she said she would be back that evening.

He had to understand where Des was coming from, he told himself, as he walked into Rathmines. The dog was jealous; it was only natural. Over four years, with the exception of a couple of intoxicated vagrants who had been sleeping rough on the front steps, no human but Lee had slept in the apartment. In the matter of copulation between humans, Des was an ingénue. On the countless evenings when Lee had arrived home too drunk to make it up the ladder, Des had been patient and companionable, and had snuggled up during the night to Lee's unconscious body, compensating with his canine warmth for the chill from the lino and possibly preventing his master from contracting pneumonia. Still, biting was not on, and biting the only woman in a decade who had fallen for Lee was not on big time. Lee had spoken sternly to Des and had explained clearly that the dog's punishment was to stay indoors. When Des had, as a last throw of the dice, sat up on his hind legs and shown his tongue, Lee had almost relented.

Eddie had called. As it was Saturday morning, he had been sober and in the *Sunday Trumpet* office, fussing in case any big, last minute news stories might make his features section redundant, stale or just plain stupid. For such emergencies, a number of even more banal and bloodless features of varying length were lying in the deep permafrost of a hard drive, awaiting their moment of life.

Eddie said, — Listen, remember Delicato?

— Just about.

— Well, he's going ahead. Launching a weekly. They're looking for writers.

— You serious?

— They want people who can, you know, really write prose, practitioners of the art. They've asked me – unofficially, of course – to act as literary consultant. I mean, nobody in here must know this, but I've told them I'd be available informally, you know, to cast an eye over the overall project. A bit like an old master looking over the shoulder of talented pupils.

— Like Hemingway.

— You took the words out of my mouth. I've given them a collection of my old pieces, and they've said they're the best they've ever come across.

— They're right, of course.

— They particularly liked 'Munching Maize in Mandalay', Eddie said. — They told me they actually salivated as they read it.

— I'm not surprised.

— I'll have to write under a pseudonym, of course.

— I understand.

— I'll keep you posted.

— Thank you, Eddie; I appreciate it.

— When the going gets tough, you know the old saying, Eddie said.

* * *

As he opened the door into the jeweller's shop, bells chimed. A stooped man in an overcoat was being served at the counter by a woman with peroxide hair. The shop was tiny and stank of furniture polish. The predominant sound was of clocks ticking. From a room behind the counter, in response to the bells, a wizened character emerged, dropping an eye-piece from his eye into his hand like a trick.

— Hello, I found these, Lee said and took out his handkerchief with the arrowheads. — I was wondering how much they might be worth.

— Fell off the back of a lorry I suppose, said the man wearily and rolled his eyes for the benefit of the woman.

— Actually, no, I found them in Goose Point, Lee said and spread out the handkerchief on the baize counter cloth.

The woman had inserted a tiny battery into a hearing aid and was handing it to the other customer. The male jeweller popped his eye-piece back in, pinched up one of the arrowheads and, his teeth glinting like a weasel's, began to examine the tiny object.

— Huh, he said, hmmmm.

Lee's highest expectation was that the arrowheads might be worth fifty euros, in which case he intended bringing Gwen out to dinner. The woman behind the counter was saying, — How's that?

— It's very loud, the elderly customer shouted. He was wearing a UCD scarf. — I need to turn the bloody thing down or I'll be deaf.

— Mr O?

— Ah, that's better.

— Mr O? Lee asked again.

— Ah, hello. It's Des, isn't it?

— It's Lee, actually. Des is at home.

— Ah, now I remember; lucky you that can have one at home, said Mr O and handed over a fistful of coins for the woman to count. — How is he at all? Did I ever tell you about my little Pablo?

— These are probably fireworks parts, my friend, the jeweller said with a doleful face. — Probably from Northern Ireland. They may well be silver, but I'd have to have them assayed and that would probably cost more than they're worth.

— They look old, Lee said. — I think they were buried really deep down and only came to the surface because of an explosion.

— Dig anywhere in this country, my friend, and you'll find some sort of a yoke that's a few hundred years old, the man said grudgingly. — Let's face it, this is an old country.

— You're a journalist, said Mr O. — You said you'd write about these bloody landlords.

— They're nice, said the woman and picked up one of the arrowheads.

— But what can you do with them? asked her male counter party with a practised shrug.

— They'd be nice on a ring, said the woman and held one of the heads to her plump middle finger and extended her arm.

— I'm not working for the paper any more, Lee said.

— They're all… Mr O shielded the woman with his shoulder, … bastards! he hissed.

— Be like a knuckle-duster, the man said.

— Or as a pendant, said the woman and trundled Mr O's coins into a till.

— Fuckin' choke you, said the man, who had to, at this stage, be her husband.

Lee asked, — How much?

— Still, we have our health, aye, said Mr O. — What more can we ask?

— Thirty would be tops, the jeweller said.

— You'd want to mind your gas meter, Mr O said, mine was done twice recently in broad daylight.

— Your change, the woman said.

— Fifty, Lee said.

— Fifty? Sorry, my friend, but I'm not in the charity business, I have to make a living, I'm only making you an offer because I heard you say you're out of a job, the jeweller said and again picked up one of the little silver heads and held it to the light.

— Forty and not a penny more. I'm sorry, but we're closing for lunch now.

He had no idea why but Lee felt suddenly attached to the little arrowheads, which up to then he had never imagined as pieces of jewellery; and what better way to remember the day he fell in love with Gwen than to give her a necklace sparkling with silver? Furthermore the jeweller's almost primal wheedling had made him suspect that maybe these objects were worth more than fifty euros. He was just about to say, thanks, so, I'll think about it, when the man behind the counter said, with a big sigh, — All right, go on, I'm an eejit, fifty it is.

— *Wait!*

Lee and the two behind the counter turned in the direction of Mr O.

— Let me see that, please, Mr O said.

— Excuse me, but I've just made a purchase from this gentleman, said the jeweller.

— You'll hand it over to me this minute! Mr O thundered and stuck out his hand.

— Listen, me oul' pal, I've a panic button here connected to the guards, said the jeweller. — Now back up and fuck off.

— I never said I'd sell them to you, Lee said.

— You asked me fifty and I said yes, the man said.

— You bid me forty, Lee said. — Let him see the little piece, please.

— You asked, fifty; I said, fifty it is. That's the law; sorry.

— Let him see them. Now.

With great reluctance the jeweller put down the arrowhead on the counter and Mr O picked it up. Mr O wore spectacles with very thick lenses which, when illuminated as now by the light, transformed his eyeballs into minute black dots. The woman said, — I'd call the guards, Harry, I'd say this is some kind of a set-up and they're in it together.

The air being expelled from Mr O's nostrils was strong and draughty. The old man put back the arrowhead and then, unchallenged, picked up the head with the piece of wooden shaft and turned it between his fingers. The jeweller, now called Harry, leaned over the counter and nudged Lee.

— Look, Harry whispered from the side of his mouth, don't let on to the wife, but I was going to make that a hundred – ok? Fifty here and fifty outside. No questions asked.

Lee's heart quickened. Harry straightened himself and said in a strong voice, — All right, sir, you've had a good look, I think. Now, if you're completely finished, we have our business to complete. Thank you. Bye-bye.

Mr O, still holding the arrowhead, turned very slowly from his inspection. He said, — I am Professor Ó Dálaigh from the Department of Archaeology, University College Dublin, aye. I believe what my friend here has found are nothing less than the sacred decorations of the Fir Bolg. Another word out of you and I'll have the Office of Public Works and the Fraud Squad in here to close you down.

He put the piece of fluted silver back on the handkerchief, bundled them all together and put them in his pocket.

— Now, if you'll excuse us, my friend Des here and I are leaving.

He walked to the door and opened it. The bells chimed merrily.

— Are you coming, Des? asked Mr O.

TEN

From the window of the den, as she munched a Pringle, Medb-Marie observed the gardener cool himself at the outside tap. He had a lean, well-muscled body, and his broad shoulders and long back reminded her of the pearl divers she had watched in Dubai. Big chest capacity was needed to make it down to the ocean bed and stay there for several minutes, collecting the pearl oysters, the boat skipper had told her, himself quite a catch, and the divers' bodies needed to be smooth and strong in order to meet the least resistance from the ocean. Medb-Marie had not been able then, nor was she now, as she took in the gardener's physique, to avoid making the contrast with Albert, whose body was covered in hair, like a dog. Years before when he had been wiry Albert-the-plasterer, his body hair had been a turn-on, but now, more than a dozen later, his sweaty back hairs and greasy mop made her nauseous.

As Medb-Marie watched, the gardener splashed tap water over his chest and shoulders. She liked his attitude too: a few weeks before when she'd been upstairs on her computer buying jewellery online, she looked out the window and saw the mongrel pissing his little heart out against one of the wheels of Albert's car. How she laughed aloud at that! How it summed up everything she thought at that moment about her husband! But then, as if Albert had heard her mockery, the loft door burst open and he came down the steps at speed, thunder in his face. *You dirty little bastard!* He lashed out with his foot and the small dog became airborne. It landed shrieking loudly, but in a corner, where it was trapped before Albert's renewed advance. *I'll fucking teach you!* He drew back his big heavy leg again. *Whoa!* He'd appeared from nowhere and caught Albert by the collar of his coat. *Leave him alone.* Albert, gaping, gasping, unbelieving, said, *You... you're fired!* Upstairs, from her gallery, Medb-Marie felt her hackles rise. He was *her* gardener! *I'm employed by the missus, sir. And you've no right to kick a little dog like that.* He stood his ground and Albert stepped back. Then, as if she was watching a Shakespeare play in the Globe, London, a place she'd read about and intended to visit, Medb-Marie saw Christiana, the Polish au pair, appear from stage left, hands to her mouth in horrified anticipation of the fight she thought she was about to witness. *No!* Christiana cried. *Please!* The gardener picked up his dog. *I'll remember this*, Albert said, backing off, quivering, and got into his car.

* * *

The droplets flashed and glistened in the evening sunlight and somehow made his skin even more succulent. Medb-Marie leant against the window frame as a rush of longing overwhelmed her. She knew when a man wanted her, always had, from the age of twelve when she had suffered the gazes of corpulent men at Fianna Fáil meetings and in the halls of GAA clubs where her father had spent most of his evenings. First she was amused by all the attention, but soon began to learn that she could use it to her advantage. All she had to do was look in a man's direction for him to leap up and buy her a Coke or, as was soon the case, offer her a cigarette, or a packet, although she had never inhaled, just knew that the whole business of her lighting up, the way she learned to pout her lips as she held the filter tip between them, had the whole room watching.

Yet sex and pleasure had not yet converged in her young mind, a triumph for the nuns who taught her, whose mission was to keep sex and pleasure on different trajectories, one headed for the coals of hell, the other for the sweet brooks of heaven.

Her education went out the window in five minutes when she met the young man who sold ice cream for his father in Bray. She was stunning that day, in a bikini top, a mini-skirt and high-heels, a beautiful facsimile of the equally stunning young Americans and Australians she'd seen on hundreds of imported television soaps. Strange, now, she couldn't remember his name, just his head of blond curls, the shape of his mouth, the innocent way he asked her if she'd like to come into the back of his van and see how ice cream was made. Although he would be the first of a legion before she met Albert, the boy with the ice-cream curls, even now, nineteen years later, occupied a sweet, special place in Medb-Marie's memory. He had assumed she knew what it was all about; and she, suddenly buzzing with irresistible feelings and wants, all at once *understanding* for the first time what was really involved, didn't want him to think she was a novice. He French-kissed her – she was still using that term! – one arm around her bare shoulders as with his free hand he closed the hatch on the disappointed faces of several prospective clients. It was all done on stacks of milk cartons and boxes of cones and strawberry flavouring. His own jeans were around his ankles and he had her knickers off before you could say Mr Whippy. The next couple of minutes had been a mixture of terror and ecstasy, of amazing revelation, of finally, gratefully and even prayerfully accepting the sublime intrusion that would make her a woman at last.

It was a measure of her dilemma that here she was, a married woman with two daughters, thinking of the ice-cream boy. All she had to do was tap on the window and the gardener would be in; she'd seen the way he had looked at her, the way he had difficulty breathing when she stood beside him, how his nipples had hardened two days ago when she'd gone out to pick parsley. She held herself and nearly swooned as an image of the bare-chested gardener, in here, in the den, the curtains drawn closed and Medb-Marie on her knees in front of him, unbuckling his jeans belt, was so vivid she could all but taste him.

She sat down to steady herself. What a stupid bitch to actually consider taking such a risk. What if he told Albert? Worse, imagine if Albert or the kids walked in?

* * *

In the kitchen she drank a glass of water from the cooler. Her father's solicitor, a conniving political bagman for whom moral compromise was a way of life and who was also her father's election agent, had seen her two days after Albert's disastrous birthday dinner. His office, located above a restaurant and within three minutes' walk of Dáil Éireann, was musty and old-fashioned with ancient oak and leather furniture, and was staffed by a couple of arthritic late-middle-aged women whose jobs were secure for life on the basis that any tiny fraction of the wheezes they'd seen pass through could bring down a government.

The solicitor, from whom the whiff of the previous night's alcohol gently but persistently wafted, was tall and gaunt. Hair grew from midway down the beak of his nose. He listened gravely as she recounted her predicament, then, when she had finished, drank from his coffee cup. Kevin, Medb-Marie's father, had confided that this coffee was always heavily doctored with Remy Martin. The solicitor smacked his lips, removed his glasses, knuckled into his eyes and said, — The last thing we want is anyone else stickin' their head into how those fuckin' flats were acquired. You understand me?

Blood drained from Medb-Marie's face and she began to shake. The solicitor said, — Ah, for Jesus' sake, Medb-Marie, will you cop on to yourself. You knew the score then, you know the score now. Count your chickens, girl, and shut your mouth.

Few people addressed Medb-Marie Barr in this fashion, but her father's solicitor, a man whose only hope of staying out of jail would be to die of cirrhosis of the liver, had known her since she was a child. She said, — How dare you speak to me like that! You're a parasite living off the work of decent men such as my father and my husband. You just sit there like a spider and suck the blood out of anything that comes near you.

The solicitor blew his cheeks out, then laughed.

— A minute ago that decent man of a husband of yours was a gobshite trying to mortgage your flats. Listen, you're a smart girl. People were put out on the streets so that those flats could be sold off the government's books. Old people, cripples, drug addicts.

He shook himself and took a sustaining gulp from his coffee cup. He continued, — Methadone-dependant families, droves of them, were shifted so that your husband, aided and abetted by your father, could bounce a few million around the world – let me think, oh yes: the Bahamas, Cyprus, the Dutch Antilles, as I remember, were all involved. Beautiful footwork; Jesus, talk about Roy Keane – this was financial artistry. No one ever saw the money in any one place for more than ten seconds.

Medb-Marie began to sob.

— You want my advice? Get Albert back on your side. What's the point of divorcing him? He's under pressure. If he says that giving those flats to the bank is just a short-term technical thing, then that's what it is.

— Those flats are part of me, Medb-Marie gasped.

— Ah, Jesus, will you get a grip, the solicitor said. — Make it up with Albert. Be generous, Medb-Marie! Trust Albert! He's one of the key men that has allowed this country to take its rightful place in the world! If Albert Barr fails, we're all, excuse my French, f-u-c-k-e-d.

— Oh God, I feel like I'm being raped by all of you! Medb-Marie cried.

The solicitor turned away, blinking. For twenty-five years he'd dreamed... stop it! Oh Christ, imagine what it would be like... God forgive me! Known her since she was a girl, but even then... Loathed that part of his mind, reviled his behaviour after each occasion of sin, and on Friday evenings dumped his entire previous week's seed depletion on a hapless priest in Clarendon Street

Church… Stop it! He was a family man, a Massgoer. He was on a committee that advocated stricter censorship…

— You're all the same, Medb-Marie said with disgust.

The lawyer expelled breath at length. Outside he could hear dead leaves rustling along the lane, the inevitable revolution of the seasons, the progression of age, the growing realisation that nothing again will ever be sweeter than youth. He looked at his watch, at his empty coffee cup, then with an unconvincing show of reluctance that time was up at last, said, — Can I speak frankly? You're a very pretty girl, but you're a saucy little bitch as well. Shut up for a minute! Thank you. You married a man, you knew what he was and you did bloody well out of him. You've still got a house that's worth a bloody fortune; I should know – I bought it on behalf of you and your husband.

— Albert paid the market rate at the time, she said primly.

— May I remind you that it was acquired from three young children, wards of court, whose parents had just been killed in a plane crash? I was their executor, after all. Listen, Medb-Marie, whether you like it or not, we're all in this together, in everything, for better or worse; it's a kind of big marriage, get it? Now Albert is starting to have it rough from the banks, and the first time he comes and asks you for something other than a ride, what do you do? You go berserk! You throw him out of the house and then run in here asking me how you can shaft him. You're some fuckin' article, Medb-Marie, that's the truth of it, some fuckin' article.

— What about my rights? she gasped. — I have my rights.

— And I have a lunch appointment for which I'm already ten minutes late, her solicitor said. — Please tell your father I was asking after him.

* * *

She fished into the bottom of the tin tube and plucked out the last Pringle. Had she ever loved Albert? A difficult question – she had been fascinated by him, certainly, and had admired him greatly to the point, in the early days, of being in awe of his ability to squeeze money from the most arid situations. He was corrupt, of course, but so was her father, so was everyone she knew; corrupt was unfair though, in a country where everyone had had to use their wits to survive for a thousand years.

She loved her father. For all his unvarnished manners, his transparent lack of education and eye for the main chance, he was her father and he had elbowed his way into the centre of Irish politics by making sure he was always elected with huge majorities. Over three decades he'd never cared what he'd had to do to achieve such universal approval from his constituents, never shirked a call for a favour from a voter, no matter how pathetic that favour might be. The term 'client politics' described exactly what her father did. The result was a political apparatus in Munster that was second to none for the high degree in which everyone that belonged to it was compromised. What would happen in his constituency when Kevin Steadman went to that place in the sky where everything and everyone was always grand, great thanks, grand, no one had ever tried to contemplate.

When Medb-Marie had given birth to the twins – when her second set of contractions had started she had screamed the house down – Albert had been at his most loveable. Misty-eyed, energised by his wife's capacity to create chaos around her, delirious with joy for his twin infants, Albert had blubbered happily, his hair askew, six in the morning, sober, kissing everyone who came within reach. He had been shorn for the first time of the kind of background conniving, quick-eyed calculating, on-the-lookout-for-the-main-chance, frankly shithouse-rat cuteness that he had never been quite able to shake off. Here he was in Mount Carmel Hospital, father of her children, a man whose foundations were made up of nothing more than love and decency. The fact that he didn't seem to mind that she was in the aftermath of the never-to-be-repeated birth process – Jesus, even now she squirmed when she saw a pregnant woman – or that his once powerfully attractive wife lay before him haggard, misshapen, without makeup, her hair dull and sweat-streaked, with two chins – enough! He had wrapped her in his arms and told her that he loved her. She loved him too, then, at least as much as she loved her father.

Of course, as her ravening solicitor had pointed out, she hadn't married a cuddly pushover who changed nappies on the side, and although for the first few years after the twins were born the warm vibrations of Albert's genuine affection for his family continued to be felt, a happy, bumbling dad who burped his kids every night could never easily square with Albert. This was a man who had, over one particular Christmas, obliterated an entire lake in a border county using illegal backfill and then had his father-in-law arrange for that same, once-pretty body of trout-rich water to be erased from the records of the Ordnance Survey.

She poured herself a Grey Goose over ice with a lime twist and added slim-line tonic, a splash. Their marriage had coasted along at the level Medb-Marie had observed in those of her contemporaries who had also married men who had become successful. (Those of her friends who had married schoolteachers and civil servants were seldom in touch any more and when she encountered them in shopping malls the occasions were distinguished only by mutual embarrassment.) The love experienced in Mount Carmel had mutated into a more long-term acquiescence of their separate roles, spiced up regularly by the liberal addition of – *things*. Not that she minded them: if she'd married a primary school teacher in Bray, which had once looked possible, it was unlikely he would ever have come in one night, half-pissed, and announced that she now owned a grouse moor in Scotland. (She still did; she'd been there once; she hated it.) And her life would probably still be a series of compromises, as it now was: separate roles, both sides subscribing to a formula for survival. It had worked for years, this way she had of being in love with Albert, her husband.

And then eighteen months ago, he became ill. The first she heard of it was when she came back from dropping the twins to school. The au pair: *You go Blackrock Clinic! Blood! Quick!* Stupid hysterical girl, what was she talking about? Medb-Marie allowed herself to be dragged upstairs to their ensuite and over to the toilet bowl. *Let go of my arm, Christiana!* There in the wastepaper basket, tissues with blood on them. Had he cut himself shaving? No, no! Christiana kept pointing to her bottom. Fighting back suspicions about Albert's darker side, Medb-Marie called the clinic.

His Porsche was still at the steps of the hospital when she got there. Over the next couple of hours, in an ambience of cheerful near-death and vile cappuccino, Medb-Marie learned of Albert's rectal polyp. He was drugged when she was let in briefly to see him, didn't recognise her as she kissed his unshaven cheek, looked no different, in fact, to the way he did on the occasions when he passed out. They were running tests, he was in no immediate danger, she was assured, although a mature female nurse confided in her that he had stumbled into the hospital in his pyjamas, traumatised, convinced he was dying.

In what she would remember as the long week of waiting, Medb-Marie saw her husband in a different light. Here was a man on whom she and her two children totally depended for the shoes on their feet. He was, arguably, now going to die, although fingers crossed and all the rest; yet death, yes, was on the table, as the consultant put it, adding, we could all die in the morning. We aren't all going to die in the bloody morning; only Albert is going to die, she said and walked out of his consulting room. She hated being taken for a bimbo. Where did it leave her and the girls? Only Albert knew the answer to that question.

No will, no provisions, everything he did had been planned on the basis that he would continue to live. She couldn't believe it! When he came home next day from hospital she tried to get him to address the problem, but he was morose beyond belief, introverted, self-absorbed: me, me, me. Moved into the spare bedroom. One day a priest arrived – a priest! – or at least some creep in white robes and open-toed sandals; she showed him upstairs and Albert kept him there for two hours! Worse, when this religious yo-yo at last emerged, shoving what she was sure was a cheque into the folds of his outfit, he had smiled confidently at her and said, — He has made arrangements.

Hope leaped in her then, for perhaps Albert had been so grief-stricken by the image of her and the girls having to live on without him that he had been unable to bring himself to discuss face to face the details that he had put in place for her.

— Tell me, please, father, what arrangements has he made?

— He wants his ashes to be scattered on the eighteenth green in Tramore, the priest said.

She stood, mouth partially open, waiting for the next instalment.

— And…?

— And then he'd like everyone to come to lunch in the clubhouse.

— What about… us? What about me and his children?

— Oh, I'm sure you're included, the priest said.

She'd slammed the door behind him and stood there, heaving, terrified. Her husband's financial entanglements were of such size and complexity that although there was always an assumption of solvency, it was never entirely assured. Sometimes, in drink, at least once a week in other words, she had grown accustomed to him looking at her with his half-crooked boozy grin and saying, Jesus, honey, this thing could all go up in smoke, you know. When she pressed him for details all he did was make motions with his hairy hands, holding them out in front of himself at chest height where they gently rocked from side to side, like flying saucers hovering.

Now that he might soon be the late Albert Barr, she could see clearly beyond the eighteenth in Tramore to a post-mortem regime of accountants, lawyers and bankers, feeding off the cadavers of his enterprises, winding up, shutting down, skimming fees, allocating her and the twins ever smaller allowances. He'd never even paused to consider them as people apart from himself. They might as well all die together as far as he was concerned.

But she wouldn't, she thought during the long week of waiting, nor would the girls. She would have her own life. When it was all over, after a decent period of observation, herself and the girls would move south.

She topped up the Grey Goose without tonic. That was then, this was now. In the end, despite everything, she had too much to lose by refusing to help him. Otherwise her life was most appealing: the house, the twins, the servants. She loved jewellery, online shopping, the way rings, brooches and bracelets, lockets, bangles, necklaces and precious beads swam up to her out of nowhere on the screen, amazing details, how did they do it, you could see the tiny ornamentations, she loved being able to click on 'add to basket', verify her pin number, send a brick of money through outer space to what she imagined was a cosy little shop in Milan or Miami, to a man with a goatee beard hammering away with a silver chisel on another priceless creation, sit back and three days later take delivery of a reinforced envelope through the post. She thought of the racehorses, the jet, the holidays, the last time she'd gone into Tiffany's and walked out with a ring that was worth more than a small yacht. You didn't need to be good at algebra. This was living.

It was easier and more manageable to direct the anger she felt for Albert towards someone else, to convince herself that Albert wasn't to blame, which he wasn't, all he was doing was trying to do his best; current events were being forced by others, she didn't have far to look.

She had despised Eric Chester from the first moment Albert had hauled him into their house. They'd just done the initial Goose Point deal and Albert had called her up and said he was bringing someone special home for a steak. On instructions she'd refrigerated two expensive bottles of white wine. Hated him from first sight; he reminded her of a horrible little GAA porter who had once tried to feel her up. This one had gloated on her without remission for four hours and Medb-Marie, who had the antennae of a bat when it came to sex, had flirted with him because she knew he was important. Whereas she normally deplored Albert's tendency to get legless in such situations, which he did again, that night it was the other man's ability to remain sober that really annoyed her. The way he sipped his wine, the purse he made of his lips, the fact that he was left-handed. He was so loathsome that he made Albert, slurring Albert with a pee stain at his crotch, look attractive. The way his eyes fed on her tits. And then Albert, as this creature eventually slithered out, pathetic Albert had been so grateful for the money that he'd lurched over to Eric and tried to kiss him on the mouth.

She didn't want to think about it. The fact that he now held the deeds to her apartments was nauseating. And yet, and yet, even as she came to terms with her compromised financial position and pushed the gardener's lithe body to one side of her mind and gasped with remembered nausea at her first encounter with Eric, she reflected on what she might have to do one day to save her husband's fortune. Could she, if everything depended on it – the jewellery, the jet, *everything* – could she in her wildest, most crazy dreams…?

Medb-Marie laughed at her ability to torture herself with an impossible hypothesis. She hadn't time for a further vodka because she was due in the Westbury in thirty minutes; Albert was sending a car. But what a thought! Where had it come from? From the fact that Eric was more powerful than her husband? From a sudden appreciation of the mortality not just of men but of their ambitions? Medb-Marie shivered. Draining her glass, she walked out through the hall and upstairs to change.

ELEVEN

Young men and women wearing headphones directed operations in the Grafton Suite of the Westbury Hotel. On a central dais the model of a town had appeared, spread out over an area the size of two snooker tables. Apartment blocks overlooked lakes and a golf course; a football stadium, complete with miniature players, could be found next door to shopping malls, schools, theatres and a grand-looking building with 'Opera House' scrolled above its façade were sprinkled throughout office blocks and towers of further apartments. A girl unwrapped plastic elephants and giraffes from tissue paper and placed them in appropriate locations within the zoo.

As hotel staff began to put chairs out in rows in front of a stage at one end of the room and as the shutters on the bar rattled up and uniformed chefs wheeled in trolleys of food, young women in good shape with false tans, wearing the skimpiest of bikinis, rehearsed stepping forward with large placards, each one with its own letter. Albert stood back to get the full effect.

GSOEOPTOINOWNDRELNAD !

A man in his twenties wearing an Oxford-cloth shirt and blue Levis held a clipboard and shouted instructions: — Svetlana! Move down one, please! Inge? You're 'w' for the love of Christ – does anyone here speak feckin' English? Consuela…

Albert, in whom the need for alcohol was suddenly gigantic, moved to the bar and pointed to the Hennessy. He looked nervously towards the door. Eric Chester had left a message on his mobile that he wanted an urgent chat before the launch began. Albert took the drink down in two gulps. What did urgent mean? What was Eric's latest demand going to be?

As nets of balloons were hoisted to the ceiling and the whiff of barbecued kebabs replaced the smell of stale drink, members of the Dublin media pack began to drift into the room. Although one or two acknowledged Albert's presence, most of them walked straight to the free bar without a glance at either Albert or the fifty-grand model of his development. A photographer with a mop of woolly hair stood on a chair and began squeezing off shots.

— Albert.

He jumped despite the brandy.

— Great model, great set-up. I really like the girls.

— A drink, Eric?

— Water, non-fizzy, lemon, no ice, said the chairman thinly. He checked left, then right. He said, — I am very unhappy, Albert. Perhaps you know why.

HUBBI's grapevine had delivered the first droplet of the rumour to the chairman in the HUBBI gym that morning. The grapevine was an impressive information-gathering machine fuelled by the naked self-interest of HUBBI's fifteen hundred employees, down to the humblest clerk in the smallest suburban branch. Thus a middle-management HUBBI executive from Terenure, who had been settling down for a drink after work in Rathmines the evening before, had overheard the barman remark to a customer that the local jeweller had been in earlier and had said that there had been a major archaeological discovery on a big building site in Goose Point.

— We have a problem, the chairman now said and flashed an eye tooth.

— A problem?

Albert cradled a fresh brandy balloon in his hand and looked bewildered.

— Apparently, the chairman said, someone's found archaeological material on your site.

— Ah, for fuck's sake, forget it! Albert said, relieved beyond measure. — That's all *covered*, Eric.

The chairman bit down and drew blood. That afternoon he had personally spent a fruitless hour on the telephone trying to reinsure the bank's exposure to Albert Barr on the international market. The market was nervous. Three per cent of HUBBI's share capital was now in the hands of MUESLI, a Zurich hedge fund whose name was an acronym for its title in German and which was betting on a drop in HUBBI's share price.

— There's going to be a media question about it, the chairman hissed. — Here, tonight. The planners will run for cover at the slightest excuse.

Albert was simultaneously overwhelmed by dread, heartburn, the need to drink more and the understanding that he needed to be sober.

— This is complete news to me, he said.

— Apparently they'll try to claim that your site is the cradle of Irish civilisation, said the chairman with a withering smile.

— That's all looked *after*, Albert said in a wavering voice, I have a report. And anyway, Kevin said it's a done deal. He has the last word.

— Kevin is a politician, Eric said bitterly. — You think if the media come the heavy with him on some allegedly priceless archaeological shit that he'll tell them to fuck off? Like hell he will. You may as well pack up these hookers and go home.

— Kevin's my father-in-law, Albert whispered and simultaneously grinned for a photographer. — He would never do that to Medb-Marie.

Up on the stage the formal part of the show was swinging into action. People with pinned-on name tags were shaking hands with one another and grinning from ear to ear as if they'd all just banked a lot of money. A man tapped the microphone and said, testing, testing. The line for the bar was growing fast as fresh media people arrived. Hacks drinking from pint glasses were circling the model town, press packs stuck under their elbows. At the door flashbulbs went off as Kevin Steadman, Minister for Infrastructure

Development, made his entrance. He'd been in the public eye for the last week, ever since news broke that a few months before he'd flown first-class return to Tokyo to inspect a Japanese parking meter. On stage a small, smiling man was now speaking into the microphone.

— Thank you. My name is Charles and I'm the media co-ordinator for Barr None Enterprises, the developers of Goose Point Wonderland, Home Was Never Like This, and I'd like to welcome you all here this evening. I won't take up too much of your time. We just have a few things to get through before I let you back to the important business.

Loud guffaws came from some hacks at the bar who had already reached entry-level inebriation.

— If you could just bear with me, thank you. Thank you. You all should by this stage have picked up your information packs. To our friends, the members of the media, I hope that you will find all you need to write your stories about this unique new project for Dublin.

This led to more raucous laughter. Journalists who covered these events looked upon the organisers with unconcealed disdain and, as a matter of principle, never ever read the contents of a press pack.

— I'd like to acknowledge the presence here this evening of the Minister for Infrastructure Development, Mr Kevin Steadman, TD…

Trickling, hesitant applause.

— … and of Doctor Eric Chester, Chairman of HUBBI, 'If You're In HUBBI You're In The Money'. HUBBI finance sustainable, quality-led developments and are the first Irish bank to introduce the generational mortgage.

Someone belched and the crowd tittered.

— But without further ado, since I know how busy you all are, without standing any more on ceremony I would ask you to put your hands together please and to welcome the force behind this exceptional development. Ladies and gentlemen, Mr Albert Barr and his lovely wife Medb-Marie!

The house lights were killed, then over the speakers came an audible click and a tape lurched into the opening bars of *Hail to the Chief!* From high in the ceiling the recently hoisted balloons, each one decorated with a large 'GP', floated down onto the assembled guests. To a man the people on the stage were on their feet, applauding. The girls who made up the letters of Goose Point Wonderland shimmered into view. Spotlights come on and from the stage wings Albert and Medb-Marie emerged.

It seemed like the whole room was straining to get an eyeful of Albert's wife. She wore a low-cut charcoal jacket with a pinstripe above a matching skirt that ended just below her knees. A gold neck band lay on her bare, tanned throat, within reach of her cleavage. Precious stones and metals twinkled and winked from her hands and ears. She was smiling brilliantly. Photographers and TV crews were crawling forward on elbows and knees like infantry, and were now unleashing a firestorm of flash photography. Albert, meanwhile, who under the unforgiving spotlights looked like someone who sold pigs' feet for a living, stood regarding his wife with mute admiration. At the bar three newspaper correspondents were helpless with laughter.

Albert, on the podium, was adjusting the microphone down to the level of his mouth. As he took out a sheaf of papers from his jacket pocket the chatter level in the room resumed.

— I'd like to start by thanking…

He was terrified by what Eric had said. He took some reassurance from the attention of the room on his wife, who radiated an almost superhuman level of beauty and, bizarrely, of the presence of her father in the audience, nodding in agreement with everything that Albert said, the same way as he did in the Dáil when the Taoiseach answered questions.

Albert's script spoke of urban regeneration and how the lifeblood of old Goose Point would soon flow again now that the city fathers had given their blessing to his panoramic scheme.

How come Eric had heard the rumour before he did? Eric, who at his most attractive resembled a disease-bearing rat, could not be trusted. Always had an agenda. As far as Albert could see every journalist present was at the bar and couldn't give a toss about archaeology.

He finished with extra, unscripted promises that his brandy-emboldened tongue flung around the room like mortars to maim hostile forces: free kindergarten education, ten-grand cash and a trip to Disneyland for the one-thousandth flat buyer and free cars for the runners up. The people on the stage, including his wife, clapped generously and the smiling, low-sized master of ceremonies stepped forward and said, — I'm sure some of you may have questions for Mr Barr.

A silence. Parish-hall foot scraping. Then up got Kevin; call him what you like, he was a trooper. Could never resist an opportunity to speak in public, of course, especially in the presence of television and a dozen reporters, however drunk. More photography as Kevin proclaimed that this kind of development was exactly what this government was all about, how his department had been very severe in their scrutiny of what was being launched today; how he, the minister, because of a certain overlap of interests not to mention emotional connections – good natured laughs; Albert could have kissed his father-in-law – how Kevin had personally withdrawn from the evaluation process so that no possible allegation of influence or favouritism could ever be levelled. He wished Goose Point Wonderland the best and looked forward to bringing his grandchildren to the zoo there.

Up bounced the smiling master of ceremonies looking left and right at the blank faces whose nostrils were twitching to the succulent aroma of the fillet steaks that lay awaiting them.

— *Wrap it up!* Albert hissed.

— Very well, ladies and gentlemen, in that case it only remains for me to… Sorry? Ah, a lady over there. Yes?

A young woman with a wad of black curls and wearing a denim mini-skirt stood up.

— Mr Barr, Cyclamen Montgomery, *The Irish Times.* Are you aware that a prominent archaeologist, Professor Ó Dálaigh, formerly of UCD, regards your site in Goose Point as having exceptional prehistorical significance? Can you please say if, during your extensive excavations in Goose Point, any items of archaeological significance have been uncovered? In particular, can you comment on a persistent rumour that artefacts, in some cases thought to be evidence of Fir Bolg habitation in Goose Point, have been discovered on your site? And if such items have been uncovered, what steps are you and your company taking to preserve these historic national treasures?

A buzz of anticipation flew around the room, although Albert was smiling as if his very favourite topic had been reached.

— I'm very glad you asked me that, ah, Cyclical. Although I never comment on rumours as anyone who knows me is aware, the protection of ancient sites and the scrupulous collection and safeguarding of archaeological artefacts has long been my priority.

He glared over at the bar where snorts of derision could be heard.

— We at Barr None have procedures on site in Goose Point, and indeed on all our sites, so that anything – and I mean anything – that looks as if it might be genuinely old is immediately reported to me personally.

Some people at the bar were already drunk enough to laugh openly at this remark. Cyclamen stood up again and said, — And has anything been reported to you, Mr Barr?

— Most certainly not, Albert replied. — Is that it?

Another hack was on his feet asking a question about the opera house, but by then the drift to the bar had become unstoppable.

Albert saw his father-in-law in the audience, a smile on his big face like a grin on an excavated skull.

TWELVE

The tight faces that gathered around the table for this unscheduled meeting of the executive committee were all fixed on HUBBI's chairman, Dr Eric Chester. Royal George particularly looked unwell: the head of markets' normally big, weather-beaten face was pasty and pinched.

— You lead off, Don, the chairman said to his head of treasury.

Chester felt queasy and apprehensive. Not even ten minutes of drooling over Inge earlier had managed to cheer him up.

Don Dunne breathed deeply, fixed everyone in turn with his fiercest glare.

— The only subject on our agenda this morning is Albert Barr, he said. — Albert Barr owes us nearly five hundred million. As we all know, his loans are in respect of an extensive mixed development in Goose Point. Additionally HUBBI owns five per cent of this development, purchased at a cost of thirty million. Our loans are secured on the site in Goose Point plus a wide range of other assets, plus Barr's guarantee. Up to a few weeks ago this looked like one of the best-secured loans in HUBBI.

The chairman looked at Fagan O'Dowd and wondered if the little bastard was actually taking pleasure in all this. Don Dunne continued, — Although the site has been prone to flooding from the Irish Sea from the outset, that problem was thought to have been solved – until three weeks ago when new leakage occurred in a new location on the site. This means that additional retaining works are now needed, but – and this is crucial – it also means that new planning permission is needed. Until new planning permission is obtained, the site is, de facto, without planning permission.

Fagan O'Dowd felt that it would be counterproductive at this stage to point out what he had said in the past. He had tried many times but all his efforts had been spurned. They hated him, these people. They hated the truth.

— A month ago Barr began to miss his interest payments, which we're currently rolling up, Don Dunne continued. — As aforementioned the outstanding amount owed to the bank this morning is four hundred and ninety million and change. Now another potentially more serious problem has arisen.

The chairman kept taking his glasses off and polishing them, as if what he was seeing was unclear.

— I think we've all read this morning's *Times*, Don Dunne plugged on. — A heritage issue has arisen in Goose Point. It is unproven, of course, but nothing threatens planning like heritage. What was previously unthinkable – that the planning authorities would reverse two previous decisions – is now a possibility according to the *Times*, apart altogether from the new permission required. The paper says that public protests can be expected.

— Your recommendation? the chairman asked.

— We have to ensure that this thing does not escalate any further, said the head of treasury. — Planning permission must be obtained.

* * *

Fagan O'Dowd had started his career with a large insurance company where he had worked his way up to manager by the age of twenty-seven. He then took what many saw as a crazy risk and joined the then tiny HUBBI as loan officer. It was Fagan who had laid down HUBBI's risk structures, who had built up the teams that scoured collateral for its true worth and gouged the last ounce of security from a commercial deal. Fagan had been crucial to HUBBI's success – and yet at some point along the way he had become philosophically estranged from the chairman. Fagan had tried on numerous occasions to rein the chairman in, to try to curtail his tendency to shoot from the hip, but he had been rebuffed. Don Dunne, who had once been his ally, now openly sneered at Fagan and Royal George patronised him as if he were an idiot.

Of course Royal George and Don Dunne were both making fortunes out of the ascending HUBBI share price. Fagan had once owned twenty thousand HUBBI shares purchased at nine Irish pounds each. When they'd risen to eleven – over a six-month period that he still remembered as the most uncomfortable of his life – he'd taken his profit and never bought HUBBI again.

Then one morning about a year ago, Fagan awoke to a sudden vision of exactly where the chairman's behaviour was leading HUBBI. Financial adrenalin had taken over the bank, he realised with horror. The chairman was giving enormous loans to madmen. At first terror consumed Fagan. Could he be so sure of his view when everyone else believed the opposite? No, he was certain: his view of the future was spot on. And for the first time in his life, in a moment of epic revelation, he saw how real wealth could be his.

* * *

— Fagan? the chairman said. — I'm sure you're just itching to illuminate us as to the security position of the Barr loans.

Fagan noted the thick layer of condescension in the chairman's voice and how Royal George and Don Dunne exchanged smirks. He referred to a thick ring-binder.

— We are secured by Goose Point, as Don has mentioned, Chairman, Fagan began. — I have an independent valuation dated three weeks ago that says if the flooding persists, and in the event of nothing being done about it, that ultimately the site may revert to foreshore. The valuers have consequently written down the value of the site to take account of such a possibility.

— To what?

— To not very much, Fagan said and looked at his notes. — In a nutshell we are out with the guts of half a billion on a flooded site that lacks planning permission.

— The worst possible scenario as usual, of course, said Royal George disdainfully. — Surprise, surprise.

— I assume you're getting another valuation, Fagan, the chairman said.

— Yes, of course, Fagan replied, but without the planning permission no professional valuer is going to be able to assume that the flooding problem is solved.

Royal George blew out his cheeks as if he was being confronted by a lunatic; Don Dunne tried to skewer Fagan with his eyes.

— We have substantial further collateral from Albert Barr, the chairman prompted.

— We have twenty-three assorted pieces of development land that are in many cases also pledged elsewhere, giving us in effect a secondary lien, Chairman, Fagan replied. — These sites are located in Drumshanbo, County Leitrim; Moneygall, County Tipperary; Borris-in-Ossory, County Offaly…

— How much?

— It's not that easy in the circumstances, Chairman, Fagan replied with his pained expression. — As you know, these properties have to be marked to their market value, and that value often resides solely in the planning permission, so if you have a site that has not yet obtained permission…

— How much? the chairman snapped.

Fagan peered down at his list, turned the page; the chairman vowed to hurt him badly one day.

— Eleven million, Chairman.

— Eleven million.

— You asked for a figure, Chairman.

— Not an awful lot, is it? the chairman said. — But we also have two blocks of apartments.

Sometimes, in the circumstances, it was difficult to be objective, Fagan thought. And yet the facts were the facts.

— Ah yes, formerly in public ownership, Chairman, he winced, transferred a few years ago to Mrs Medb-Marie Barr, agreed in recent weeks to be mortgaged to us.

— Fifty, sixty flats, the chairman said, I secured them myself, they're worth a fortune.

— A masterly stroke if I may say so, Royal George said.

— Only you could have done it, Chairman, said Don Dunne.

Fagan said, — Actually we're still going through the process of finalising the mortgage…

— Fifty or sixty flats, the chairman repeated calmly.

— Yes, Chairman, but…

— In the centre of Dublin. They have to be worth twenty million in a nuclear war, the chairman said as Royal George shook his head from side to side in disbelief at the intransigence he was witnessing.

— Chairman, I have to tell you that we've discovered a possible title defect in the original conveyance to Mrs Barr, said Fagan. — Seems corners may have been cut at the time she acquired the flats; the whole deal was done in haste, perhaps due to political pressure, there was a general election coming up, the transaction seems to have been signed off over a May bank holiday weekend…

The chairman blinked.

— … and Revenue may also be taking an interest in what happened back then. There were possibly some offshore shenanigans. In addition we're told the Criminal Assets Bureau may be taking a look…

— How much?

— Hard to put anything on them at the moment, Chairman; sorry… Fagan said.

Royal George folded his arms, crossed his legs and looked out the window.

— What else do we have? the chairman enquired. — Barr has guaranteed all his loans. What does he own, in other words?

The plastic-covered pages of the ring binder were turned once more. Fagan really did feel genuine grief that what he had predicted was now coming to pass.

— With Barr's personal guarantee, his assets are in effect ours, Fagan said. — These include half a million shares in HUBBI that are showing a profit of about three million…

— At least he's got balls! Royal George interjected.

— … several retail units in shopping centres in Dublin and Cork, a house in Inchigeela…

— Where?

— Inchigeela; it's a place in County Cork, Chairman.

— Go on.

— A speedboat, a duplex in London, six Sean Scullys…

— What are Sean Scullys? barked the chairman.

— Modern art, Chairman, said Royal George. — They're in our vault, not really my taste, but … a box at Leopardstown Racecourse, several expensive cars, a few hundred thousand shares in one of those new hotels we financed in Temple Bar, two memberships of the K-Club, a dozen racehorses, a hundred thousand in wine, a share in a jet. A greyhound in Wexford…

— How much?

— Forty-five, fifty.

— Is that it?

— That's all we've been able to uncover at the moment, Chairman, yes.

— Bottom line, the chairman rasped.

— We can recoup sixty-five million from Barr, tops, Fagan said.

— And he owes us five hundred million, the chairman said. — Fucking wonderful. George?

Royal George had acquired a 70-foot-long yacht the year before for three and a half million, which he kept moored in Palma, and about which he kept quiet in Dublin. Now a picture of the boat's graceful lines kept intruding into his mind. He said,

— We made just short of four hundred million last year, Chairman. Were we to take a hit of the size being discussed, which

I believe is ludicrous by the way, we'd report a loss of around fifty million for the year. We've never reported a loss before, as everyone is aware. The negative market reaction in such a case can be well imagined.

— We have accumulated reserves of a billion, the chairman said.

— Yes, and we would have to dip into them substantially to maintain the dividend in such a scenario. Even if we maintained the dividend, the share price would be severely impacted by announcing our first ever loss, Royal George said.

— Impacted by how much? the chairman asked.

Royal George cringed.

— Hard to say, he said, but I asked our brokers to run a computer-based bear-case scenario; purely hypothetical, I need hardly add.

— And?

— HUBBI shares could dip 50 per cent, Chairman.

— I see, the chairman said.

The people at the meeting would go on to describe the moment that now gripped the little group as surreal: out of body, unreal, not actually happening, weird, unnatural, they would later say.

— There's another problem we have to address, said Royal George reluctantly. — Our shares are being sold aggressively short. At least three large hedge funds that we know of have stepped up their short selling of HUBBI in the last two weeks. The most prominent is MUESLI, based out of Zurich.

There was a tremor in Royal George's deep voice as he articulated an issue that everyone knew was top of the chairman's list of the despicable.

— These short sellers will get burned, of course, their arms will get torn off, Royal George hurried on, but in the short term we don't want to help their case by announcing bad news. Which is why the kind of hysterical talk we've been hearing this morning from the head of risk is so counter-productive. You're talking us into a loss, Fagan, which I'm sure makes you happy!

— Chairman, that's very unfair… Fagan began.

— Go on, George, said the chairman tersely.

— Were we to write down the Barr loan as we've been discussing and show a loss of that magnitude, it might be seen as a sign that the market had topped, Royal George said. — Other assets in our loan portfolio might come under pressure. We might have to make further write-downs. When this starts no one knows where it might end. The short selling could increase.

— Bottom line? the chairman said from clenched teeth.

— Bottom line, we *cannot* write off this loan, Royal George replied.

The chairman knew what had to be done. Over many years he had prepared for a day like this; this was the kind of test he had been born to take. It was simply war, and in war you had to fight to survive. He addressed the meeting.

— So what in essence needs to be done here? How do we get back to where we were just a few weeks ago? I'll tell you how. We need to remove the obstacles to the new planning permission on Barr's site that have suddenly arisen. A month ago this was a site worth at least five hundred million. Am I correct?

— Absolutely correct, Chairman, Royal George and Don Dunne said as one.

— What are these obstacles? the chairman asked. — The unexpected appearance of a possible heritage issue on the site, as outlined in *The Irish Times*, which may cause problems for the planning authorities and at least two government departments. Barr's father-in-law is Minister for Infrastructure Development and has extensive powers – need I say more? So the only problem we have here is a problem with the media. It's a *media* problem. Anyone disagree?

Fagan wanted to say, the media is simply *reporting* a problem, we need to deal with the underlying issues and we need to get our fucking money back as quickly as we can; but he knew it was too late to say such things, so he remained silent.

The chairman said, — Last night I took a look at the institutions that manage the pension funds for the principal Irish newspapers. Their funds are heavily skewed in favour of Irish banks. A 50 per cent drop in our share price, which would be bound to affect other banks as well, would be ruinous for these funds. Don, I want you to get onto the chief executives of every one of these pension funds and make sure they fully understand the position. I have no doubt when they do that they will contact the chairmen of the newspapers and advise them accordingly. The same applies to commercial radio and TV.

— But Chairman… Fagan began.

— *What?* the chairman snarled.

— Nothing, Fagan mumbled.

— I'm glad to hear it, said the chairman with undisguised venom. — Next up, as an extra precaution, I examined our loan books to see exactly how much we are owed by certain newspapers. Take the Valentine Group, for example. They owe us a hundred million on a revolving facility that's due for review in two months. That scenario can be spread right across the industry. I doubt if these papers are going to risk their financial well-being for a couple of cavemen.

Royal George nodded gravely and murmured, — Hear, bloody hear.

— Finally, the chairman said, one of our junior internal loan officers came up with this little nugget of information. A certain Miss Cyclamen Montgomery has applied to us for a one hundred and ten per cent generational mortgage of three hundred and fifty thousand to purchase a house off the South Circular Road. The loan is currently pending approval.

Royal George actually clapped; Don Dunne fixed Fagan with his most evil stare.

— So let's stop digging a hole for ourselves, the chairman said with the fervour of a zealot. — Let's start concentrating on the opportunities that this position has created.

There was a time when Fagan would have said, listen, I agree with all that and I admire your tenacity, Chairman, but what we should be trying to do is to lower our loan exposure here. Barr has missed interest payments – instead of loaning him even more money, what we should now be doing is realising the assets we have. The Goose Point development can wait.

But the chairman, on his feet, had begun to pace.

— I want the lifeblood squeezed out of the bastards that are short selling HUBBI, he stated in a rising voice. — I want all the bank's property assets revalued using only firms that are sympathetic to our vision of where our property's true level lies. Use those firms that owe us money. My estimate is that our true worth is at least a few hundred million north of where it stands on our balance sheet – anyone disagree?

Fagan, in his mind, was already packing.

— Two: I want half of our pension reserve, currently in government gilts, cashed in and invested in our own shares. I estimate four hundred million is available. I mean, why deny the pension fund the opportunities that ordinary people have to invest in our brand – eh? Let's hit these hedge funds right where it hurts them – in the marketplace. Let's squeeze the shit out of them.

— Alleluia! Royal George cried.

— Three: I want to immediately start buying back our own shares on the market using our cash reserves, up to a value of five hundred million. The fewer shares on the market in potentially hostile hands, the lower the risk to the bank's share price.

— Shouldn't this strategy be first run by our board of directors? Fagan asked. — And shouldn't we also tell the Financial Regulator?

— I will look after our board of directors, said the chairman thinly. — They will stand four-square behind my strategy, believe me.

Especially since they're all in HUBBI up to their necks, Fagan thought. He asked, — And the Financial Regulator?

The chairman exchanged glances with the two other members

of the executive committee. Royal George shrugged and said, —
We've never had a problem before with the Financial Regulator;
why should we have one now?

— I want to hit the people who don't share our vision, the
predators who've been selling us short, the chairman said. — We
screw the sons of bitches, we impale them on the very weapon
they've chosen to use against us!

— Amen to that! Don Dunne said.

The chairman's eyes were blazing now, his hands reaching out
in claws as if to catch the bank's enemies and physically destroy
them.

— 'If You're In HUBBI...' he cried.

— '... You're In The Money!' Don Dunne and Royal George
chorused.

— Fagan? the chairman blazed. — I didn't hear you...

— Eric, Fagan said sadly, I think you've gone stark raving mad.

THIRTEEN

Half asleep, he remembered the time shortly before he got married when his father took him for a drive. Dad was getting on in age then, yet he still liked a car with a walnut trim and a racing steering wheel, in this case on a cream coloured Bristol: a lovely six-cylinder two-door saloon with a body styled by Zagato. They drove up into the Dublin Mountains and parked in a gateway with a view down over Greystones.

— You must be very excited, Dad said.

Lee answered that he was, which was true. The prospect of possessing Tallulah in a legal sense was very exciting. Dad said,

— Life is a strange jalopy.

Lee smiled. Dad always said things like that when he wanted to give advice.

— But nothing in life is as strange or as important as deciding on the person you are going to marry, Dad said. — It's a decision whose wisdom, or the lack of it, will affect every day of your life. At the time you make that decision, you are young, your revs are high, your fuel tank full. You don't need a roadmap, you think. As far as you can see, the road is straight ahead.

Dad was looking at Lee intently.

— But no road is straight, Lee. Some are crooked but then straighten, and some are death traps. It's very hard but you have to try and see beyond the first bend in the road.

Lee often wondered in later years when the road with Tallulah got really bad — when, in fact, they ran out of road — if that was what Dad had been trying to tell him in the mountains. Or if Dad had been trying to tell him something else, if in fact he had not been alluding to Lee and Tallulah at all.

Tallulah had been beautiful, but in a delicate, very breakable porcelain way which changed with her moods, and sometimes even with the light. Medb-Marie Barr's beauty, for example, was spectacular beauty; she was beautiful at all times, even on those mornings when Lee noticed the Latvian cleaning lady hauling out a box of empty Cristal bottles for Christiana to take to recycling. Even hungover, which he could sometimes sense she was, Medb-Marie was hypnotic. She commanded him, queen-like, scarcely seeing him as she spoke. And yet something unsettling lay behind her beauty, an almost destructive quality that made Lee fear for her.

Tallulah too had commanded him, not queen-like, but by turning up and down her visible level of displeasure like an erratic thermostat. In the end she had not been very nice to Mum, hadn't bothered to visit her in hospital even though she'd only been down the road from St Vincent's, pleaded headaches the whole time, said hospitals and death terrified her. At the funeral she'd been completely out of it and midway through the service had to be helped out.

How she had sucked Lee dry, spending his money on art which she had subsequently stolen, on absinthe, Consulate and laudanum. Then, in a single devastating weekend – one weekend! – she had taken off forever.

Gwen's beauty, although not as obvious as that of either Tallulah or Medb-Marie, trumped them by a distance. Gwen's beauty was an inner thing, the expression in her translucent, oyster-grey eyes, the way she felt his pain, her quiet intelligence, her calmness, and the fact that with Gwen the sex was better than he had ever known it before.

He had not been surprised to hear that she had once been married, although why this was his reaction, he wasn't sure. Her husband had been a surgeon, she told him, a man with a busy daily list who believed that all of life's problems could be expedited with the scalpel. She had foundered, parched of intellectual stimulation, and the surgeon had run off with a Filipino nurse. Gwen had studied Freud and Jung. A few boyfriends had appeared, but none had stayed the course. The last one was four years ago, she told Lee as she kissed his throat and moved her knee up between his legs.

She liked him to hold her close for hours after they had finished, as they dozed off, his nose in her hair, his chin in the little cradle made by the bones of her shoulder.

He felt at ease and happy. He had for lonely years looked on Sundays as days to kill, hour by hour, sitting with his headphones on, waiting for the midday Angelus before he started to drink. The Sunday before, which he had spent almost entirely in bed with Gwen, had been a day in which he had grudged each passing minute.

* * *

He wondered if he should tell her of the startling dreams he had been having ever since he met her. It seemed mildly dishonourable to take advantage of her professional expertise without paying a fee, as if Gwen was, say, a housepainter with whom he was sleeping, and he was now asking her to touch up the kitchen. At the same time, if she had asked him for advice about something she was writing, notwithstanding that no evidence existed that she was writing anything, Lee wouldn't have minded giving it; and so he began to tell her about the very strong dream he had had the night before, in this very bed, as she slept beside him.

— You don't mind? he asked.

— Why should I mind?

— You might think, I don't know, you might feel… you know, the last time we discussed such matters, I was your client.

— You still have to get to know me, she said.

— It involves a dream in which a voice calls out, 'Come back!'

— Okay.

It was indeed his mother's voice, he was sure, Lee told her. The memory of Mum's voice was strong and insistent; even as he spoke, Lee could hear her shouting out the words. His dream had been of Whiskey, a white West Highland with a button nose that Dad had given Lee as a present for his third birthday. Funny, but until the dream it had been years since he'd thought about Whiskey, adorable Whiskey who had slept in a basket at the foot of the bed in little Lee's room.

— He was exactly like the white dog on the label of the bottle of Black & White Scotch, Lee told Gwen.

In the dream, during which all action is skew-ways and present tense, Lee is holding his mother's hand as they walk into Donnybrook to the grocers. It's a cold day in winter, there's snow on the ground which makes Whiskey hard to see as he bounds ahead, disappearing, reappearing, sniffing at the tyres of parked cars and lifting his leg at every one of them. Lee wants to run ahead like Whiskey, and reacts with anger when Mum tells him that he has to hold her hand.

— If you don't stop being bold you'll get no sweets, is what Mum says.

Suddenly, in the black-hole technology of dreams, Lee is standing with his father watching a man dig a grave in the back garden. A misshapen potato sack is placed in the grave. Lee's mother is standing on the stairs in the house. She screams, COME BACK!

— And that's the dream, Lee said.

Gwen stroked his face with the tips of her fingers, something which he had fantasised about her doing during their formal sessions. She said, — What happened to Whiskey?

— He was run over by a bus, Lee said. — In Donnybrook, I think.

— Why do you think that?

— I remember once when we were going to Mass Mum saying to Dad, 'That's where poor Whiskey was killed by the bus,' and Dad saying, 'You say that every Sunday.'

— What do you think happened? Gwen asked. — What are you remembering, do you think?

Lee said, — I think, although I can't be sure, that the first part of the dream, where Whiskey runs ahead, was when he was killed. I assume Mum saw him running out under the bus. She screamed 'Come back!' at him. I must have seen it happen.

— That's awful, Gwen said.

Lee lay back and looked up at the ceiling. He said, — And yet it's not Whiskey I feel sorry for. It's Dad.

— Your dad?

— Strange, isn't it?

They lay in bed listening to the wind build up outside and the rain lash into the window. Des, on the sofa below, snored lightly. Gwen said, — You think your mum was calling after Whiskey, yet she's inside on the stairs, not on the street in Donnybrook.

— I know, Lee said.

Later, as dusk came prematurely, they grilled anchovies and Lee chatted to Gwen again about Mr O and the arrowheads.

— You should have heard him in the jewellers!

Wind shook the house and she cuddled in beside Lee.

— There was a time when I'd have jumped at the opportunity to write a piece about something like that, he said. — But I never want to go back to that, ever. I'm a new man.

— Hmmm, and I like that new man, Gwen said and began to work her fingers up under his T-shirt.

She must have got up early next morning because Lee woke to the smell of kippers grilling. He came down the ladder and kissed her on the neck. She was standing in the galley, reading *The Irish Times*.

— Hello, he said, his eyes still glued with sleep.

— Hey! Gwen said. — Listen to this!

* * *

Every day of the summer holidays young Con Ó Dálaigh made his way out by bicycle from Dundalk to the Cooley Peninsula to watch seabirds, aye. Along Cooley's steep cliffs, the air crackled with ozone as gulls and hawks hovered and hunted. This sunny landscape, which young Con came to call his own, was the property of the Buck family; men of military tradition as Con's grandfather, Gearóid Ó Dálaigh, had explained to him. Gearóid, or simply Gerry Daly, as he had been back then, had been the stable groom in Minister's Peak, the Buck residence on Cooley.

Granddad used to talk about the quality of the Buck dung, aye, the stable manure, you understand, because in those days they hunted four days a week, both sides of the border, the Colonel and Lady Primrose, which meant eight hunters in full livery, aye, which is what granddad was there for, you understand. Eight hunters in full livery produce a lot of dung, but quality dung, and all of Dundalk would be queuing up to get a couple of decent shovelfuls for their roses, because no rose prize was ever won on Cooley in living memory that wasn't reared on Buck dung.

Young Con, freshly returned from his twitching sessions on the cliffs, heard about the great battles that had taken place on Cooley, the countless landings, sieges, battles and episodes of indiscriminate butchery that had torn the place apart for at least four and half thousand years. The Buck estate, which had once extended to fifty times its present size, had been awarded by Elizabeth I to a cavalry officer named Buck, who had distinguished himself by slaughtering most of the inhabitants of Cooley during one particularly unpleasant weekend in 1587. The land out there was soaked in blood, according to Granddad Ó Dálaigh, and the Bucks had always been in the middle of it.

— A terrible family for fighting altogether, Granddad had said. Aye.

The old colonel was well-known around Dundalk for his projects that always ended in failure. There had been the disastrous plan to produce honey – tens of thousands of unwanted glass jars still cluttered up one end of the hay barn; five hundred beehives were sold off in a job lot – the peregrine-falcon breeding project and, financially the most ruinous, the conger-eel project. By the time young Con Ó Dálaigh had begun to come out to the cliffs of Cooley in search of kittiwakes and gannets, the colonel had retreated into a private world of manuscripts and fossils, shells and scrimshaw.

On the cliffs one day, Con heard a human cry. He hurried to the source of the problem and found a tall, elderly gentleman sprawled on his back. Ach, yes, the old man was in agony; he had badly twisted his ankle in a rut. Con, who suddenly realised that he was looking down at Colonel Buck himself, tried to get him to his feet, but the colonel was too tall and young Con too small for the purpose. Casting around for something the better to bear the colonel's weight, Con suddenly spotted the outline of a long staff lying half buried in the centre of the very rut which had caused the colonel's fall. Gouging it out, he thrust it into the colonel's hand and they hobbled for home.

— And there it might all have ended, said Mr O. — That might well have been the end of it, indeed.

Colonel Buck was a hoarder. Rather than jettison an implement of such happy consequence, he carefully stored away the wooden staff and a few months later took it out and cleaned the blighter. What emerged from the encrusted clay of his makeshift crutch was an ancient length of wood engraved with decorations which, archaeologists in both London and Dublin confirmed, was a section of a doorpost from 2750 BC. A message was sent to Dundalk. Young Con Ó Dálaigh cycled out to Minister's Peak and the colonel proudly showed him the results.

— I remember seeing the engravings, Mr O said and smiled. — They were beautiful – hunting scenes in the main. Very detailed, aye.

From that moment on, young Con Ó Dálaigh set out on the path of truth and discovery. It would turn him into an archaeologist, his education paid for by the Colonel and Lady Primrose, and subsequently into Professor Ó Dálaigh, Head of the Department of Archaeology, University College Dublin.

The Cooley Doorpost, which the Buck family subsequently presented to the National Museum, had one wee problem, however. It wasn't from Cooley. A succession of palaeogeologists, epigraphers and fossiologists were adamant that the origin of the doorpost was Dublin Bay – its sedimentary composition of tiny prawns, found only in that body of water, proved it beyond doubt. Mr O made it his life's ambition to find out if they were right.

Over forty years, discoveries by Professor Ó Dálaigh in and around Cooley included silver fragments, a map drawn in ox blood on hide from the pre-Christian era and, from an executor's sale of a cottage outside Dundalk, an old sugar tin containing an eighth-century illuminated scroll, executed by a scribe working under the instructions of St Scrotus.

— They all pointed to one thing, Mr O whispered.

Lee held his breath.

— I had discovered the Fir Bolg! cried Mr O and shook the table with his bunched fist.

It's two thousand years before Christ, a long time ago. In Greece, merciless temple builders have scoured the northern seas and brought back shiploads of white-skinned slaves to their sultry kingdom. These poor wretches toil under the hot sun and the whips of the oppressor, hauling stones on their backs in leather hides, falling, dying, surviving, breeding. One thing they never lose sight of is their green, cherished isle, the place they were snatched from. Its position is fixed in their heads like the structure of the stars. They toil, they dream.

— Lord Almighty, think of their courage! Mr O said.

Then one day, in an act of ingenuity unsurpassed even by the Israelites, these slaves sail away from Greece in crude boats sewn together from the same leather stone bags with which they have toiled for the stolen generations. The Fir Bolg – the men in bags; the first Irish diaspora – are back! God alone knows the hardships of their journey – across the Mediterranean, through the Straits of Gibraltar, up across the Bay of Biscay – they cannot be stopped – they battle around the tip of what today is Cornwall – they are salmon, glued to their destiny and to their destination. At last they reach the sacred land that spawned them centuries before. The Fir Bolg are home!

— Although folklore persistently places the Fir Bolg's arrival in Ireland around 2000 BC, the Cooley Doorpost pre-dated that event by three-quarters of a millennium, said Mr O gravely. — This means that the Cooley Doorpost belonged to the ancestors of those who had been taken into slavery by the Greeks in the first place.

Apart from the carbon-dated Cooley Doorpost, hide maps also illustrated a settlement on the coast, with mountains to the south, and several small islands just off the coast, south and north. Moreover, a faint but proportionately accurate map of the coast placed the settlement exactly in the place where modern-day Dublin now stood: Goose Point.

Then there was the manuscript, which although executed millennia later, was probably copied from older parchments, themselves the heirs to oral tradition.

On each day of the moon's being full, the king sat down in his palace which lay on the plain by the sea, and conferred with his noblemen. As night fell, only the moonbeams catching the scales of the salmon leaping in the water could equal the splendour of the silver on his table.

Goose Point would have been an obvious choice. First and foremost, security: access to the sea, but also the means to prevent hostile landings. The Dublin Mountains to the south provided their own defence. From the point of view of weather, Goose Point sheltered the settlement from the worst of it.

— And now these, Mr O said and spilled out the arrowheads from Lee's handkerchief.

Professional artists, skilled in working with ancient images, had two decades before extracted the tiny details of the arrows depicted on the Cooley Doorpost and had extrapolated them into detailed illustrations. Mr O opened a book containing a number of large, coloured and detailed drawings of arrowheads, all of them identical to the tiny silver heads now lying on the table.

— We have found it at last. We have found *Cathair an Airgid*, said Mr O. — We have found the silver city of the Fir Bolg.

* * *

It was strange to walk into the reception area of Valentine Newspapers and not proceed through the hip-high metal turnstile and hear the electronic click as his security pass was digitally scanned. He felt suddenly excluded, albeit from a place whose absence from his life he had spent the last month celebrating. The writer in him, for now he had a story worth telling, the writer in him wanted to be through the turnstile, up there in the middle of the action, at his keyboard, on fire.

Behind the chin-level reception counter sat two women that Lee had never really noticed before. One, a female with short, straight black hair and a nose stud, looked at him as if he might have something contagious, then picked up the phone to call Eddie.

Through the reception lobby a steady flow of employees moved in both directions. They all seemed in a hurry, even the ones going out for a smoke to the pavement. One or two recognised Lee and waved to him nervously, but no one stopped to chat. The curse of the excluded. Why did he mind? He hated this place and all it represented, and yet... A small, broad man of thirty-five or so, dressed in a black shirt and red tie, like someone playing the role of Al Capone in a Christmas play, clicked his way through the turnstile. He was Sam O'Sling, the editor of the *Daily Gael*, a Cork journeyman who had made it big in Dublin and whose current position depended entirely on his ability to ruin decent people's reputations. Lee hated this place, these creatures like O'Sling who fed off decent people's lives – and yet… Dick Bell, the towering managing editor, Eddie's nemesis, came thrusting into reception, belly like a spinnaker, fishing out a cigarette. Lee shrank into a corner where that day's *Daily Gael* was piled six feet high. Bell looked like an angry bull despite his tailored voluminous shirt with French cuffs and diamond-studded gold cufflinks. He glared in Lee's direction for a terrifying moment, then carried on outside, where he lit up, creating a little area of quarantine around him.

— Pssssst!

Eddie grabbed Lee's arm and dragged him out through a side-door used for deliveries. The rims of Eddie's eyes were red and ruptured and his face had been shaved only in parts. Walking rapidly from the building, glancing back several times until the smoking area was lost from sight, he lit up a cigarette for himself, took half a dozen frenzied drags, stubbed the glowing tip with his yellowed thumb and pocketed the butt. Propelling Lee across the road, they burst in through the doors of a coffee shop. Eddie ordered a latte for Lee and a triple espresso, Java-Mocha blend, for himself, and angled into a table at the back from which he could keep the entrance under observation. Flowering paranoia, the child of alcohol. Sipping from his polystyrene mug, grimacing elaborately at the hot, sweet-spicy hit, Eddie said in a low voice, — We're all going down in there, it's like Cambodia under the Khmer Rouge, no one is safe.

His whole body shook, sweat swam in a torrent down his face. Lee could see himself, a few months before, toxic, half mad, hiding in the jacks, trying to remember old prayers, pleading with time to speed up so that he could decently slip into a wine bar and order his first, mercifully cool, blessedly restorative glass of the day.

— It's carnage, Eddie whispered from the deathbed of his tortured soul. — It's the fucking Holocaust multiplied by a thousand.

Dolphin Valentine himself, the proprietor, had started coming in, an unheard-of event, and had taken up residence in Dick Bell's corner office. Dick had been forced to relocate down the corridor to an office with only one window, Eddie confided. A bloodbath. Ten per cent of the people on that floor had been let go, *kaput!* No notice. The proprietor refused to meet the unions but the outgoing staff reported daily horror stories upstairs as Dolphin Valentine savaged Dick Bell. Eleven thousand copies of the *Sunday Trumpet* from the month before had shown up in a deep trench on the border. How many more were missing? A pilot group had been formed to examine whether the *Trumpet* could be used for wall-cavity insulation. A rumour was going round that the international press agencies were withholding copy to Valentine Newspapers because they hadn't been paid for six months. Dick Bell, like a wounded, rabid dog, was roaming the lower floors, foaming, feral, looking for retribution.

With fresh coffees, Lee tried to redirect the conversation. He took out a copy of the previous day's *Irish Times* and opened it to an inside page.

— Eddie, look at this. You see this?

Eddie needed his quivering index finger to guide his eye. He didn't want to throw up in here, coffee was driving him mad, cups beyond counting that morning alone, caffeine shrivelling up his organs, rusting his brain away, despoiling his skin, every time he passed water he smelled like Indonesia.

— So? he said. — What the fuck is it?

— I have the inside story, Lee whispered as Eddie, like a dehydrated invalid, stared at a close-up of Medb-Marie Barr. — I have conclusive proof that Mr Barr is lying his head off. This site is to Irish archaeology what Mecca is to Muslims – the most holy place on earth. This is the biggest story you'll ever break.

He seemed not to have grasped even a small part of it, so Lee took out the reasonably distinct photographs of the arrowheads that he had taken with a Kodak throwaway, and a large colour picture of the Cooley Doorpost.

— Eddie! Wake up!

Times were, he had thought this kid and himself would make a great team, like Woodward and Bernstein, England and Carew, or maybe the other way around sounded better, alliteration had always been his strong point. Now he was terrified someone might walk in and find him actually talking to an ex-employee; he'd spotted a few already, a sub-editor from the *Eclipse*...

— It's got everything, Eddie, it's got money, the sexiest woman in Ireland, Dublin's biggest building project, a massive cover-up. And not only do I have the heritage angle in the bag, I *work* for these people.

— You...?

— I'm their gardener.

Eddie took out his cigarettes, realised where he was, re-pocketed them. Out there, from a place he sought to be, a region of cool reflection and well-being, where the gears of his mind engaged with smooth perfection, from a mossy glade of absolute sobriety, Eddie heard a tone he had been long awaiting.

— Their gardener?

— That's right. I know these people. I can write the whole personal-interest side of the story as well – their lifestyle, their wealth, their barbecues. I clean up their empty bottles, Eddie!

It was the groundwork that he'd laid down over the years, the sheer hard work it took to mould talent into coherent copy, that had brought this kid to where he was. Without him, without Eddie, he would never have developed the nose for a story, Eddie told himself feverishly. Talent always came to the surface in the end, even in a city destroyed by war. This could be Valentine Newspapers' Washington Fucking Post Moment! He'd celebrate tonight, a couple of glasses of *vino blanco*, but not too many, he wanted to retain editorial control. A surge of hope. Yes! Heaven was like the bar in the Ritz Hotel in the Place Vendôme, Paris, France, as the great man probably once said.

— Eddie? Eddie!

Eddie's head was going from side to side, the way it did when he was revved up.

— Kid, I want to hear it from the beginning! he whispered in his crazy way. — Nothing left out, no poetic licence, as it really is.

FOURTEEN

Albert nearly choked. There was his death notice, in the paper. He actually thought that his chest was going to seize with terror, as if someone had poured concrete down his windpipe. He stumbled from his office, found a pub with a snug and drank brandy for the day.

The things the media did, given half a chance! He was turning a wasteland into a paradise and all that this bitch could write about was ... was *what?* Nothing! There was nothing down there in Goose Point. A leaking pit. His whole life and career were on the line – and what had she written in the paper? The cradle of Irish civilisation. Men in bags? At first he'd thought it must be a joke. And such a sanctimonious bitch! He'd wondered later how she might react to a straightforward bribe, although *The Irish Times* was full of Protestants and they were different. Albert had never had a satisfactory deal with a Protestant, that is if you left out the women he'd dealt with over the years in Germany and Scandinavia, many of whom had told him they were Lutherans, which Albert was pretty sure made them Protestants even if they were on the game.

He hated the media, like many a man. The money he'd spent over the years, not just on advertising but on pouring drink into the bastards, was obscene. They only wanted to destroy, never took a risk themselves, begrudged people like Albert who had made it big, fed off the delusions of fools who bought newspapers in the first place.

Sometimes he fantasised about what would happen if Kevin ever made Taoiseach, or even Minister for Justice; the measures Albert would make sure were taken to cut the media down to size. Mandatory jail sentences for reporters who breached stern guidelines. Paid informers in press rooms and selective use of torture for miscreants would become standard. The possibility of internment too, and if the bastards wanted to go on hunger strike then – rock 'n' roll all the way to the graveyard, folks!

After the formal part of the launch he'd spent more than a grand at the bar in the Westbury in the hope that the drunker the hacks became, the less likely they were to remember anything. Poured Grand Cru Classé down the throats of more than thirty of the bastards, many of whom, garrulous and incoherent, were sprawled on piles of discarded Goose Point press packs. Some of them, pissed beyond realising who he was, had whispered to him in the vilest language what they would do to Medb-Marie in bed.

When he eventually got home Medb-Marie had retired. He'd actually planned a small celebration dinner in town, just the two of them, but she'd got fed up waiting for him. In the den Albert sat down in dread to watch the nine o'clock news. Was it fair that he was miserable on what should have been the greatest day of his life? He fell asleep before the news came on and woke up just in time for the weather forecast. He briefly considered: taking Viagra, returning to the piss-up in the Westbury, watching a porn movie, buying a new Porsche online, surfing the net using the password one of the lads had given him which enabled holders to correspond in real time with Nigerian call-girls, having a fry.

He got up at last and opened a bottle of the most expensive wine he could find, to make a statement – to the hacks, to God, to the world – and began to drink it with chilling deliberation. He shuffled through the usual stacks of unopened mail.

The S&P 500 seems to us 'coiled', as they say, for another spring upwards.

Our Vietnamese 'Napalm' Property Fund is showing scorching year-on-year compound gains of close to one hundred per cent!

Dear Mester Alber Barr: What does have the Siberian white hares and New York silver futures got in common?

He took up the whole bundle of correspondence – bills, flyers, magazines and circulars – stumbled out to the backyard and threw them in the bin. He stood for a moment, confused by the rush of cool air, tingling as the night pricked at his skin. Despite the cloying pollution of sweet yellow city light, some stars were visible.

What chance had he, Albert from Tramore, a speck, of influencing the passage of great events? Maybe there had been a settlement long ago in Goose Point where men like him – settlement builders, all of them – had also stood out on a night such as this and felt humbled under the spread of heaven. As it had always been. How often in the years between that faraway time and now had cities risen and fallen, kings ruled and died, men tried and failed? Thousands and thousands of times. Ambition was laughable, when you saw it like that. Why should he be afraid of what anyone wrote, or said, or did? They could bring him down, but he would rise up again. Albert walked out into the centre of the cobbled yard. This was where his destiny began and ended.

— Fuck you all! he shouted from full lungs. — Fuck you all!

Some lights came on in the house next door.

— And fuck you too! someone shouted back.

He laughed. He felt immortal.

* * *

The trouble with handing in his notice to Medb-Marie Barr before he filed his article and saw it published, as Gwen insisted, was that although based on admirable principles, the decision was flawed insomuch as it supposed an outcome that was not absolutely guaranteed.

— You mean, they might *not* publish my piece? he asked, wide-eyed and derisive. Currents of excitement darted through him. This was what he had been born for. — They're getting the hottest story of the year, Gwen! Eddie is delirious.

Outside, across the road in the park trees swayed wildly in a sudden wind. Slowly but surely winter was coming in.

— Write her a letter, Gwen said. — Post it tomorrow after the paper comes out.

— I'd prefer to look her in the eye, he said.

— Do as you will.

Lee loved Gwen. He knew his life would forevermore be the now, the future and BG – before Gwen. BG was a place he never wanted to revisit, a nightmarish bewilderment of drink, years of uncertainty, sadness, guilt and suspicion. It would take him years to get to know her the same way she knew him, but he relished the prospect of doing so. In the meantime he loved her for her warm and uncomplicated sexuality; her erudition in all things, but especially when it came to matters concerning him; her enthusiasm for his projects and her love. He had become a vegetarian.

Before he sat down to write the piece that would change his life he had dragged her across the park, through closely knit groups of bespectacled Chinese and turbaned Sikh families with prams and heavily swathed Muslim women pushing replete shopping trolleys. Out a gate on the far side that formerly he had never used, he led her up a road of two-storey, semi-detached houses with basements until they came to one with moss-covered steps, which they carefully descended. His arm at her elbow, they proceeded along the side of the house where dense briars and ragwort, gigantic dock leaves, ferns and ash saplings sprouted and sprang from walls and cracked paving slabs. Vertical steel bars protected the windows and were twined thickly with ivy. Lee rang the bell. Gwen shivered. After a few moments they could hear lusty swearing as a series of locks were tumbled, one by one. The door opened.

— Mr O!

— Who is it?

— It's Lee. Mr O, this is Gwen.

He wanted her to hear it from Mr O himself; not that she wasn't convinced already or that he felt she doubted the story he had to tell, but he wanted her to hear the passionate conviction in the old man's voice as he spoke about prehistory and this great new discovery.

The kitchen was long with a low ceiling and as damp as a crypt. An aged gas cooker stood in one corner beside an enamel sink. On a central table covered by a plastic cloth lay an egg-streaked plate, a batch loaf with green spots and a half pound of butter. The flagstones oozed tuberculosis.

— Well, the fact of the matter is, I grew up on the Cooley Peninsula, aye…

Gwen loved Lee. During the two years of their professional relationship, in the lonely aftermath of her own divorce, she had increasingly looked forward to their weekly sessions. From the wreckage of his life she could discern an enduring innocence that she found irresistible. She loved his unquenchable spirit, and the fact that he bore no grudges. He wasn't bad looking either, which didn't hurt, and on several occasions in her own dreams, which she had recorded in a journal, speculative images of Lee Carew without clothing had been noted. Of course she had accepted that as a client no future could exist between them, and so when he failed to appear any more she was almost relieved.

Now, together, she was much happier than she had ever been. At times she feared that he did too much to please her, for everyone needed to live for themselves as well as others, but his enthusiasm for her was boundless and she surrendered happily to the blissful moments.

She felt, too, that one day he would write the book he so often spoke of but never seemed to engage with, but that the catharsis needed for such an achievement had yet to be reached. It would however, she was sure, be a good book when eventually he got round to it. Meanwhile she feared that the project he was now pursuing was inappropriate. It would draw him back into the world from which he had so recently been delighted to escape, a place that had always made him unhappy, into the company of people who were unworthy of him, into that side of his life ruled by chaos and destruction.

Gwen reached over and squeezed Lee's hand. This basement place and its old occupant were all about the past. She wanted to be outside. She didn't care about the Fir Bolg or where their settlement might have been or whether they had ever existed. She wanted to feel the sun on her face.

* * *

Instead of sending a letter of resignation Lee composed a text to Medb-Marie, saying he would not be in the next day since he was going to the dentist. It was a lie he hated telling, since he had teeth and gums to die for. He sent the text. He then sat down and wrote the piece.

At six that evening it was done. The article ran to over three thousand words, which for Valentine Newspapers would be epic length; and yet, Lee mused as he re-read the piece, this was epic material; this was huge. The paper would run it over three, perhaps even four days. Goose Point, as Mr O had said, was more significant than Newgrange, Wood Quay and Clonmacnoise rolled into one. This was the seat of Irish civilisation! No other country in Europe could claim to have reached back so far into the annals of time and come up with such rich proof of its beginnings as now lay within Ireland's grasp. To build apartments on this sacred place would be criminal, scandalous, immoral and in contravention of our duties under international law, as Mr O had put it. Goose Point should immediately be declared a World Heritage Site. All building work should cease permanently. Planning authorities should be advised of their liabilities to the past and the dead. A national day of celebration should be declared – Fir Bolg Day.

Lee had watered down some of the professor's more animated suggestions and had concentrated on the evidence provided by the arrowheads. He had called the financial correspondent in the *Trumpet* and had ascertained the effect that halting all work on Goose Point would have on Barr None Developments and their lead bankers, HUBBI. Hypothetically, of course, as he put it.

— I hope it's hypothetical, the woman journalist said. — I have a thousand HUBBI shares and if what you're telling me is true then they've loaned nearly half a billion on a site that's never going to be developed. They only made four hundred million last year. Work it out for yourself.

A tremor of sympathy for the consequences his story might have on Medb-Marie Barr shot through him, and a brief but instant scenario formed in his mind: Medb-Marie on her knees, in the spinach, pleads with him not to publish his story, Lee's belt buckle level with her face, Des to one side, barking...

Goose Point was only one development of many where Albert Barr was concerned, Lee felt sure. These kind of people had money everywhere, and anyway, as the financial correspondent had said, it was the bank that would suffer, not the Barrs.

Earlier, Lee had taken a trip to the National Museum to see the Cooley Doorpost for himself. He had stood at the glass case for thirty minutes and observed the unmistakeable shapes of arrowheads etched into the post's long shaft. He had also interviewed a spokesperson for the museum about the Fir Bolg and their significance to Ireland. The man's eyes had gone misty as he had spoken of the epic journey from Greece and of the body of mythical work that had been collected from folklore. To now locate these artefacts in a real place, to venture that the city of silver might not be just a myth but a historical fact, would lead to joy unconstrained.

— They were the champions, the man said and his eyes brimmed with feeling. — Without them we wouldn't exist. They were the hardy lads, have no doubt.

Lee sat back, re-read it all once more, then, attaching the pics of Mr O to the email, he pressed send.

* * *

At ten-thirty next morning Eddie was in the DART on his way into work. He watched the sand dunes in Royal Dublin, then the sea; a train slammed past in the opposite direction; Eddie jumped.

He always felt like this in the mornings except on Sundays and Mondays, his days off, when he slept till three; those days he felt like this in the afternoons. Tried to keep to coffee until the evening Angelus when he slipped down the street, all his copy not yet filed, his proofing almost but not quite completed, in by the side door, the sharp smell of a licensed premises before the customers got settled in, a small moment of benediction for the prescience of the ancestors who had cultivated the rich secrets of grapes. Back to the office to tidy up and sign off – God, did he feel better! – then twenty minutes later, downstairs again – and away! Those first delicious early evening hours in the foothills, the regaining of confidence and health, the words that he had spent the whole day trawling to find now coming instantly to his tongue. The wit and the laughter, the insights – Christ, he could see the whole planet in X-ray, understand every problem and know how to solve it. People flocked to him. In those hours he was God-like.

It wasn't being drunk that was sublime, it was getting drunk. Brought to mind his poor father, a professional actor all his life, Norman England, people used to say he sounded more like an era than a man. A lover of Dimple Haig, God rest him, lovely tenor voice, sang for little Eddie, sang in the wee hours, even when the mother locked him out he sang to her from the street. Eddie's earliest memories were of sitting on the old man's knee by the coal fire, rain lashing against the window, smelling the Dimple on Dada's breath as he crooned one of Tom Moore's melodies.

The train was held up short of Connolly and Eddie was suddenly hit by the dread panic of vanished memory. The evening before, when he had come back upstairs after his customary post-Angelus break, the piece had been there on his computer; yes. He had read it with mounting excitement, that much he remembered. It was amazing, he had thought; it would blow the town apart; it was the scoop the Valentine Group had lacked for the past five years. But what then? What had he *done* then? Printed it out, almost certainly; but if so, where was it? He had no further recall of the evening, the span of the many hours that had followed had left no impression on his mind. Like the Starship Enterprise he had entered a time warp at around seven-thirty the night before and at ten the next morning had been deposited in his bedroom in Howth. Nothing in between, not a flicker. He could have been to New York and back or had a heart-lung transplant for all he knew. Jesus.

We go forward, Monte Cristo! as his father used to cry, taking the *en garde* swordsman's position. We move on! It was still a great story, the kind of journalistic coup that got advertisers on their knees to marketing departments. Yes. It was like an exclusive on the moment of bloody creation. The train lurched into Connolly. He needed a lot of coffee and medication, he needed to forget that he couldn't remember, he needed to find the power in his fingertips again, the ability to turn this piece into a work of art. He would, and could. Think of how the master would have done it, there must have been many nights lost even to his memory, which hadn't stopped him. Nor would it stop Eddie now, not with that kind of shining example to lead him forward; he might even break his rule and have a drink at lunchtime; with this behind him all would be different. When the going got tough…

* * *

Lee arrived at two sharp. The reception woman used the point of her tongue to remove a piece of undigested food from her eye tooth as she dialled Eddie's number. Lee felt the rush of power, which was suddenly and unstoppably replaced by the urge to pee. He excused himself abruptly, asking the woman to tell Eddie to wait, and ran fifty yards down the street to the coffee shop. He needed to have his bladder checked out; that, and to find out why he found it necessary at such times as this to pee sitting down, which he now did at length. He could imagine Eddie back in reception, fretting, wondering if there was a problem. Out in the washroom he wet his hands and ran them through his hair, to give it a bit of body and bite, because you never knew, Eddie might well want a picture over his by-line, might even have Mick the Pic standing by.

He should call Gwen, he thought as he charged up the street and back into the reception area. She had texted earlier to wish him luck, but had also cautioned,

DON'T LET THEM PROMISE U THINGS AND THEN STEAL YR STORY. REMEMBER HOW THEY TREATED U BE4

A young woman of uncompromising bosom dressed in a mini-skirt and tan knee-boots, was standing in the centre of reception, looking at her watch. As Lee made his entrance, the security woman gave her the nod.

— Lee Carew?

— Yes?

— Mr Bell would like to see you.

— You mean…

— Right now. Sign in please and come with me.

— Where's Eddie?

— With Mr Bell, she said.

He was shaking as he printed his name, then signed, and his friend behind the counter tore off the top copy, slotted it into a plastic holder with a lapel pin and tossed it to him disdainfully. How foolish people could be, he thought. How she would long in the years ahead, in the unlikely event of her still being employed here, how she would crave to be saluted every morning by a household name on his way through the turnstile. Saw you on *Prime Time* last night, Lee! Brilliant! Lee has never forgotten the days when he was nobody, when this dyke sneered at him, when she wrinkled up her nose stud at him. He ignores her, as he has for the last three hundred mornings, and she sinks further down into her pit, crushed, bleeding for his recognition, obliterated by his inaccessibility.

— Please try to hurry, his guide said as Lee fumbled with the name-tag pin. — Mr Bell hates to be kept waiting.

Through the turnstile and down to the banks of lifts. Had this top-heavy functionary read his piece, he wondered? Most likely had, but had been sworn to secrecy. The whole paper had probably been embargoed, including the political and financial correspondents, after being briefed at a special editorial conference. By now the sub-editors too would be in on the scoop, checking the layout and coming up with a front-page headline. WELCOME HOME, LITTLE MEN! was Lee's personal choice, although he wondered if the management might even go so far as to bring the editorial forward onto the front page, a move reserved for such things as the outbreak of war. If so, would his pic be above or beneath the editorial? They stepped into the lift. Lee said with a little smile, — Busy up here today, I bet.

The girl closed her eyes, as if she thought he was trying to chat her up. Lee said coyly, — I'm sorry if I have increased your workload this morning.

Her look was one of genuine curiosity, which did not surprise Lee, these people knew how to act. She asked, — Have you ever met Mr Bell before?

— No, Lee said, this is the first time – for both of us.

He had already decided to pass if Dick Bell offered him coffee, or even a drink; the last thing Lee wanted to convey up here was the impression that he might have a weak bladder or a weakness for alcohol. On the other hand, now that he had given up drink, he wondered if Dick Bell might think less of him because he was a teetotaller.

Then there was the whole business of titles. How should he address this man whose name in the building was synonymous with sudden death? Dick sounded a bit raw, too pushy, whereas Mr Bell sounded servile, especially from a writer with the authority of a scoop behind him. Best not to call him anything, Lee concluded, best just to smile confidently and let him make the running.

The lift doors hummed apart and the first thing that Lee noticed was the quiet. Down in features, even when no one was there it seemed loud with stored up voices and tension, but up here on the twelfth floor all was hush. His way was barred by a further young woman, this time holding a clipboard. Everything notable about her seemed to have been done with a sharp instrument: her blonde-grey, wet-razor-cut hair, her little tits, stiletto heels and cutting eyes.

— Lee Carew?

Lee made a joke of consulting his security pass and saying, — Yep, I think so.

She rolled her eyes at the other woman and said, very tightly, — Mr Bell is waiting.

She turned and walked with killing steps in the direction of double mahogany doors about twenty yards away.

Men like Bell always had these devoted people working for them, men and women who gave nothing away in advance of crucial meetings. But this was good! Dick Bell would not have bothered calling Lee upstairs if he didn't like the story. If Dick hadn't liked it – how could anyone not *like* it? – he'd have let Eddie deliver the news. Young individuals of both sexes with sharp haircuts were everywhere as the doors were approached, their heads inches from the screens of computer terminals. This was the heartbeat of Valentine Newspapers. The woman pushed both doors in ahead of her without breaking stride. In the distance, at the end of the corridor, Lee saw a man he thought was familiar, something about the way the top half of him stooped, ducking into an office. Lee heard the office door click to, just before they passed it. Around the corner, further double doors were presented. At these, the woman paused and knocked, then entered.

— Lee Carew, she said and stood aside.

* * *

The layout of the office said everything: three windows with views to Croke Park and the decaying streets of the north city, leather chairs like those used on TV chat shows and an enormous coffin-shaped table. The first person Lee saw was Eddie. Eddie was holding on to the arms of his chair and looking dead ahead, eyes popping, like someone about to be electrocuted. Beside him sat

Sam O'Sling, fidgeting nervously with his red tie. At the top of the table, one ankle cocked up on his opposing knee, sat Dick Bell. Bell's hair was black, his small head somewhat out of proportion to his body, and his mouth, when not in use, reposed in an expression of the most extreme displeasure. Lee's eyes were drawn to the managing editor's cufflinks, seen previously in the lobby but at a distance: the gold and diamonds were set in the shape of miniature pianos, suggesting a softer, more musical side to Dick Bell than Lee had imagined. Dick Bell said, — What the fuck is this?

He was stabbing his finger towards the table on which Lee now saw the pages of his copy lying, fanned out. Eddie had ceased to breathe. Dick Bell shouted, — Hey, freelance piece of horseshit! I asked you a question!

— It's, ah, the piece I, ah, filed last evening, Lee replied, adding, Mr Bell.

— Don't ever fuck with me, Carew, you understand? Dick Bell said as if Lee had just told him he wanted to ride his daughter. — When I asked you what this is about, I meant, what bunch of tree-hugging, trade-union-infected scabs put you up to this, eh? Who told you to write it? I want to know whose agenda this is, dammit!

He hit the table so hard that a substantial bronze statue of a man about to launch himself from a diving board jumped. Lee said, — No one told me to write it. It was entirely my own decision, my own research, my own work, sir.

— Like fuck, said Bell with contempt. — Was this little rabbit's arsehole involved?

He was sneering at Eddie.

— I, ah, I, ah, showed it to Eddie, yes, but I, ah, I... Lee stammered as he tried to find a way to protect both Eddie and himself.

Bell turned to Sam O'Sling and said, — And he sent it to you.

— I got it just two hours ago, boss, I was in late, my daughter's first communion... Sam began to say.

— You people nauseate me, Bell said as his mouth plunged into a rictus of revulsion. — You make me want to puke. Maybe that's what I'll do, you little gobshite! All over you!

Eddie, to whom this remark had been directed, was trembling. Lee said, — What is the problem here, Mr Bell?

— I'll ask the questions! Dick Bell yelled. He gathered in breath noisily through his nose and went on, — This little piece of cowardly fly-fishing suggests that two of this country's most illustrious entrepreneurs, Albert Barr, the developer, and Eric Chester of HUBBI, are somehow involved in covering up the origins of a crowd of cunts from Greece, the whatever you call them…

— The Fir Bolg, Dick, Eddie said.

Dick Bell's enlarged eyes came to rest on Eddie. He continued, — … who some off-the-wall old arsehole of a retired UCD professor thinks we're all descended from. Meanwhile, somehow, someone in this building leaked the substance of this bucket of shit to a flysheet that's apparently been started up by a nigger who…

Bell struggled to find the means to articulate the next piece of information.

— … who up to recently worked as a roadside vendor for this newspaper group.

Lee stared and felt his lifeblood slip away. Dick Bell had moved his hands to the side of his desk and twitched out a page of newsprint from beneath a file. Lee saw a newspaper masthead,

SAINT PATRICK'S PEOPLE

and beneath it, the headline

MASSIVE COVER UP!

Lee didn't dare look at Eddie. Dick Bell said, — It's your piece, Carew, chapter and verse. They just ran it off without even bothering to edit out such phrases as 'sources close to the investigation have told the *Trumpet*' or 'a spokesperson for Ireland's national museum emphasised to the *Trumpet*. In other words, we're all over this piece of shit like a rash. And you know what? Albert Barr's lawyers have been on here this morning. The man is hysterical. He says he's going to sue this paper for fucking millions.

— Even if it's true? Lee said.

Dick Bell stared at Lee, then said with terrifying restraint, — There's no story here. I've just spoken to the minister who oversees all this kind of fuckology. He says there's no substance to any of the facts on which this story depends. Clear?

Made brave by a sudden blinding headache and the need to pee, Lee said, — I don't think you're right, Mr Bell. I think there's some big cover-up going on. I think that a significant archaeological find is being kept quiet and that Barr's Goose Point site happens to be the site of the Fir Bolg's City of Silver.

They were all staring at Lee. No one had ever spoken to Dick Bell like that. Lee took a step forward.

— This could be a sensation, Mr Bell. Forget the flysheet – how many people have read it? This is *our* story. This could put the *Gael* and the *Trumpet* back on top where they belong.

Bell twisted his mouth into a sort of horny smile and said, — Yeah, yeah, yeah, but who are you humping in here, Lee? Huh? What little piece of ass did you ask to look over your piece of history and then she passed it on to the guy she really wants to ride her, one of the spades who works on this abortion – who? Or is it, he? Eh?

— No one, I swear, Mr Bell.

Bell was doing quite a complicated trick with a pencil, making it walk in and out across his fingers. He turned to Sam O'Sling.

— Do you know who leaked this stuff?

— I told you, boss, I got in late, and I've never met this character here before, said Sam in his sing-song, nervous way.

Without moving his head, Bell's eyes slid over to Eddie. Eddie said in a panting voice, — Swear to God, Dick, on my children's lives.

— Jesus, I don't believe this, Bell said and splintered the pencil.

At that moment a mobile phone began to ring. No one moved, as if to claim ownership of the source of this sacrilegious interruption would be terminal. Then Dick Bell jumped to his feet, rummaged in his trouser pocket and with the phone pressed to his ear and the shattered pencil held like a dagger, left the room saying, — Yeah, sure, sure, just a minute, yeah, okay, okay.

Sam O'Sling put his head back and closed his eyes. Eddie, who was declining Lee's attempt at eye contact, badly needed a bottle of Chardonnay, or a vat by the looks of him. Sam said, — You're out of your mind.

— Sorry?

— You're out of your mind if you think you can fuck with these people, he said as if talking from his sleep.

— I understood they wanted a story that would sell their papers, Lee said.

— Look here – Lee, isn't it?

Sam checked towards the door for sign of Bell.

— Lee, you and me and Eddie here, we're just fucking sprats in a big ocean, get it? We're nothing. You saw Dick. Dick is a little bigger than a sprat, but not much. You think he likes his job? You think he likes the fact that everyone on the face of the earth thinks he's a cunt? Of course he doesn't. But he has no choice. Why? Because there are big, big sharks who control these waters – big fucking fish the size of train engines, get it? – and they're the ones who call the shots.

Eddie, who looked like a man who had just lost both legs in a car accident, said, — Listen to Sam. Please, Lee. I've got a wife and seven young children and a mortgage.

The revelation that Eddie was the father of seven children was startling, if not terrifying, and seemed for some reason as if it might also be illegal. Sam said, — This is not your fault, Lee, but this morning you got up the nose of some very big fish, get it? You're lucky to be alive, I'm serious. Just do exactly whatever the fuck

Dick wants, and I'll speak to him on your behalf about a really decent fee. How does five hundred sound? Not bad, eh? Good boy, there you go. Ssshh.

Bell burst back in through the door, his face dark as tar. He shouted, — Get out! Get out!

They all made for the door and Eddie actually shielded his head with hands.

— Not you, Dick Bell snarled at Lee. — You, you stupid lazy bastards. Get out!

Dick Bell sat, plonked his feet up on the table and said, — Sit down, Lee.

Lee lowered himself into the chair Eddie had just left, all too conscious of the symbolism.

— Lee, I've been thinking.

Something beyond the reptilian entered Bell's face as soon as he tried to smile, as he just had. He continued, — I like your stuff, Lee, it's got a bit of class. You wrote that fish piece, am I right?

— The medal in the mackerel? Lee said, unable to control his rush of pleasure. So they really did read his stuff up here.

— Yeah, yeah, the medal in the mackerel, Dick Bell said, again with his twisted grin. — It was shit, but don't get me wrong, it was class shit. Eddie tells me you want to write a novel.

Lee nodded, unsure if he was being insulted or complimented. Dick Bell said, — Don't we all, Lee, don't we all. But, hey, if it ever happens, I'll make sure the review is okay, understand? Of course you do. And I'll tell you what – how about a profile of you with the book in the *Trumpet*, eh? Big pic, respectful copy – what do you think, Lee? I can make things happen around here, yeah?

— Thanks, Mr Bell, said Lee with genuine gratitude.

— It's what we do for our friends, said Dick with unexpected charm, we look out for each other, yeah?

— Sure, Mr Bell, but…

— So, listen carefully, this is what you're going to do. In the next hour you're going to write a fifteen-hundred-word piece for me, okay? We'll run it on tomorrow's front page. The story will say the following: today's report in certain quarters – I'm not giving these black bastards the satisfaction of even naming their flysheet – you'll say that this story suggesting a link between the site in Goose Point and archaeology is complete bollox. Sketch material for a novel you're writing was stolen and ended up in these certain quarters being quoted as fact, yeah? You'll say that reliable sources – we'll provide them – have confirmed that the only artefacts found on the site were made in Hong Kong within the last twelve months. The Department of Infrastructure Development is issuing a supporting statement saying that Goose Point is of no historical significance whatsoever and that the possibility of any city, let alone a silver city, having been built there is absolute zero. We will run the Department's statement in full, in a box, beside your piece. You'll get paid a grand, yeah? Any questions?

Lee suddenly remembered the tall, familiarly stooped figure he had glimpsed out in the corridor as he was being led in here. He said, — One question, Mr Bell.

— Go ahead, Lee.

— What about the truth, Mr Bell?

Dick Bell began to gyrate slowly in his chair, like a large snake in the process of digesting a medium-sized dog. He snapped, — What do you mean?

— The truth, Mr Bell.

— The truth? Dick Bell cried. — What is the truth? And stop calling me Mr Bell! Call me Dick.

— The truth is the opposite of a lie, ah, Dick. It's the real thing; it's what actually happened as opposed to what didn't actually happen, it's…

— I know all that, said Dick Bell tightly and looked at Lee with the sudden attention of a vivisectionist. — But which of us is arrogant enough to claim we have a monopoly on the truth, eh? I mean, take the Gospels. You know the Gospels, Lee? You're a Christian, yeah?

— Yes, I think so.

— Good, I might have guessed but I still had to ask because nowadays you never know with people. We're talking Matthew, Mark, Luke and John, right, Lee?

— Right, Dick.

— Those boys are the truth, aren't they? I mean, they were the fucking eyewitnesses to the greatest story ever told, blah, blah, blah, wouldn't you say?

— We say, 'It's the gospel truth'.

— Exactly! Dick Bell roared with laughter. — 'The gospel truth'! You got it exactly right, Lee!

Dick got up and came around to perch on his desk so that Lee was eye level with his crotch. The managing editor lowered his big unpleasant face and said, — So how come if they're gospel truth that they're all different?

— Different?

— That's right, Lee. Sure, the overall copy gives the same result, no problem. It's like a football match. Romans, 1; God, Nil. I mean, they crucified him, yeah? But what happened after the match? I'll tell you what happened – these holy reporters filed different stories. You'd think, for example, that the virgin birth would be hold-the-front-page material, wouldn't you? You bet your ass you would! VIRGIN GIVES BIRTH TO GOD! Jesus Christ, I'd call that a two-hundred-thousand print run, Lee. So, how come this great scoop is only reported by Matthew and Luke, eh? And not by St Mark at all – why? Was Marko on leave? Was he playing offside that week? Was he detoxing in Jerusalem? And hey, Lee, by the way, St John actually denies that it happened at all! No hold-the-front-page as far as John-boy is concerned. So what's the truth?

Lee shifted uncomfortably.

— Or how about Jesus' baptism, I mean surely that's a page-one story as well? SON OF GOD BAPTISED IN RIVER JORDAN. Ticket-only event, would be my view. But hold on, St John doesn't even mention it. Oh dear, I wonder why not? Did it not happen?

And if not, are Matthew, Mark and Lukey-baby liars? So what's the truth? By the way, Matt & Co say Our Lord's ministry ran for a single year, whilst good old John says it was three. They all differ on what actually happened at the Last Supper too – just like restaurant critics, Lee! So where exactly is the truth in these gospels? They're the gospel truth, after all. Which of them is right?

It was the kind of question that Lee knew he should allow Dick to answer, so he said, — You tell me.

— All right, son, I will. You see, all of them are right and none of them is right, Dick said with thrusting intensity. — Why? Because the truth is simply a point of view. Truth is a flawed and dangerous concept that has created evil dictators and led to the deaths of millions. The word I prefer is trust. Trust involves people, whereas truth is like daylight – it's forever changing. Trust is permanent. Get it?

Dick had rested his hand on Lee's knee, just parked there, but there nonetheless. Lee said,

— Could you, ah, run me through how this affects the Goose Point situation?

— Easy, Dick said, slapping Lee's thigh and getting up, hands thrust deep into his pockets. — We have two conflicting positions, two teams, if you like. One of them says the arrowheads are from the pre-Christian era, the other claims they were made in Hong Kong. The *Daily Gael* goes with the Hong Kong team. Simple.

— But with respect, Dick...

Thunderclouds had moved back in across Dick's face. Lee ploughed on, — ... with the greatest respect, Dick, the Hong Kong theory is not the truth.

Dick looked at Lee for a moment or two, then went over to the window where Lee could hear him letting off a stream of swear words. He swung around.

— I'll go to fifteen hundred, he said, but that's the top. Cash, if you want. Now go and do it. Go!

— I'm sorry, Dick, I...

— You want the fee agreement in writing, yeah? Okay, I can do that too.

— It's not the money, Dick, it's the story. It's my story and I can't kill it like this.

Walking towards Lee, his face alarmingly incandescent, in a voice that gathered force like a dangerous wind, Dick said, — You get downstairs and you write the story I want you to write or so help me God I'll strangle you, do you understand? Do you fucking understand, you retarded arsehole? You go out that door and you go down to the shithole where you turned out the garbage you've been dishing up here for years, and you tell our readers that the city of silver is a story made up by bum boys like yourself. Do you understand? Do you?

Lee, feeling strangely light-headed, said,

— I'm sorry, I can't do that, Mr Bell. Dick. Sorry.

PART THREE

FOUR MONTHS LATER—January 2007

FIFTEEN

He looked out the window and saw the snow falling gently over Manhattan. So quiet, so beautiful. Kids building a snowman as their parents watched, couples walking through Central Park, arms linked, pinpoints of snow on their fur hats. Dog walkers, their hands full of leashes, in a moving knot of fur-jacketed canines. It was hard to believe how well he felt! The clinic in Arizona offered the world's most complete medical check-up *plus* a five-day detox for only six grand. Not that he'd needed the detox, but since Medb-Marie had given him the whole package as a Christmas present, he'd gone for it. Never thought he could feel so good, not to mention the effect five days on carrot juice had had on his testosterone. Towards the end the little Mexican masseuse had nearly driven him crazy.

Yet, one of the many things he'd sworn as he came through the storm of recent months was: no more of *that*, *ever*, end of story. He'd even resigned from the Los Desperados away games; some of these younger fellas could drink twenty pints. Christ Almighty, the whole Goose Point business had put years on him, if he drank twenty pints he'd need oxygen. Kept in touch with his mates, though, got the gossip on what was moving, the government infrastructural projects coming up, the new investment angles on places like India; you'd need an atlas in your hip pocket. A couple of the lads were quietly talking of putting sites on ice, slowing down, just as a precaution, straws in the wind; not that Albert was unduly worried: deposits on nearly two hundred apartments in Goose Point had been taken in the weeks coming up to Christmas.

— How's my big boy?

She'd crept out from the bathroom and was pressed to him, warmly and wetly, rubbing herself against him in small, abrasive movements.

— Hmmmm.

— Look at that snow.

— Isn't it beautiful? he said as he smelled her cascading hair.

At times, particularly in the weeks after the Goose Point launch when the threat to the site by environmental pressure groups had overhung all their assets, he had feared for her reason: a mere word or a glance could send her into a cyclone of rage; terrifying when it happened, an eruption as if from nowhere, usually with Albert as its target. She had been drinking more too, sometimes starting at lunchtime. Although she liked sex when she was drunk, once or twice when they were out together, when he was into his third or fourth drink, Albert had suddenly realised that his wife was wall-eyed. Taking her home under such circumstances had its compensations, but these occasions had the capacity to hurt Albert's business. For example, in November, although this was an exception, at a fork supper to celebrate the election of the newspaper tycoon Dolphin Valentine to the board of HUBBI, a bash at which two hundred selected guests drank champagne and ate lobster in the HUBBI penthouse, Medb-Marie had passed out during Eric Chester's keynote speech. Only the personal intervention of Valentine himself had prevented pictures of Albert's beautiful wife, dead drunk amid a platter of lobsters, from making page-one news next day. Who you knew was everything in life. Using the same network of media contacts HUBBI had killed the Goose Point Fir Bolg story stone dead.

Like many men who are themselves heavy drinkers, Albert was uncomfortable to see such weakness replicated in his wife. He worried that whereas he could handle alcohol most of the time – he saw himself as just one of the lads, part of a national movement, really – when women fell into the grip of drink it meant trouble. Men got drunk but women became alcoholics.

His secretary, with the greatest of respect, had drawn his attention to Medb-Marie's credit-card transactions. She was spending twenty-five grand a month, and often more, buying jewellery online. Which explained the flat, reinforced envelopes that had been showing up. Although she was bleeding off his cash through a hundred little wasteful pinpricks, at a time when Albert had been revising his cash-flow projections every other day, it was not possible to confront her about this expenditure. If she went berserk just because he looked crooked at her, what would she do if he suggested she take her foot off the cash pedal for a month or two? Then, one evening she got a fright. Fell asleep in her night-dress by the fire and was awoken by the smell of her nightdress burning. She got it in time, but she was shocked by what had nearly happened. She told Albert.

Together they consulted a shrink in London who came highly recommended, a man with shoulder-length hair who charged three hundred an hour. London was discrete; no one knew the Barrs in London. Albert booked a suite in the Savoy for a week in November and the consultant had seen Medb-Marie every morning for two hours. On the penultimate day Albert had met this man privately in his rooms on Harley Street when Medb-Marie was having her hair done in Bond Street by the top stylist at Vidal Sassoon.

— Mrs Burr's frequent, violent loss of temper is consistent with her highly unstable borderline personality, the psychiatrist said. — She is an only child, brought up by an indulgent father. Mrs Burr is, 'spoiled', he said, hooking his fingers artistically in the air.

Albert narrowed his eyes and decided that this character didn't get out much.

— Furthermore, if alcohol is added to her already volatile personality, then an extremely dangerous situation could be provoked, the man said.

— This is my wife you're talking about, said Albert thinly.

— Which is not for a moment to suggest that she is not also charming, accomplished, loving and, of course, very beautiful, the psychiatrist hurried on, perhaps with one eye on his as-yet unpaid fee.

— What do you suggest? Albert asked.

— Mrs Burr needs to see someone like me in Ireland, the psychiatrist replied. — She will benefit from long-term therapy. That said, however, by far the best you can do, sir, is to continue to 'love her unreservedly' as you have already assured me you do.

Albert paid the fee in cash and then took Medb-Marie out for a slap-up lunch. He would continue to 'love Medb-Marie unreservedly', no question about that, but he was damned if he was going to let any Irish shrink near her.

Even now, looking out from the Plaza at snow falling over Manhattan, Albert's heart skipped when he thought of it all. Weeks of further scrutiny by civil servants, that Kevin had benignly overseen, and hairy-faced archaeologists, and dick-heads from the Office of Public Works – what an industry the past had spawned! – crawling over the Goose Point site for the thousandth time. Often in the intervening period, albeit in places no one could see him, he'd gone down on one knee and given thanks to Kevin Steadman and to God, in that order, for the fact that the problem had been contained.

In the weeks coming up to Christmas, as the pressure eased, he had put his wife's and children's needs first. Not that he hadn't done so before but with Goose Point as good as sorted and as real sales began to take place and the cash began to flow again, he could devote real time to them. And he had. Stayed home some weekdays, brought her shopping to Paris – Jesus, the woman could spend money! – went for long walks on Killiney beach with her when he should have been at board meetings. He bought the whole family bicycles costing three grand and a trailer to go behind the jeep, and even tried to use the bikes one weekend down in County Wexford, but they had to turn back at Gorey because of traffic.

Now here they were in New York in the snow together, in excellent health. Thank God. By the time they got home Kevin would have signed off on Goose Point once and for all, granting the development unequivocal planning permission by ministerial order.

* * *

— What time is it?

Albert looked at his watch. — Nearly twelve. We've lunch booked in that place on Madison Avenue for one.

— Call them and tell them two, said Medb-Marie.

He turned around and she looked down at him and said, — Wow!

— God, you're gorgeous, he said as they kissed.

— Carry me, Albert, she said.

He picked her up and weaved his way past the breakfast trolley. She had become more pliable in recent weeks, demanded less in bed from him, a gift in itself, had begun to trust Albert more and to take what he said at face value. This was a softer Medb-Marie, which was not a reference to her increased poundage in recent months – she said two; he guessed six or seven – but to her more rounded beauty. A good trade off, no doubt. The crazy woman who wanted a rainforest one moment and the next was hysterical had all but disappeared. In her place was a going-on-plump, very pretty, luscious, sexy and sometimes tipsy lady of forty.

On the bed, in the bed, the theatrical snow at both windows, she pushed him back and sank down her head. Oh God, life was good, if only you had the guts to hang in there! Did everyone who made the rich list have to fight as hard as he had? Fought not just the system, including the media, shits to a man, and the rancid bankers, and the horrible little auditors, not to mention the bastards in planning offices and architects and valuers, but the whole shambolic Irish medical system that had failed to support him when he was most in need. In the months leading up to Christmas when he was trying to deal with his wife's health he had become convinced that he had a brain tumour. Headaches like you could not accurately describe and dizziness when he lay down, and also when he stood up, and a blurring of vision, nothing to do with drink, more the inability to focus on such things as demand ultimatums and letters from solicitors. He was particularly repulsed by the surgery needed to get at brain tumours: they cut half your frigging head away! Flew to Milan without telling Medb-Marie to see the doctor who looked after the Dalai Lama, and the man had prescribed Nurofen Plus. It was beyond a joke. Albert had broken his rule and paid two grand for a large lady who was only available when she came off the last shift of the chorus in La Scala.

Medb-Marie knelt, swung her leg over and straddled him, sweet as melting butter.

He could laugh now for he could see that he was as healthy as a pig, but his mind had tricked his body into believing otherwise during the Goose Point crisis. He could indulge the luxury, at last, of imagining what it would be like to be both rich and old.

— Oh, oh, oh, you're like iron! Medb-Marie cried.

He was too, thumbs-up to carrot juice, imagine what he'd be like if he stayed off drink for a month. New York, so good we say it twice, as the luggage porter had joked, had been a brilliant idea. So exciting. Last night at the Met, he'd already forgotten the name of the opera, Medb-Marie had proved that a three-grand gown was worth every penny. Even Albert could look good when he put on a tux. People had stared.

— Jesus, oooh!

Whether or not he'd pony up for the three-year-rent-guaranteed triple penthouse off Broadway, eight per cent per annum yield, which was the real reason for coming here, he hadn't yet decided. HUBBI again, this time with a new developer discovered by the bank's New York office, wanted to tear down an existing skyscraper and pop up another one twice as big.

— Ah! Albert! Ah! Ah!

The opportunity was being offered to a select few, pals of Eric's as that little shit had put it – didn't matter if he was, the guy oozed money. The drawings of the place were awesome, towers soaring into the clouds like rockets, piercing the heavens, and at the top, laid out in white leather, a dozen penthouses each with its own gym, cinema, private roof garden and shared helipad.

— Ahhh! Ahhhhh!

Ninety-eight-per-cent geared, of course, which was standard HUBBI, which still left them looking to the likes of Albert for half a million dollars, of which Albert was being offered one-hundred-per-cent funding based on his existing guarantees. It meant that he could acquire one of these yet-to-be-built penthouses without putting his hand into his pocket.

— Medb! Mar-ieeeeeeeeeeeeeeeeeeeeeee!

She dropped her head to his chest, her nose in his black bushy chest hair, and exhaled emptyingly. She would adore a penthouse, she had said, although since he'd have to rent it out to cover the interest payments, he wondered what was the point? Would it beat the Plaza? Hardly. But it will be *ours*, darling, she'd said. She slipped down beside him, pulled up the sheet. He kissed her nose. The snow fell thickly and beautifully.

He'd sworn that when the final planning permission for Goose Point came through he'd stop punting. Not just a prayerful wish following a near life-threatening situation, more a signal from his gut. People of no substance, Polish immigrants for God's sake, flipping Dublin apartments within six months of buying them. Bricklayers with properties in the sun, garbage-men driving brand-new cars, typists talking about three weeks in the Caribbean. Mares' tails in the blue skies of the Celtic Tiger.

— Do you love me, Albert?

— I'm crazy about you.

— You don't think I'm too fat?

— I like you the way you are.

— So you do think I'm fat.

— Honey, I think you're the most beautiful piece of ass I've ever laid eyes on.

— You sound like an American.

— I'm serious.

— I'm going on a diet when we get home.

— You're crazy, you know that? You look amazing.

— You don't think I look fat?

— I told you.

— Am I?

— No. Look out at that snow.

It was time to call a halt. He wouldn't buy the penthouse. He'd tell her he was getting his solicitors to look at the contract, which he would do, then he'd quietly pass. Something to do with tax, he'd say, if he had to, although by then she'd have forgotten about a penthouse in Manhattan. Time to slow it all down at home as well, apart from Goose Point, of course. Albert would survive; many wouldn't. The gut message was totally recognisable even though he had never experienced it before. It had to do with the barely discernable way in which the pace of the boom had suddenly slowed; it was connected with the increasingly strident assertions by elected representatives and estate agents that all was well; it was reflected in the foxy words of economic media commentators who clearly didn't want to be the ones to ruin the party, but who nonetheless wanted to be on record when it all ended. It could be smelled in the bite of higher interest rates, in the inexplicably easy money that was being made on the stock market. The man who serviced Albert's car reported he would soon have made enough money from HUBBI shares to retire.

— Let's go for a walk in the snow, he said. — In the park.

— I need boots, she said.

— Then let's buy you boots and then let's go for a walk in the park, he said.

* * *

Dun Julio's steaks were flown up every day from Buenos Aires – Direct from the Pampas! as it said on the menus. Foot and mouth disease my arse, thought Albert as his knife glided through the thick, pink meat. Ireland was too regulated, too up its own backside trying to conform. If meat like this was what angel dust and growth hormones produced, then bring it on!

— We should ring home and make sure everything's all right, said Medb-Marie.

As a slowing-down experiment on this trip Albert was only turning on his Blackberry for an hour each evening to retrieve messages.

— They're fine, they're grand, said Albert, masticating, as he revolved his index finger at the wine waiter. How come he had never truly appreciated the Zinfandel grape before? *Rich black cherry scented with a hint of spice.* Christ, there were so many things he had yet to do, his mind was so full of other information that he felt he'd been abused by the system, by life. He doubted if his father had ever tasted wine, not to mind Zinfandel. What a grape! He'd started actively fantasising about buying a small vineyard somewhere in California, moving over there, growing old with Medb-Marie among the undulating rows of vines. In his mind he kept seeing her dressed in low-cut dungarees holding a pruning shears. Why not? No language problem like in France or Spain, lovely weather; he'd have to cash in most of his Irish stuff first, but that had always been the plan. The waiter brought fresh wine balloons and Albert sniffed and tasted.

— Will you call them now? she asked again.

— Hmm, lovely. What love?

— I'm worried about the twins.

— Why are you worried, pet?

— I don't know. I was thinking when we were out in the park in the snow, how they would love it over here, said Medb-Marie. — I saw parents with their children, playing.

— Ah, you're such a sweet little baby, he said. — I love you.

They raised the new glasses. She said, — I hope they're not snowed in or anything. Christiana may have been trying to call.

— I bet it's not even snowing in Ireland, Albert said benignly. — I'll bet you…

— Ring up and find out.

— ... I'll bet you a ride, he whispered.

— Albert!

— Joke.

— Two years ago all our pipes froze.

— Your man is coming in, isn't he? The gardener? Chopping wood? He can shovel the snow if there is any.

— The diesel froze too, remember? We had no heating for three days, she said.

— I'll never forget the winters in Tramore, and we had no snow, he said. — Damp. It killed my mother, you know.

— That man in one of my flats was dead for a month before anyone found him. Over here they don't seem to mind about weather like this, she said.

When the plates were cleared menus were snapped open in front of them.

— Do you do *crêpes Suzette?* Albert asked.

— Yes, sir!

— *Crêpes Suzette* and a bottle of Bollinger, Albert said and winked at Medb-Marie.

— Right away, Mr Baah!

— We'll be pissed, she giggled.

— Then do you know what we're going to do? he asked.
She smiled.

— We're going to go back to bed in the Plaza, said Albert triumphantly.

Her anxiety about the twins, the house, home, was part of the new, softer woman that had emerged since he'd given more time to her, he believed. She was more caring of others, mellower, less selfish, less vain, and as a result of these improvements even sexier than she'd ever been. Moreover, the old Medb-Marie would have stamped her foot about the telephone call and he would have been forced to make it, to ruin this intimate moment in the restaurant, because when she got on to the children she would then speak to them for twenty, thirty minutes each about the same things, over and over, about nothing, really.

As waiters brought over a serving table and ignited blue flames that shot three feet in the air, and the nice thumping pop of a cork leaving a good bottle of champagne was heard, Albert knew he was in the place of ultimate achievement. Right there, right then. This was what he had been destined for from the moment of birth. For this prize of enlightenment and peace he had fought all the hard battles, grafted, screwed, cheated, lied, slaved, tussled, clawed, screamed. For this he had lain awake on a thousand nights watching rain drip from a soggy ceiling, drunk himself senseless times beyond recording, plastered a million rooms, licked a million arses, jumped twenty rungs of the evolutionary ladder, begged, cajoled and entreated men half his quality, watched better men than him die of hunger, wept a million tears, died so many times it was scary. For this moment.

His eyes were drawn to the leaping, aromatic flames. Through the blue fire, out in the small bar of the restaurant, he could see a group of businessmen watching something on television, guffawing. The waiter doused the flames, laid out the pancakes on two plates and served them elegantly, whilst another poured the champagne. What had happened? Albert wondered with sudden unease.

— Albert?

Something had happened. He could sense it in… in the way the men out there were laughing. Something… ugly about what they were doing. What did it matter to him? But it did, somehow. It did.

— Albert?

— I'll call now, he said, fishing out the Blackberry and turning it on.

— I hope Christiana hasn't put them to bed yet, Medb-Marie said.

He saw he had a stack of messages and began to retrieve them. One by one. As his pancake was getting cold.

SIXTEEN

Looking out on the little damp park it was hard to imagine, he thought, that warmth and sunshine could ever return, or that the bare shrubs and trees, now ghostly menacing shapes, could become bushy and verdant again. At six-thirty in the morning the yellow glow from the street lights struggled to penetrate the enveloping mist. Gwen slept peacefully, her head turned towards him on the pillow. Below on the sofa Des too was awake, an extension of his master's metabolism.

This was happiness, he knew, this little unit that had somehow formed and held. The week before Christmas Gwen had finally moved in. A big statement. Turned in her own lease, hired a truck and helped Lee to load it. She'd put her stuff like wardrobes, the clothes she hadn't worn for years, a pine dresser and a dining-room table into storage, which was cheaper than keeping two flats. Christmas dinner of hake, prawns and octopus by candlelight; a walk on Sandymount Strand afterwards, to acknowledge the crucial part the beach had played in their lives; the soaring certainty of each other's company as they drove home. Great sex.

Sex with Tallulah had been a brittle business, even at the best of times, overshadowed by the fear that she might shatter, which emotionally she had often done, as if her failure to achieve orgasm for herself or to ensure one for him was a sign of epic failure. Sex with Tallulah became something that had to be ambushed or kidnapped, which was how she liked it best, at times when it was least expected such as when she was on the telephone to her mother – what a bitch *she* was! – or if the plumber or the electrician was working in the other room. What excited her was the idea that they were doing something dangerous. Tallulah? *Yes, mother?* What's that funny noise? *Oh, it's, oh, it's oh, it's nothingggggg, Motherrrrr!*

He seemed to have lived all his life in the shadow of abnormality until he'd met Gwen. She could contain in separate and equally sweet parts of her the wisdom of ages, deep love and the wild passion of a madwoman. He no longer worked up juicy fantasies each time he encountered Mrs Barr; rather he had become an observer of her idiosyncrasies, which confirmed for him, almost daily, how lucky he was to have found Gwen.

His present to her for Christmas had been the Bach Cantatas and she had given him a writing course to be carried out by correspondence. Not that he'd activated it yet; he needed to find time; the old story. However if he didn't make the effort he knew now that he'd have less excuse than before. It was incredible that she believed in his talent for, apart from a few poems he had shyly shown her, all that existed of his writing were a few issues of the *Trumpet* and one copy of the first and only edition of *Saint Patrick's People*. She had been so calm about all that, that he had wondered at the time if she realised the magnitude of what had nearly happened. But then in the weeks that followed he understood that she had never really felt that Valentine Newspapers was the place he belonged nor, deep down, had she approved of his ambition to make his name on the back of cheap exposés. She was right, of course, because now that he had finally terminated all contact with that contorted world, his happiness had truly soared. He didn't read newspapers any more. They never watched television.

One night in the week coming up to Christmas, Eddie had telephoned. Lee reckoned that the office Christmas party was probably taking place since Eddie's slurred voice was relayed to a background of carol singing, paper hooters and the occasional lewd comment from voices that Lee vaguely recognised.

— It's as if Josef Stalin is in the building, Eddie whispered with an edge of madness. — You think I'm kidding?

— Sounds bad, Lee said.

— Even someone with a total command of the English language, with an unerring grasp of narrative form, would struggle to describe it, even I'm struggling, even…

— Eddie...

— I'm taking notes, Eddie said, dropping his voice even further.
— I'm keeping a diary about what's going on, recording every detail. I'm not in this business for nothing, you know. Dick Bell has lost three stone – three fucking stone! Need I say more?

— Is he sick? asked Lee and wondered if he sounded too hopeful.

— This *place* is sick! Eddie hissed. — Advertising is drying up, used to be ten pages of property ads, that's down to two. They say that Valentine is trying to sell his shares to Murdoch, it's that bad. They've even started making us clock in and out when we take a piss!

— I'd like to meet you for a drink sometime, maybe after Christmas... Lee said in a tone that suggested closure.

— They bought him out! Eddie cried with renewed derangement. — He got fifty grand!

— What?

— Swear to God on the heads of my kids! Fifty grand! Eddie shouted.

— Who?

— Who the fuck do you think?

Lee didn't have it in him to hang up on Eddie.

— Hey, Eddie, take it easy, ok? Try not to be so upset.

— Shipped him back, part of the deal, I don't even know what part of the dark continent he comes from, Eddie said hysterically.
— But what about his old pal? What about all the evenings I spent advising him, teaching him all I know? Is that the way I should be treated? Fifty fucking grand!

— Eddie, you're a great man and a good friend. You should go home now.

— Listen! Eddie's tone changed the way it did when a shaft of semi-sobriety pierced the darkness. — We can do this, you know? *We* can do it, you and me. We're a team, kid: my skill, your talent. Listen – *listen!* Don't you dare hang up! – that story is still out there for the taking, you know? What a story! You still have it on computer, right? They'll have to buy us out as well!

— Eddie, I'm out.

— We'll make a fortune! I guarantee it!

For another few minutes he tried to be respectful of their relationship, and then he did hang up.

* * *

The week before Christmas, Lee and Gwen had walked around to see Mr O with a view to inviting him for Christmas dinner. It took Lee a few moments to realise that it was the same house as before: the steps down to the basement were clean, the handrail painted, the weeds that had previously sprouted from walls and cracked paving slabs were gone, as were the bars from the windows. The flat's front door was now a cheerful yellow. Lee, who along with Gwen had taken the precaution of wearing two pullovers, knocked. One lock clicked to and a young man wearing jeans and an open-necked shirt appeared.

— Hello?

— I'm looking for, we're looking for Mr O, Lee said.

— Ah, the old gent who used to live here.

— Yes, said Lee with a sudden feeling of dread. — I thought he still did.

— He's gone, said the new occupant. — I think to a nursing home in Drogheda or Dundalk or someplace, but I could be wrong. You're the third person to come looking for him.

Over his shoulder Lee could see a different space to the one he remembered, this one bright and airy. He could feel heat.

— You don't know which nursing home? he asked.

— Sorry, mate, I don't, I'm just telling you what the postman told me.

Lee felt the weight of change heavily, as if all that had happened so recently was now out of reach; which of course it was, being the past.

— He didn't leave any belongings, did he? Lee asked. — You didn't come across a package of little silver arrowheads, like tiny ornaments, by any chance?

— Sorry, no, we took the place unfurnished, the man said.

— If you do find anything or hear where he went, here's my number, Lee said and wrote it down.

— Cheers, thanks. Happy Christmas.

— Happy Christmas, said Lee as he and Gwen walked back towards the steps. He turned back.

— By the way, who else was looking for him? he asked before the man closed the door. — You said there were others.

— No idea, said the man, re-emerging. — About two days after we moved in, there was a young woman. Didn't leave her name. Big head of black curls is all I remember. Then a few days after that a fellow in a black coat, a businessman of some kind. I didn't like the look of him. Tried to sort of interrogate me. Sod that, I thought. I closed the door.

— Good for you, Gwen said.

— You're not from the guards or anything, are you? the man asked.

— No, we're just friends of Mr O's, Lee said. — Sorry for bothering you. Merry Christmas again.

— Have a good one, mate, the basement-flat occupant said.

* * *

He bent over and kissed Gwen's nose. Since the Barrs had returned from wherever they'd been – five days early; a family funeral, Christiana had said; from out the back Lee had observed the comings and goings of stretch limousines – he was working only half-days. Coming in at eleven to chop wood and cart it inside the house, leaving at three. He turned to Gwen, shaping his body to hers and closed his eyes. He'd meant to get out the *Golden Pages* and telephone nursing homes in Drogheda and Dundalk, but he'd never got around to it. Soon, he thought, he'd do it soon. He still saw the arrowheads as a bracelet or brooch for Gwen.

It wasn't true to say that he'd done no writing, he just hadn't shown the little he'd written to Gwen. But he'd shown it to Eddie and after several weeks Eddie had sent it back rewritten. Lee wasn't quite sure if Eddie had got it quite right, though.

She came from a place as far removed from Andalusia as chalk is from cheddar. Smoked weed. Nothing to do with gardening. Joints using the innards of a Consulate and quality hash picked up from a one-legged newspaper vendor. A black man. Because she liked the colour of his skin.

He frowned as he read it – he had never actually read anything written by Eddie before.

But this is now and that was then. She only lit them with nine-inch matches. Stared for hours at the glowing ash. And her throat was dry. She drank ice-cold beer from a beer bottle by the neck.

He wondered if anyone reading it might recognise Tallulah.

Six months she'd buttered sandwiches near Euston Station for a slave-driving Armenian Jew. Then her long lashes quivered as she delivered salmon on open brown bread one day to an advertising agency. Glided across the foyer. Marble everywhere and women thin as celery. As she sniffed the air. He was walking towards her, two-day stubble, hairy forearms, a young campesino.
'I knew it,' he whispered. 'Come here.'
So she did.
Six weeks later, shacked up in a trailer beside the Great Pyramid of Giza, making a commercial for soap.
'You are Queen Cleopatra now,' he intoned.
Muy bien, *she thought and snorted softly as a filly foal.*

* * *

— Lee! Lee! Wake up! You're having a nightmare! Lee!
— Oh God, oh God, oh thank God…

Sweat covered him as he sat up, the sheet soaking, his hair drenched.

— Ah, darling, she said, come here.

All the images still lingered, like ghouls at dawn, peering through the bars of jail windows, crowding out towards the edge of the campfire of his memory. She put her arms around him.

— I'll get us some coffee, she said.

— No.

He was terrified, exhilarated, tongue-tied, amazed and bewildered. How *could* it be? And yet, it made sense as never before. The words spoken, the faces of hate and recrimination, the subsequent voids now accounted for – he could finally understand everything, or so he thought. The hurrying advent of death, the conveyance of property and the mindless years of slowly dying love were suddenly terrifyingly clear.

— Tell me, Gwen said.

He shook his head violently, unsure if he was yet awake.

— I'm about five or six, very young at any rate, I'm upstairs in bed. It's late.

Drumming on the roof, which must be rain, the lights are all on downstairs. A Christmas tree.

— It's Christmas Eve!

Except the house is not the house Lee grew up in, but the house he bought when he married Tallulah. Laughter drifts upstairs. Mum and Uncle Dickie are in the drawing room and little Lee has gone to bed early, because he's so excited, because it's Christmas Eve.

— I hear a key in the front door, and I know it's Dad, so I jump out of bed and run to the landing. Dad's been working late in the garage, he's even working today, on Christmas Eve. He talks a lot about the year end.

— Boy, am I hungry. Anyone home? Dad calls.

Little Lee peers through the spindles, just as Dad walks from the hall to the drawing room. Lee presses his head as far as it will go because he wants Dad to see him, because when Dad sees him he takes the stairs in twos and there's a chase, and Dad always pretends not to know where Lee has got to when all the time he's back in bed, under the sheets, hiding deliciously, waiting, waiting… And Lee wants to tell Dad so much this evening, wants to tell him what Santa Claus is bringing and about the present Lee has bought for Mum.

— GET OUT OF MY HOUSE!

A loud crash. A scream.

— GET OUT OF MY FUCKING HOUSE!

— *Ah, no, ah, no, please! No!*

First Uncle Dickie appears, teetering backwards, ginger hair awry, one hand to his scarlet face. Dad next, sweeping the air in front of Uncle Dickie's head with his clenched fists.

— GET – THE – FUCK…

Mum appears, half falling, arms outstretched. She cries again,

— Ah, Jesus, no…

Despite the fact that it's raining hard Uncle Dickie stumbles out without bothering to get his topcoat. Dad stands there fighting for his breath, his grip on Mum's arm. She's screaming,

— Let me go! LET ME GO!

Dad's holding Mum back but she's trying to follow Uncle Dickie out into the rain. Lee is crying, although he scarcely knows it as he tumbles down the stairs. He catches hold of Mum too.

— Why? Dad asks her. — *Why?*

She looks at Dad as if he is a stranger.

— BECAUSE I LOVE HIM! she screams.

Dad drops his hand away and Mum gets up. Lee suddenly realises what she's going to do.

— Mum, please, no, he cries. — Please. It's Christmas.

Mum looks at Lee but he's not sure that she even sees him. Slowly, she gets up. She walks to the hall stand, takes her coat down, puts it on. Then she folds Uncle Dickie's coat over her arm, turns and walks out into the night. Lee tries to follow her, but Dad has him wrapped in his strong arms.

— Come back! Lee cries. — Mum! Mum! COME! BACK!

SEVENTEEN

Throughout the flight home from New York he could not expel the image from his mind. He would never come to terms with it, never; and as for Medb-Marie – Jesus! Bad enough having her hysterical in the restaurant, but then when they got back to the Plaza, with Albert making non-stop telephone calls to arrange seats up front on that night's direct Aer Lingus flight to Dublin – he would have preferred British Airways via London, but this was a crisis – not to mention funeral arrangements, press releases, the exigencies of a post mortem – when they arrived into the suite and there in front of them, before their eyes on a forty-inch, pop-up, slim-line television, was… was *it!* Obscene did not even approach the fitting description.

And this before any of the real complications were faced. The political and financial complications, the lack of information – of any information! – that would last for days. Cut off on the flight home from communications, a blessing for the vortex of his mind, watching his wife peacefully sleeping, Albert tried to work out what he had done to deserve this.

He was probably better off when all was said and done, Kevin, probably happier than being drunk and morose every night, although no one could be certain about that. But surely not even his most bitter enemy could have wished him the end he came to. Dying on live television, choking to death on the wishbone of a chicken during a televised food fare in the RDS to promote Irish farm produce. It didn't even fall within his ministerial remit, as Medb-Marie kept shouting afterwards, as if her father's very public death should have been suffered by another member of the cabinet.

He was the Minister for Infrastructure Development! YouTube had
received over five million hits for the spectacle, which had
apparently then been pirated into dozens of languages and
reconstituted as a standing international joke, masquerading as a
spoof ad for, among others, Ireland as the gastronomic capital of
the world, and Kentucky Fried Chicken. Kevin, who had spent
years trying to get his face across to the West Cork electorate by
means of posters on a thousand hoardings, at the moment of his
death and for twenty-four hours following it, became more
internationally famous than George W. Bush.

On the flight home through the unresponsive night Albert,
after two bottles of red wine, had tried to fraternise with the spirit
of his father-in-law. What had Kevin known of life outside the
boundaries of his constituency? Or of how grand life could really
be? Drink was all he had ever wanted, bottles and barrels and tanks
of it, trying to blot out the hardship of the past. Great-grandson of
a seasonal potato-picker from the north of England who had
arrived in Cork and put a local girl in the family way, then built a
penetratingly damp cabin of mud and seagull shit. Kevin had
grown up there in the midst of arthritis, lung diseases and a life
expectancy in the low fifties, had spent his formative years lugging
bales of seaweed up from the foreshore in Ballylickey which his
father then brought into Bantry on a donkey cart and sold for
fertiliser.

Medb-Marie had persuaded her father to apply for planning
permission to build a modern, comfortable hideaway with Moorish
arches, terracotta tiles, ox-blood walls, portholes, picture windows
and a swimming pool. In their failed three-year battle to halt the
project An Taisce, the self-appointed, so-called environmental
watchdog, had likened the proposed house to a marooned Spanish
prostitute. A bad move. They'd been no match in the end for Kevin
on his home turf. The old man, God rest him, had convened a
special meeting of the county council and rammed the permission
through, calling in decades of political favours in the process. He

had fought like an ape when he had wanted to, Kevin, God rest his soul.

* * *

No one had prepared them for the chaos in Dublin Airport. Despite the fact that it was six-thirty in the morning, despite the fact that Albert had pulled strings to have them brought from airside through a side door – it had all been arranged, but the moron who was meant to meet them had slept it out – a hundred media people fought with each other in the arrivals hall to capture the arrival home of the beautiful millionairess daughter of the world's briefly most famous recently deceased politician.

— Medb-Marie, how do you feel?

— This way, Medb-Marie!

— Will you ever eat chicken again, Medb-Marie?

It was astonishing how good she looked right across the media spectrum, a goddess really, although Albert was beyond caring at that point. Her proud good looks, as she made her way to a car outside arrivals, were not only a tonic for those who feared the effects of bereavement on the appearance but also provided the necessary trampoline to re-orbit Kevin's exit from this world for another twenty-four pitiless hours.

Nor could the Irish print media, even the po-faced broadsheets, resist dropping everything from their front pages in order to juxtapose the pictures of the hauntingly beautiful Medb-Marie and her tele-visually fuzzy, choking father. He died again, every hour, on the hour, including lunchtime and following the Angelus, and in every paper the picture was always of Medb-Marie's thigh, tantalisingly glimpsed as she got into the car at the airport, as if to prove once and for all that anyone who had ever claimed that prurience didn't sell copy could go shit in his hat.

* * *

Kevin had lived for most of the year in a semi-detached house on a quiet road in Rathgar, except when he was chauffeur-driven down to Munster for his monthly constituency clinics, or during election time, or for the summer holidays.

The six o'clock news bulletin was being read on the radio as Albert drove up the road where Kevin had lived and saw the garda traffic cones, the government drivers in a huddle, smoking, and the yellow flash of garda jackets at the gate. The news was all about stock market price declines and severe financial difficulties in the American housing market, followed by confident declarations by the Irish government of the country's robust fiscal health. Albert was forced to drive two hundred yards further on before he found a parking space. He swore aloud as he trudged back along the footpath in the bitingly cold January evening. He had forgotten his overcoat.

Medb-Marie was resting at home, as indeed was her father, as the newspaper notices composed by Medb-Marie had put it. The undertaker had gingerly suggested 'reposing' but Medb-Marie had insisted on 'resting' since that's how she now saw the poor man, at long last after his long journey, 'resting in his residence'.

Albert sidestepped a refuse bin that suddenly loomed from the shadows. She had never been more attractive than she was in grief, Albert accepted. It was a caveman type of thing, to be drawn so powerfully to her vulnerability, to want to protect her, and not just protect her either. It was as if Medb-Marie had been stripped bare by Kevin's death, as if somehow only her quintessence remained, an almost childlike radiance, even innocence, combined with outstanding physical good looks. It couldn't last, of course, but it brought home to Albert that his wife's tender qualities did in fact exist, and that it was up to him to eke them out and nurture them. She was devastatingly alluring as she sat, winded by events, tame, her hair awry, eyes red, beautiful unmade-up face streaked by her tears, which Albert had the night before kissed away. So beautiful, so salty, her essence on his tongue, he had wanted her more than ever right then, but had had the sense to realise that the need for sex at such a time was very likely a one-sided thing.

As Albert hunched in towards Kevin's residence the guard at the gate threw him a sideways, downward glance. The front door was open. Kevin had lived here, a widower for eighteen years, during which time the place had never been painted, nor the staircarpet replaced, nor the furniture upgraded. The deceased minister's sister and her husband had moved in on his death at Medb-Marie's request, and now stood in the cramped hall, solemnly greeting the arrivals. Munster people, they were large, like Kevin had been; in the case of the brother-in-law, enormous, like Kevin, an ex-guard, in this case one who had moved into property development in the Munster heartland in places where Kevin's political influence had teeth. Albert, who had been here earlier writing a cheque for the caterers, whispered to them that he appreciated their continued presence, their solidarity at this difficult time.

— Albert.

The Minister for Finance was pressing hands, elbows, his head bobbing gravely, his jowls quivering, his eyes jumping to see who was over the next person's shoulder. He murmured, — We'll see few like him again.

— I might want a word in a few days, Albert said.

— No problem, ring my secretary, the minister said. — Things alright?

— I think so. What do you think? Albert asked. — Of things generally?

— Pewwwwwwwwwwhhh! said the minister and blew air.

Albert excused himself and shouldered past men and women whom he normally saw only during election times into the front room off the hall where the blinds had been pulled down, the furniture cleared and a double bed installed. Between the muted light of two smoking candles was the improbable sight of Kevin in bed wearing his best Armani double-breasted suit, his white shirt from Clery's and a silk tie, made up in a knot the size of a small red turnip. At the bedside sat the son and daughter-in-law of the receiving party outside, replicas with twenty-five years removed; Kevin's new custodians. They smiled at Albert and he smiled back. Ollie, Kevin's sister's son, looked just like old pictures of Kevin from thirty years before. He played football for his county and was something of a celebrity in Munster, although he currently worked as a junior planning officer in one of the councils in the greater Dublin area. The young pair looked completely at home, as if the exclusive ambience produced by a fresh corpse laid out in candlelight was a perfectly normal place to spend their Saturday night.

A couple of elderly females, dimly remembered from the day of his wedding, smiled kindly in Albert's direction. He strolled over and peered down on the bed at Kevin's chiselled jaw, the noble waxen face and the tweezered nostrils. You'd never think, he reflected in wonder, that the man laid out here had not drawn an entirely sober breath for twenty-five years.

Even though he didn't want to, Albert lightly and briefly laid the tips of his fingers on Kevin's brow, cold as a windowpane, and then knuckled both his eyes, muttering, — Goodbye, old pal.

He shuffled from the bed, confident that his actions and words would be reported back to Medb-Marie.

I never saw Albert so upset.

It's not like Albert, but he was blubbering.

Albert will really miss Kevin, you know.

You could say that again. He made his way across the hall and opened the door of the kitchen. Conversation fell outwards like a collapsing wall. Albert stepped in and closed the door behind him. A perspiring middle-aged waiter dressed in black waistcoat and bow-tie poured wine into glasses which stood on a tray held by a young woman of Eastern European appearance. Another, larger woman whose hair was gathered up in a scarf, was carving with gusto from a joint of beef. A line of people of mixed age and gender, all smartly dressed, inched towards the beef dispensary. Albert recognised three cabinet ministers, a handful of junior ministers, property developers like himself, political stalwarts of both sexes from Munster, a few departmental secretaries, the governor of the Central Bank, a man who was something big in Europe, the president of one of the farming organisations. Beyond the line, in one corner of the elongated room in a huddle of suits, smoking a cigarette and drinking a pint of Guinness, stood the Taoiseach of Ireland. Albert took a glass of red wine and stood alone, away from the food line.

— Albert Barr!

A gnarled, dishevelled, hollowed-out man with wild hair and demented eyes drove Albert up against the wall.

— I'll give you three guesses!

Albert inhaled long hours of beer and whiskey. He had no idea.

— I give up, he said.

— Ah, fuck it, don't give up! Albert, it's me!

— Give me a clue.

— *Playboy*? the man said, then fell back in a spasm of mirth. — *Playboy*, Albert! *Playboy*!

Seized by unaccountable dread, terrified that this might somehow really be his own wake, not Kevin's, Albert tried to step back, but the wall stopped him. His assailant grasped him by both shoulders.

— Billy! the man shouted joyfully. — Billy Maidstone, the golf pro from Tramore, Albert! Billy from Tramore!

— Jesus Christ, Billy, Albert said, although the drunken man in front of him caused no ripple of recognition in his memory. — What the fuck are you doing here?

— I got a job in Cork in eighty-two, Billy said, and this man here, this man in the next room…

Billy abruptly burst into tears.

— … Kevin Steadman got me permission to build my house.

— It's okay, Billy, I understand.

— And he got Billy junior into the guards, Billy said and blew his nose noisily. — Oh God, I'm sorry, I came up on the train, I read about you in the papers, Albert, about all the nonsense you've had to put up with from gobshites. I'm proud of you.

Albert looked left and right. He said, — Thanks, Billy.

— I used to leave those magazines out for you, you know, Billy said and winked. — You were a divil, that's for sure, a feckin' little divil.

He made the universal forearm sign associated with sex three or four times, guffawing loudly. Albert suddenly recognised him. It was the way he'd pumped his forearm, the same gesture that had been lost in the decades. Albert could, terrifyingly, smell the chamois, see the flickering eyes of young girls that had gathered like moths in that little space, ogling at Billy who spent his summers trying to crook his middle finger up between their legs.

— You were a little whore for it, Albert! Billy bellowed.

— Jesus, Billy, keep it down, Albert said.

— Get out of it, Albert, I knew you when you had head lice, son, Billy said.

— What, ah, what are you doing at all with yourself these days? Albert inquired uneasily.

He felt as if he had been catapulted back through time, with all the attendant nausea of motion sickness.

— A bit a this and that, Billy said and snaked a drink off a passing tray. — I give lessons, do a bit a caddyin'. I have a tenner each way on Harrington to win the Open this year at five hundred to one – what do you think?

Albert was about to reply when opposite him the press of suited men around the Taoiseach melted and the man himself walked across to Albert, his hand outstretched.

— Albert, so sorry, so sorry, he said.

— Thank you, Taoiseach.

Albert angled around so that his ancient provider of pornography was excluded. He said, — You're great to be here, Taoiseach.

— Where else would I be? the Taoiseach asked. — What a character, what an operator.

He was a mid-sized, bullet-headed individual in his late fifties with large dissembling eyes and a small red puckering mouth. He said, — He never said much in cabinet, but he didn't have to. I always knew what he was thinking.

Albert decided to take this remark as a compliment to his late father-in-law.

— He'll be hard to replace, that's for sure, he said.

— Taoiseach…

Billy, the golf pro, had inserted himself between the two men.

— … Billy Maidstone. A great fan. I'da died for Kevin.

— Thanks, good to meet you, Billy, said the Taoiseach.

— This is some little divil here, this character, Billy said. — He'd get up on a stiff breeze.

— Is that so? said the Taoiseach with a grin.

— On a clipped hedge! Billy said. — I hope you're looking after him, eh? Givin' him a bit a work, eh, Taoiseach?

— Billy, why don't you get us a couple of plates of the beef? Albert said.

— Oops. Understood. On my way, Mr Barr! Billy said and clicked his heels before stumbling away.

— How's your good wife? asked the Taoiseach smoothly. — I thought she'd be here.

— She's at home; she's exhausted, Albert said as he noted how the Taoiseach's nostrils had dilated when he mentioned Medb-Marie.

— Ah, God love her, the Taoiseach said. — She's an extraordinary lady, your good wife, I'll see her at the funeral of course, but I remember her from elections down in Munster years ago before she was married. We used to have great old craic altogether.

This was news to Albert, for although Medb-Marie had never mentioned the Taoiseach in conversation, she had sometimes made references to election campaigns, comparing them to warfare, and the late nights that were involved, and the drinking. And everyone knew what went on in warfare. Maybe, Albert thought, just maybe, this was like opening a drawer and finding a long-forgotten deposit account.

— She often talks about you, Taoiseach, he said.

— Ah, God, we were great old pals, said the Taoiseach and his eyes brimmed with sincerity. — I often think about her.

— I'll tell her that, Albert said. — She's been very much tied up in our Goose Point development, you know.

— Oh really, I see, the Taoiseach said.

— It's been hard work ironing things out, but we think we're on the way now, Albert said. — Goose Point is the big one.

— We're in uncertain times, for sure, the Taoiseach said.

— There were, you know, heritage issues down there that Kevin was aware of, Albert said.

— I know, we all have to be very careful these days, the Taoiseach said.

— But I think on balance he was happy with what his officials found there, Albert said. — Or at least didn't find, thank God!

— I know what you mean, said the Taoiseach.

— I think he was happy, Albert said, I mean, I didn't hear to the contrary, although it's been hard to find out what's going on in his department, you know, since Kevin choked.

— Jesus, the papers gave you a hard time over his death, the Taoiseach said as his large eyes emptied. — That was dreadful, dreadful for your good wife – but who's surprised? I mean, you've probably seen what they're doing to me on this extraordinary rendition?

— No, I hadn't seen that, Albert said and swore bitterly to himself as the fish slipped out of his reach. — We've been in New York.

— What am I to do? the Taoiseach asked. — Ring up Bush and say, hey, George, how's Laura? I'm the best, thanks, George. By the way, next time one of your military planes lands in Shannon, we're arresting the whole crew. Eh? I mean, let's be honest here, does anyone in Ireland give two shits if tomorrow morning a plane refuels in Shannon and it's carrying some bloodthirsty little Arab on his way to whatever-they-call-it Bay in Cuba, eh? Who's looked after little Ireland best for the last sixty-five years? The United States of America or Amnesty fucking International, eh? Jesus, we're bad enough without declaring war on America.

— You're dead right there, Taoiseach, Albert said as he saw Billy listing across the room with plates in his hands.

— I'll see you at the funeral, the Taoiseach said, nodding, reversing. — Tell your good wife I said how very sorry I am.

It would never be the same again, Albert realised as the Taoiseach went back into the safety of his huddle; the finality of death had never been quite so explicit. It was amazing that it had taken him all these years to appreciate that when a powerful man dies, his power dies with him.

EIGHTEEN

It had just gone seven-thirty on the morning of Kevin Steadman's funeral when the chairman picked up the phone and called HUBBI's stockbrokers. He had been down to the gym, waited in vain for Inge, then breakfasted alone in his office, scanned the papers and gone over his schedule for that day. Markets were jumpy. The day before HUBBI had traded as low as twenty-nine. You could look at it this way, the bank's broker had told him, a few years ago when we traded at twenty-nine we were all delirious. Yes, but that was on the way up, the chairman thought. That was when the biggest loan that the bank had made was a couple of hundred million, secured on half of Grafton Street.

The opinion pieces in the morning papers were all reporting the economic news. It was pathetic. For the last five years the markets had risen like Christ from the tomb and the op-ed pages hadn't run one opinion piece about this astonishing fact. He needed to make a decision right away on the price at which HUBBI went in again and bought a further suitcase-full of its own shares. This could be the buying opportunity of all time.

At nine o'clock he was due to open a children's ward in a hospital, the HUBBI Ward, complete with soft cuddly toys and deposit savings books specially designed for the under-10s. Then the funeral at eleven-thirty. The chairman had a bad feeling about Kevin Steadman's death. It was as if a rotten but nonetheless crucial pillar on a bridge to safety had been removed.

He pressed the key on his phone's fast-dial and a trader in the stockbrokers picked up.

— Chester here.

— Hold the line please.

You'd think with an account like HUBBI's that they'd tell him what he needed to know.

— Eric?

— Yes?

It was the stockbroking firm's managing director.

— I was just going to ring you, Eric.

— Just wanted to hear how we're trading in the pre-market, the chairman said.

— That's what I was going to ring you about, Eric.

The chairman blinked. He listened, then he laughed.

— You mean twenty-eight, he said to the broker. — *Twenty*-eight.

Twenty-eight hurt, but then maybe he should buy again.

— Eighteen last traded and offered, the broker said.

— *Eighteen?*

— There's been a massive sell-off, the broker said. — The hedge funds are having a field day.

* * *

Analysts were unanimous, in retrospect, that the share price slide in HUBBI began in the weeks leading up to Kevin Steadman's death. That first sell-off had been nothing dramatic, in fact most punters used it as an opportunity to get back in and bring down the average cost of their HUBBI shares; not least among them the bank's own thoroughbred stable of shareholding clients to whom the standard 100-per-cent loan for this purpose was advanced. And yet in retrospect the analysts would say that the selling volume had been huge.

So too in mid-December did the HUBBI board of directors make various HUBBI share purchases, ranging from a hundred thousand shares up to, it was rumoured, two million in the case of Dolphin Valentine, the newspaper magnate, HUBBI's newest director. All bankrolled by the bank itself. And if HUBBI's directors were all wading in, then surely it would have seemed odd for the bank's own pension reserve to stay on the sidelines; it joined the rush, as did the fund created with the bank's reserves to reduce the outstanding share capital in the market. Not to be left out, most of the bank's employees, from the head of treasury down to the uniformed porter on the ground floor, already up to his chin in debt, drew down fresh lines of credit from the bank and bought HUBBI shares, even then rising again toward heaven; but not before the Eric Chester Charitable Trust had snapped up a block of three million shares at a price said to be the low point traded on that particular day.

The stock market bounced and the pubs around Grafton Street echoed into the wee hours with the laughter of easy money. The short sellers were getting squeezed to death! Put it to music and you would have a number-one hit, everyone in HUBBI laughed! This was what success tasted like! Those few who had doubted Dr Eric Chester's financial creation slunk away and gnawed their knuckles.

For a week or so those travel agents who specialised in the most exotic and expensive locations could not cope with the business. But where previously such a price-bounce in HUBBI had exceeded the old highs and made new ones, this time, as the price clawed its way back upwards, it was hit by a renewed tidal wave of short-selling orders – mostly out of London; the Brits, as usual; fuck them, everyone said; although a big short seller in Switzerland was equally to blame. The price quickly broke down through its important support level of thirty euro per share. It did pop back up of course in the weeks before Christmas, prompting the forecasters employed by Dublin stockbroking firms – young people with hair gel and degrees in economics – to come out with a unanimous price target of forty euro a share for 2007. This prompted a new wave of buying. The offices closed for Christmas, in Ireland a ten-day affair. What no one foresaw was the sell-off on the second Tuesday in January. At one point that day, the day on which Kevin Steadman's coffin lay in Donnybrook Church, HUBBI traded as low as seventeen.

* * *

— Our share price is causing us problems, the chairman said.

No one at the executive committee meeting needed the chairman to explain that if a bank lent someone the money to buy its shares at thirty-five, and the share price was now eighteen, that the bank had an exposure of seventeen euro per share; or that the investment was showing a loss of nearly 50 per cent; or that unless the borrowers shored up the loss, the bank was exposed to the underlying loans.

It was eight-thirty and outside the day was fine. People were heading down to the shops in Grafton Street for the New Year's sales, the Irish Tote had reported that all betting turnover records had been broken over the holiday period at the Leopardstown racecourse. Many people were still in the Caribbean or in Cape Town. Life was proceeding as normal.

The chairman wondered where Fagan O'Dowd was. It was most unlike the head of risk to miss an emergency meeting of the executive committee, especially one taking place under such circumstances, yet Fagan O'Dowd had sent word the day before that he had been called away on urgent personal business.

The chairman said, — Essentially the message I want to convey to the market is that fundamentally we are a completely solid, well capitalised, liquid, solvent bank. We have an excellent, well-performing, well-secured loan book. We're in good shape.

He paused to allow the chins of Royal George and Don Dunne to dip in approval.

— The contraction we are seeing originated with American banks who invested in US mortgages and are now trying to offload their investments, the chairman said. — We have no such investments, not a cent, not one penny. We are completely clear and uncontaminated.

— And thank God for that, said Royal George. He had aged in recent weeks, for like the others around the table he had believed in the strength of HUBBI's share price the same way that a child believes in the tooth fairy.

— And yet we are being sold short day in, day out, the chairman said. — We are being sold short as if we are up to our necks in these American loans. Where has the famed wall of investor cash gone? We need to attack these short sellers and obliterate them. The hedge funds that are responsible for our share-price collapse are deliberately putting the savings of investors at risk for their own selfish ends.

— Well said, Chairman, said Royal George. — We should approach the government and get them to talk about the national interest. Outlaw short selling by statute. Nothing like the threat of jail to make these bastards think again.

He had spent the last weeks, including Christmas week, devising defence strategies with stockbrokers, travelling on gruelling roadshows around the UK and the US, trying to persuade institutions like HUBBI not to sell their HUBBI shares. He said,

— It wouldn't do any harm at all, excuse my frankness, if a couple of these short sellers had the shit beaten out of them.

— Is that an option? Don Dunne asked seriously. — Who exactly are we dealing with here?

— Most of them are based in London, Royal George said, but the most aggressive by far is the MUESLI Hedge Fund, based in Zurich. MUESLI is killing HUBBI.

— We need to counter-attack, the chairman said. — We need to send the likes of MUESLI running. What about our pension fund?

Don Dunne's expression was tight.

— Our pension fund owns a lot of our stock already, he said. — As does the bank itself. We've spent seven hundred million buying back our own shares, all at higher levels. We've eaten into nearly all of our cash reserves.

— And yet we're making good money on our day-to-day business, the chairman insisted. — Our cash flow is excellent, the vast majority of our loans are performing, and we're fully secured on some of the choicest property in this country and elsewhere.

—We're going to bounce from here, I guarantee it, said Royal George vehemently. — HUBBI will soar in the next few days. 'If You're In HUBBI, You're In The Money!'

— It seems, Don Dunne said, that there are people out there, including hedge funds and other institutions, who do not believe in the value of our collateral. They believe that our property assets are overpriced. I'm told that this MUESLI outfit has even published a table of our most vulnerable loans.

— Where the hell are they getting their information? the chairman cried. — They seem to know more about our business than we do!

Royal George and Don Dunne sat back, puffing out their gills. Fear was not a usual emotion in HUBBI: sixty-five successive quarters of increased earnings had engendered unlimited optimism and insatiable greed, not to mention arrogance, pride, smugness and a sense of overweening superiority; but not fear. Fear was new.

There came a knock to the boardroom door. It was the chairman's personal secretary, a normally robust lady in her mid-fifties, although at that moment when she appeared she looked reduced, ashen-faced and near to tears.

— Yes, Concepta? the chairman barked.

Meetings of the executive committee were never interrupted.

Concepta approached, inclined her head so that her lips were near the chairman's ear, and for what seemed to everyone else like a very long time, whispered into it. Eric Chester sat bolt upright in his seat.

— Well, fuck me pink, I didn't think he'd have the balls! he exclaimed.

The faces around the table peered at the chairman.

— It seems, the chairman said disbelievingly, that *Morning Ireland* has just broadcast a story about how Fagan O'Dowd has gone to work for MUESLI.

NINETEEN

The limousine made its way sedately beneath the bare trees of Ballsbridge to Donnybrook church. The morning was crisp, the branches still etched with frost, the sky blue.

He would have appreciated a morning like this, Albert thought. *Nothing like a sharp, cold morning to clear the head.*

Medb-Marie had lurched between bouts of abject grief and terrifying temper tantrums that morning. One moment she was clutching to her heaving breast a badly framed picture of Kevin, sitting in the kitchen of the house in Inchigeela after a night's drinking, a lopsided grin on his face; the next she was screaming at one of the twins for not putting her tights on straight. The old Medb-Marie was back, which was somehow reassuring.

She had made some pretty outrageous demands in the run-up to that morning. She had insisted that a cardinal preside at the Mass, even when it was established that all the Irish cardinals were in Rome electing saints or otherwise engaged in hagiography. She told Albert that she wanted Celine Dion to sing at the Mass, and when it was pointed out that that singer was on a tour of South America, she collapsed weeping.

She had engaged one of Ireland's foremost dress designers to clothe herself and the twins for the funeral. At the same time she commandeered the jet and sent it to London to bring back the hair stylist from Vidal Sassoon, as if the dozens of daily commercial flights that operated between the two cities were unsuitable for such a purpose.

As the limousine neared the top of Ailesbury Road, Medb-Marie suddenly called up the florist on Albert's phone, and when the man ventured that fifteen minutes would not be enough time in which to change the altar flowers from white lilies to white roses, she launched into abuse that even Albert found shocking.

The main thoroughfare in Donnybrook was marshalled by the gardaí, who had formed a corral with crowd barriers and pushed the assembled members of the press back across the road to Donnybrook bus station. As soon as the Barrs' car arrived, however, the two gardaí on duty were swept aside by a stampede of snappers, sound engineers, radio reporters and television crews as they thundered over to the church in a blitzkrieg of flash photography. Cameramen from half a dozen TV stations, including a crew from Korea, where chicken sales had taken a nosedive, fought to get beneath Medb-Marie's black veil. They screamed questions at her and then tried to isolate the twins as a consolation prize, a manoeuvre that Albert thwarted only by kicking a sound operative in the back of the knee. Albert, Medb-Marie, their children and Christiana, the au pair, were eventually bundled through the church porch by gardaí and the doors were bolted.

The hushed church interior was already crammed with mourners: the front pews lay empty and the entire cabinet sat, starting three back, on the left-hand side. Kevin's mahogany coffin with brass handles and a prominent crucifix stood at the foot of the altar. Albert, with his arm around Medb-Marie, led her up the nave. From the corner of his eye he could see the Taoiseach nod gravely. The twins and Christiana preceded Albert and Medb-Marie into the foremost pew.

He had done his best to find out if the man who lay coffined three yards from him had in fact done what he had promised in respect of Goose Point; he could find out nothing. No one returned his calls; no one in Albert's office had any record of a decision being communicated. And yet as much as he now cursed Kevin to an eternity without alcohol, Albert clung to the fact that, over many years of conniving and skulduggery, Kevin had never let him down.

A long line of priests – Albert counted eighteen – followed by an archbishop filed up to the altar and the sung Mass began. For

Albert the proceedings were a blur of organ music, arias and lofty readings, during which time his mind performed ceaseless calculations about the effect on his cash flow of the forecasted EU reduction in interest rates. A rousing performance by a thirty-strong choir from Mount Anville signalled that the finale was approaching. Then, amid clouds of incense and pealing organ music, Medb-Marie collapsed.

She lay in the nave by her pew, face up, neatly aligned with her father's coffin. Her expression was set as if in alabaster. She was hastily scooped up and carried into the sacristy by staff from the undertakers and two junior ministers, and laid out on the bench normally reserved for altar boys. Albert, distraught to the edge of reason, tried to tap life back into his wife's face, to shake her alive, as her two daughters shrieked in unison, and Christiana, lovely, normal, dependable Christiana, raised help on Albert's mobile phone. Albert wished he could fall down himself, unconscious, and wake up in six months' time, perhaps on a desert island, preferably alone with his medication.

In through the outer door of the sacristy suddenly came the florist at the head of a team of assistants, their arms full of white roses. Perhaps not fully understanding the true nature of unfolding events, they set down their delivery adjacent to where Medb-Marie was laid out, transforming that part of the sacristy into a Brahman wake. All at once the room was a gaggle of disrobing, staring priests, jostling with each other for a view, making telephone calls, offering advice, suggesting she be given altar wine, although not the wine that had just been consecrated.

— Give her air, lads! Stand back and give her air!

The sacristy windows were opened; a disastrous move, for the press, which had been tipped off that there had been further developments, now arrived in force, some of their zoom lenses poking three feet and more inside. Half a dozen burly young priests wrestled the windows down and snapped home the catches. The ambulance service had received so many calls that several ambulances arrived outside simultaneously, further adding to the pandemonium and leading one impetuous reporter to send in a clip suggesting that a pandemic was taking place. As Albert left the sacristy briefly to accompany Kevin's coffin from the church, he passed the archbishop sitting quietly in a corner, sipping from a noggin of brandy.

With an oxygen mask strapped to her lovely face Medb-Marie was stretchered out from the sacristy to a waiting ambulance, oblivious to the screams of the media.

— Was it the grief that floored you, Medb-Marie?

— How do you feel now?

— Tell us what it's like, Medb-Marie!

And from the man who had not been replied to at the airport but who was determined to pursue his angle,

— Will you ever eat chicken again, Medb-Marie?

She regained consciousness in the ambulance before it drove off, as Albert kissed her gently. He told her to take it easy and said she wasn't to worry, that everyone and everything would be grand.

* * *

Two days later the story had disappeared, replaced by a train crash in India that killed hundreds and then by an earthquake someplace. Albert was free for the first time in a week to address the real consequences of Kevin's death, which could be summed up by the question: did Kevin sign off on Goose Point before he died, or did he not?

He could still find out nothing. The void that had been left behind was petrifying, since Albert had spent most of the last ten years with access to all parts of government. Even when he was out of office Kevin had kept his lines of communication open, had flattered and cajoled pliable civil servants, and had kept in touch with ongoing public contracts.

It was weird having no one to call. At first Albert tried to speak to the first secretary in Kevin's old department, and failing that to the man's assistant, and so on down through the pecking order until he would have been grateful just to chat to the cleaning lady. No one took his call, no one called him back. It was as if Albert too was dead, as if Kevin had carried Albert off with him.

The position was repeated with the planning authorities. A minor official, a woman, perhaps trying to get Albert off the line, hinted that a letter may indeed have been sent; Albert spent half a day rummaging through litter bins at home and in his office, searching in vain for the letter he feared had been thrown out. When he called the woman back he was told she had gone on annual leave.

He tried to call the Taoiseach, then the Minister for Finance, but got no further than their respective switchboards. How could everyone be so ignorant about such a vital ministerial directive? He considered asking Medb-Marie to phone the Taoiseach, recalling the old days that had been alluded to during Kevin's wake, but one glance at Medb-Marie's bitten nails and tense face made him abandon the notion.

At the same time he became aware of other happenings in the world of business which up to then had not seemed possible, since Kevin's lost decision was at the centre of Albert's world. Gradually, in the recesses between futile telephone calls made and incoming calls evaded, Albert saw a steep erosion in the values of stock market indices in both America and Europe, and heard the first talk of a problem with mortgage assets in Florida and California.

He began to re-examine his mail from the usual sources that he had put in a pile pending the discovery of Kevin's decision.

We see the recent pullbacks as fertile ground to sow new positions.

For once America's problems are Europe's opportunity. There is no chance that this contagion will spread. Now is an amazing time to add to your portfolio.

Dear Mr Albert Barr, we have been guiding clients through choppy waters in US real estate for two generations. Please fill

up the attached form, making sure to print your details, and
make your check payable to us at the bank listed below.

Someone had cut out an English newspaper piece about HUBBI
and sent it to him.

HAS HUBBI'S CHESTER HIT HUBRIS? Smart analysts
in Eire are betting that the psychedelic property and banking
bubble that has put bog men on Bond Street is about to burst.
Sitting on top of this pile of leprechaun manure is Dr Eric
Chester, a man who had pigged his way to the top. Holders of
shares in HUBBI, Chester's Hibernian hallucination, may
find their way to the lifeboats blocked as more evidence emerges
of Chester's ludicrous loans. 'He would take vomit as
collateral,' said one source who asked not to be named.

Albert's heart beat like a trapped bird's. He had not looked at the
price of HUBBI shares for two weeks. He clicked on Bloomberg
even as he reached for his indigestion pills.

* * *

When the envelope arrived in his office next morning – so casually!
– it arrived along with flyers, invoices, proposals from property
touts, Mass cards for Kevin and an invitation to subscribe to Fianna
Fáil raffle tickets. Albert had seen the words 'Office of the Minister
for Infrastructure Development' and had almost swooned. An
expert by now in the conditions suitable for cardiac arrhythmia,
this almost certain confirmation that Kevin, the old fool, had failed
to issue the ministerial order before he died would trip the heart of
a pedigree bull. Locking himself in his ensuite, trousers at his
ankles, he ripped open the letter, at the same time launching a
stream of invective against Kevin, HUBBI, the department, the
Irish planning system, the Fir fucking Bolg and the people of
Ireland descended from them.

It took a moment for the sense of the short, two-sentence letter
to become clear. Athwart the bowl, he read it twice more.

DEVELOPMENT AT GOOSE POINT

A chara
I am directed to inform you that a ministerial directive allowing the above project to proceed was signed on the 8th inst. 2007. A copy of this directive is attached and was conveyed on the 9th inst. to the relevant planning authority.
Is mise le meas,
[indecipherable]
Principal Secretary

THIS LETTER HAS BEEN PRINTED USING RECYCLED PAPER

Albert shouted so loudly and at such happy length that a secretary, suspecting the worst, knocked assertively on the ensuite door.

— Mr Barr? Are you all right?

— I'm absolutely wonderful! Albert roared.

Placing down the letter on the toilet cistern with all the care of a priest handling the Host, he sprang to his feet and, dragging up his trousers, leapt in the air. He was there at last! He was free!

Almost immediately his feeling of incomparable relief was replaced by guilt: he had maligned a dead man, a good man, the grandfather of his children. Not alone had he failed to trust Kevin to deliver his promises, but he had failed to respect his deceased father-in-law for the heavy price he had paid, up to and including his life. For a moment Albert felt the need to cry, and did so, quietly. Sorry, Kevin, he thought, sorry old pal, I let you down, I should have known better.

He wiped his damp cheeks with the cuff of his jacket and vowed that he would name the planned rose garden in Goose Point for his dead friend: THE KEVIN STEADMAN ROSE ENCLOSURE. He read the precious letter for the fifth time. The garden would be a beautifully scented oasis planted with roses whose names embodied Kevin's many virtues: Honesty, Compassion, Good as Gold. To hell with the cost – although the size of the rose enclosure would have to be reduced from that in the original plan, since

Albert now reckoned he could get five extra retail units into that part of the scheme.

Goodwill radiated from Albert as he made his way from his office, startling the already anxious secretary with a kiss to her cheek, using the thumb of his right hand to text the much abused florist and order a large bouquet for the female office staff. He waved the letter at the operations room of hunched shoulders and fearful brows and called out,

— We have full permission on Goose Point! It's been confirmed!

They cheered, God bless their decent hearts! They all had mortgages and car loans and villas-in-Tuscany loans and were, like the rest of humanity, living well beyond their means. The news on this piece of recycled paper and its attachment was like an injection of adrenalin into their faltering consumer dreams. Kevin, in death, had given life to the hundreds of men who would work on Goose Point, and to the thousands who would live there. It would not be going too far to say that Kevin had given his life for the future happiness of others. Kevin was, amazingly, a saint.

Outside on his way to the Porsche, having dropped fifty euros into the hat of a Romanian beggar – she said, 'God bless you, Sir', and Albert had felt like God – he called Medb-Marie. Christiana answered.

— Where's madam?

— Madam asleep. Will I wake?

— No, Jesus, no. Listen, Christiana, give madam message, yes?

— Yes, I listen.

— Tell her, tell her…

A big fat gulp rose into his throat and he was suddenly blubbering all over the phone.

— … tell her that Daddy… that Daddy came through in the end!

— Mester Albert?

— Sorry, sorry Christiana, I'm all right now. Just tell madam that, that Daddy came through in the end, she'll know what it means.

— Daddy. Come. True.

— Yes, in the end.

— In the end.

— Great. Thanks Christiana, see you later.

Why had he doubted that moment in New York when he had held all life's happiness for the first time? Now that he had grasped it again he would never let it go.

He had calls to make. Everywhere he looked, at newspapers and television, or when he listened to the radio in his car, the news had seemed like messages intended for him alone. Christ, the media didn't half gorge on a little financial crisis when they got a chance! He was out of that now. Okay, he was losing money in the stock market, but where the big one was concerned he had come through hell and out the other side. It wasn't just the material benefits of what lay ahead either, his rewards were in the warm feeling of his steady heart, in the knowledge that his digestive system was functioning smoothly and in the renewed surge of blood to his loins.

TWENTY

Media commentators and government regulators, lawmakers, law enforcers and a Dáil Select Committee would take hundreds of hours to sift through the minutes of HUBBI executive committee meetings, searching for the telling moment when HUBBI ceased to be run as a bank and became an extension of Eric Chester's personality. Such investigative work would become vital to a government-appointed Tribunal of Inquiry established to find out who exactly, at which meeting and when, had agreed that HUBBI should purchase altogether seven hundred million euros' worth of its own shares on the open market. Did those present at such meetings realise that HUBBI was already doomed? That they might as well have withdrawn the cash and burned it? Who, if anyone, spoke out against HUBBI chairman Eric Chester? Why was the board of directors, a clubbable bunch of HUBBI debtors in the main, all heavily exposed to HUBBI's share price, why was this gang of nodding yes-men not assembled more regularly, if only to rubber-stamp Eric Chester's disastrous decisions? Why had the Financial Regulator not intervened?

In the course of his three-hundred-thousand-word report on the matter, printed in five volumes, the director of corporate enforcement would use the word 'megalomania' thirty-two times.

* * *

The chairman never grasped what was truly happening in the market. He believed the share-price slump to be an aberration, a technical black hole in the fabric of an otherwise perfectly sound structure; and so he bought another million shares for his own account, which was an understandable reaction for someone who had unrestricted access to what still looked like an unlimited supply of cash. For a few days he looked like a genius, but that was nothing new.

What was new was that four days later when the shares briefly traded at twenty-one he sold the million he had bought a few days before, along with another million.

The analysts – that rag-bag of media hacks, bank-sponsored economists, chartists, hedge-fund managers, pension-investment gurus, commentators employed by stockbrokers, plus a veritable army of amateur armchair investors who had spoken of nothing else but money for a decade – these so-called analysts broadly agreed that Eric Chester's sale of two million HUBBI shares was the penultimate blow to the fairytale. On hearing the news the market went into meltdown. Chester had to issue a statement pointing out that he still was by far the biggest individual shareholder in the bank, an unenviable position as the shares quickly dropped to fourteen.

He instructed his head of treasury to step up the share buy-back operation; fourteen would never be seen again, he insisted; and he was right. Over a three-week period as the market sank ever lower, HUBBI, like a mythical beast, spent almost all of its remaining energy devouring itself in an effort to stay alive.

On the day the market learned that HUBBI's head of risk had gone to work for the hedge fund most prominently associated with short selling the bank, the party was finally over.

* * *

The HUBBI disaster was, of course, merely a sideshow in a slow-motion international drama, a transcontinental financial convulsion, involving the same worldwide audience that had witnessed Kevin Steadman's death.

An attempt was made by the HUBBI board to issue legal proceedings against former head of risk Fagan O'Dowd. A German newspaper claimed that O'Dowd had been providing MUESLI with inside information on HUBBI for over a year, allowing MUESLI to punt with confidence against the beleaguered Irish bank. O'Dowd, the tabloid article claimed, lived with his wife and children, who had recently left Ireland for Switzerland, in a castle outside Zürich. A dozen staff were employed within and outside this lakeside residence. Fagan O'Dowd's estimated worth, according to the paper, was in excess of €50 million.

This attempt to indict the bank's former head of risk was overtaken by the abrupt resignation of Dr Eric Chester from HUBBI and the appointment by the Irish government of an interim chairman and CEO to the stricken bank, whose shares were by then trading at three euro.

The first action of this government appointee was to instruct all of the bank's loan officers, and the loan officers of its subsidiaries, to issue possession proceedings against all HUBBI debtors whose payments were in arrears.

One such subsidiary was the Patriot's Building Society.

TWENTY-ONE

— We're so lucky, Gwen said.

— Hmmm?

— I said, we're so lucky.

— Is it raining?

— Not being torn apart by all these business problems. Not owning anything that can be torn apart. Imagine if we owned bank shares.

— I told her I won't come in if it's raining, Lee said.

— Cosy as toast here together. Hmmm, that's nice, hmmmmmm! Oh, please, please rain, Gwen said.

— One day they're going around with faces like death on them and she's screaming so loud at her children, at the au pair, that I wonder if she's really sane, Lee said. — Next day she's like an angel. Yesterday your man gave me a big grin and asked how Des was.

— D'you fancy her?

— Six months ago he tried to kick Des to death.

— You do fancy her.

— What?

— I've seen her picture, Gwen said.

— He has a private jet, you know. He drinks wine that costs three and four hundred a bottle.

— Her tits put me to shame.

— Whose tits?

— D'you like my breasts? Come on, now. The truth.
He put his nose between them, nuzzling with his beardy chin.

— Would you like me to have tits like her? Gwen asked.

— You've never met her.

— I can be her if you like, Gwen said.

— I'd hate to have all that money.

— Come here, gardener man, lick my muffin.

— Gwen Forbes!

She laughed and kissed his nose. — But it's true, isn't it?

— Yes it's true. Money makes you unhappy.

— I mean, that you fancy her.

— Christiana says she's a lesbian.

— Scored her? The au pair?

— Christiana has a boyfriend. Your one has given her the eye, though.

— Would you like me to be a lesbian?

— It doesn't bother me.

— Bi, maybe?

— People like that lose ten million, twenty million, it means nothing to them, Lee said. — They've always got plenty more stashed away.

— Well, go on!

— Is it raining?

— Hard to say, it's still dark, maybe a light drizzle. Do you think she'd fancy me?

— Everyone fancies you.

— And you, gardener man. Oooooh! I wasn't being seeeeeerioussssss!

Later, post-coital, dreamy, sipping tea, warm and happy, he said, — Ever think about a family?

— Here?

— On this earth.

— Children mean money, Gwen said.

— Funny, until I met you I thought I'd had an ideal childhood, Lee said. — Now I realise that no one was happy. My mother was screwing my father's brother and she ran away with him. My father was so unhappy he probably crashed his car on purpose and killed himself. I drank away ten years of my life.

— Children mean we need a better plan, Gwen said.

— This is no good?

— Good for the three of us; you, me and Des.

— D'you remember that whole Fir Bolg business? he asked. — The excitement of it? I actually believed I was going to be famous.

— You still will be, she said. — I believe in you.

— Thank you.

The situation couldn't go on like that forever, he knew, however blissful. No challenge. In order for them to live on indefinitely as they had for six months now, it would require one of them at least to have, say, a serious addiction problem; but Gwen neither drank nor smoked and Lee hadn't touched a drop for nearly a year. In the absence of substance abuse, in the aftermath of epic loving, and in the presence of sexual fidelity, not to mention monogamy, the human spirit demanded more of him than to be a gardener, and more of them than to live in a crummy bedsit. The human race was cursed by ambition.

She never mentioned the fact that he had not yet activated his Christmas present, or if she by now expected him to be sending off drafts of his writing with self-addressed stamped envelopes enclosed to an address in Birmingham. He sometimes heard his muse – or at least that's what he thought he heard – like a note of music. Sooner or later it would come to him, a knowledge that was both thrilling and terror-inducing, like the imminent arrival of death for someone who believed absolutely in the afterlife.

— I need to get a job, he said.

— You have a job.

— I need to change, he said. — I'm going to tell her today.

— It's raining, Gwen said and he could feel the warm rounds of her knees.

— Do you know something? I feel bad about leaving them.

— Do you have to?

— Yes, I do, Lee said.

* * *

Albert sat for forty-eight hours on the news of what the Patriot's Building Society, a subsidiary of the imperilled HUBBI, intended to do. Drained to a place beyond misery, cut off from cash, beset by medical complications, he dimly realised that he was a tiny casualty in a worldwide drama that he was powerless to control. His lawyers promised a spirited fight to fend off the building society in the courts, even as they cautioned that Albert's arrears were a problem. He needed to make a payment of at least two hundred thousand. The trouble was that he could not do this. Normally he'd write a cheque, then ring the bank and ask them to look after it; or flog a couple of apartments; or hammer some of his debtors. Eric Chester had disappeared and HUBBI was closed to Albert and everyone else until further notice. All his assets were mortgaged, and anyway, the property market was in sudden freefall. And the people who owed him money had also mysteriously disappeared. Normally other banks would have taken up the baton, based on Albert's track record and political connections, and he had indeed made calls to bankers who had within the last twelve months vied for his business; but they all told him that no new lending was happening. The world was suddenly a cash desert. Banks were not even lending to one another.

He'd sat that morning in his study, listening to the twins as they feuded their way through breakfast before they made their way out to school. It was his failure on their behalf that hit him hardest, the realisation that a time might soon be reached where no one would realise or care about the great struggle of his life, the journey from Tramore to here. And back. He could not actually believe that he might be going back.

He would of course fight to the bitter end, but since the Patriot's Building Society was on the brink of issuing legal proceedings the chances that the media would get hold of the story were too high. He had to tell Medb-Marie.

* * *

As he got out of his car the little dog ran over to him and sat up beguilingly on its hind legs. Albert had come to accept the presence of this animal and occasionally even patted it, but today he was too distracted to pay attention to someone else's dog.

He couldn't believe that this house – his home – might in a few months' time be owned by someone else. The hall was empty and smelled of furniture wax, which meant that the daily help had recently passed through. Albert clenched his teeth and proceeded towards the kitchen. He had worked so hard to repair their relationship and now he was about to wreck it again. Earlier that morning she had smiled at him in a way that was a signal she wanted to flirt. Albert was still fascinated by her complex, almost botanical structure, her opening and closing, an exotic flower that demanded his unflagging attention.

The kitchen was empty. He went back to the hall.

— Albert?

He looked up. She was standing on the landing above looking down at him. She was wearing a silk robe and her hair was gathered so that it fell forward over her left shoulder. A small, playful smile on her red mouth meant that, yes, fuck it, today of all days she was ready for midday sex. She adjusted her stance so that the outline of her body could be discerned through the robe, and asked softly,

— What are you doing home so early?

Albert took a deep breath. What would be wrong with giving her what she wanted, right now, and *then* telling her about the house? As she made her way down the stairs the folds of her robe lapped back and forth across her thighs. Albert winced each time he saw her flesh. In her hand she was carrying an empty glass tumbler, in the base of which Albert could make out a tiny umbrella lying on its side. This meant that she had been drinking *pina colada*, which she used to do in the old days when she first got the sun bed, and following which she was always as randy as a goat. Albert could not believe the extent of the misfortune over which he was straddled, for despite everything, her mere proximity was giving him a hard-on. She caught his lapel, floated her eyes up from the depths of their liquid sockets and murmured,

— How did you know your big bold girl wants her botty smacked?

Albert was hyperventilating. The smell of alcohol on her breath was like a musk exuded as a prelude to propagation. She came in close, fitting the contours of her body to his, insofar as a reasonably trim woman could achieve this in an upright position with an overweight man, and nestled her cheek close to his as she whispered in his ear, — I want a baby I want a baby I want a baby I want a baby I want a baby I want a baby...

Albert lived through a moment of wild rapture in which the drumbeat of the jungle replaced the calamity of his life, and he reached down and seized the two firm cheeks of his wife's buttocks and lifted her, whilst she with a little jump locked her legs around his waist and secured her heels on each other. They kissed deeply and hungrily as she ground into him with all the restraint of someone being rescued from drowning. In this configuration they teetered back towards the base of the stairs, on to which he lowered her, and as he did so, her robe fell open and the full glory of Medb-Marie Barr née Steadman was revealed to her husband's tormented gaze.

Reaching for the belt of his trousers she pulled him towards her, but Albert was riding on a carousel of vividly conflicting emotions, chiefly sex and death. Even his resurrected lust was overridden by the belief that, regardless of how she would benefit from this encounter, if she ultimately believed that he had taken advantage of her he would suffer even more. Reeling away, staggering backwards, he came to a halt by the fake antique hall clock and cried out, — I can't!

Entire weather systems crossed his wife's lovely countenance in bewildering succession. She shook her head and said, — *Can't?*

Albert went down on one knee, although he remained strategically out of reach, and said, — I have something terrible to tell you, Medb-Marie.

Medb-Marie now went through the tricky business of trans-forming her position of wanton nakedness into one of domestic respectability, and at the same time preserving her dignity that had been in no small way imperilled by the rejection of everything she had so recently offered. At the same time, as she stood up and belted up, the meaning of what had just been said caused another bout of thunder to enter her face. Her mouth plunged down in outrage and disbelief and she asked, — Are you now going to tell me that you're gay?

Albert, whose hard-on had disappeared quicker than an angel at sunrise, actually began to cry. He said,

— Ah Jesus, no, Medb-Marie, it's those fuckers in the bank and all the shite that's going on in the papers about credit and the economy. The bastards are going to try and sell our house.

Medb-Marie Barr didn't do dumb, but for a second she did a very good imitation of dumb: she cocked her head to one side like someone listening for the latch of a distant door, then said, — Oi don't think I 'eard tha', Albert. No, ducky, Oi didn't 'ear it a' all.

— We'll come out of this stronger and richer, Medb-Marie, said ashen-faced Albert. — We'll look back on this in years to come and we'll laugh.

A low droning sound arose from deep within Albert's wife as if, unlikely though this was, a swarm of bees had materialised inside her. She swayed where she stood for a moment, then, as the swarm gathered volume, abruptly turned her back on her fish-faced husband and made her way in strides at once determined and distracted towards the kitchen. Albert followed Medb-Marie, his hands outstretched in the manner traditional to supplicants, his mouth opening and closing as he endeavoured by means of inadequate words to mend the unmendable, or even to make himself heard. She was a good ten yards ahead and with each of her steps he could see the calloused undersides of her bare, well-shaped heels.

The back door crashed open as she left the house and Albert hurried after her, since he now feared that she might do herself harm, entering as she was the winter elements like the inmate of a secure institution who has escaped at bath time. Albert watched helplessly as Medb-Marie, her robe billowing up either side of her in the draught created by her passage, marched straight over the yard to where an axe lay imbedded in a block surrounded by timber. She grabbed the axe with both hands and yanked it free. As if the entire hive was erupting at that moment from her mouth, with a hideous roar she raised the axe high over her head and with demented strength rushed at her husband.

Albert half slipped as he turned to run and the axe landed on yard stone with a ringing blow and a shower of sparks. Recovering, shouting platitudes, Albert regained the sanctuary of the kitchen, turned the key in the door and reached for his phone. The blade of the axe splintered the lock and the door flew in. Medb-Marie was strong and well made to begin with, but now madness pumped her arms like relentless pistons. She advanced on him, swung high and with a scream came down where his head had been a millisecond before, shattering beyond repair a walnut floor-to-ceiling storage unit from whose ruptured interior fell tens of little glass spice jars. Albert shouted,

— Medb-Marie! Stop! You could kill me!

As if goaded on by his words that somehow belittled her intent by clarifying it, Medb-Marie attacked again, the axe flashing through the air in deadly parabolas. In the drawing room Albert pushed a leather sofa that had cost eight grand between them; she brought the axe down so forcefully that the sofa keeled away in two halves from the point of the blow.

His wife's partial nakedness now filled Albert with as much dread as it had done with lust just minutes before. He decided to make a run for it. Turning and running down the hall towards the glass-panelled hall door, he could hear her grunt with the effort; he ducked. The weapon whistled past his ear and sailed through the stained glass and filigree motif of the door like a guided missile. Albert dragged open the ruptured door, leapt out and, still fumbling for his phone and shouting for Christiana, ran around the back towards his car.

He was within ten paces of the Porsche when he realised he had left his keys inside. He doubled back through the yard and was just short of the ruptured back door when Medb-Marie appeared at the other side of it. She was screaming at him. Albert turned and ran back the way he had come. He heard her closing. A frantic yapping had started down at ankle level. He heard a voice saying,

— No, Des! Come here!

But by then the dog was between his feet and Albert was pitching headlong on to the woodblock.

* * *

When Lee heard the rumpus he had been in the potting shed, preparing the words he would say when he handed in his notice. He wanted to do it properly, to give her an opportunity to replace him. She would probably try to get him to change his mind, but he had the words ready to politely decline.

Screaming was not unusual around the house, but this seemed more excessive than normal. As he entered the yard Mr Barr was at the back door, but turned abruptly and began to run in the other direction. Des ran forward, barking excitedly.

— Des, no! Come back here!

The big, shambling figure of Albert Barr was pitching forward onto where Lee had earlier been chopping wood. Only then did Lee see Mrs Barr. She was holding an axe in both hands over her head. Lee's first thought was: where did she get an axe? He watched, amazed and frozen, as she swung the axe down into the back of her husband's head.

— Oh Jesus, Lee said.

Mrs Barr was walking back to the house. Lee rushed forward, pulled the axe free and was instantly covered in blood. He saw Mr Barr's body twitching.

— Someone get a doctor! Lee screamed.

He turned to the kitchen door where Christiana had just appeared.

— Christiana, get a doctor! he cried.

Christiana, hands to her mouth, backed inside. Lee made to follow her, every part of him red and sticky.

— Christiana... he began.

— Get away! Christiana screamed. — Murderer!

EPILOGUE

FIVE MONTHS LATER—
ARBOUR HILL MEDIUM SECURITY PRISON, DUBLIN

It was another bad summer, which at least made it seem as if someone was rooting for him. He looked at his watch although he didn't need to: during daylight hours the whistles from the trains in Heuston Station marked the hours of the day and he had laid down their timetable in his head.

He found it peaceful in the grey block Victorian surroundings, particularly in the chapel. The iridescent stained glass behind the altar, which had been done by a student of Harry Clarke's in the nineteenth century, allowed him to glide into the past as he gazed upwards into the folds of Ireland's history. The interior of the chapel was laid out in a crucifix and at first, during the early months, he had felt himself nailed to events, vilified, the central player in a national sensation that only finally seeped off the tabloids when the banks started to go bust. He came into the chapel to relax when he wasn't writing.

Visitors were seen in a room overlooking a quiet garden, whose rose beds he tended and whose razor-edged borders he maintained. He had started a salad patch as well, a source of wondrous curly-heads, rocket and butter-heads, earning him regular thanks from the prison governor.

— I may persuade them never to let you out, the governor joked, before adding, the way things are outside at the moment, I think we're all better off in here.

Apart from the once a week that she was allowed to visit him, her appearance the only outright guarantee of his sanity, and apart from his legal team that were planning an appeal, and various representatives from bodies concerned with prisoners' rights, no one else had come. Except once. A man describing himself as a friend, and then as the features editor of a Sunday newspaper, arrived unexpectedly in the visiting room. When he declined the visit, a note:

> *I would bet my professional reputation that there's undoubtedly an audience out there who want your side of the story. Your own words, from the heart. No editorial interference, you have my word on that. I envisage a piece in the first person, say, fifteen hundred words, a writerly piece, nicely turned. We would pay €350, but I daresay I could get them up a bit. By the way, do you think we could get a pic of you in prison garb?*

Some things never changed. He dwelled less on what would happen when he got out than on how to live richly in the meantime. Writing every day had transformed the way he looked at time – it no longer lay heavily on his conscience. He relished the internal seconds and, having written a thousand words, was amazed that three hours had passed by.

He was amazed too, even as he wrote, about some of the things that had come to pass. The Goose Point development, for example, looked as if it might indeed be turned into a World Heritage Site, just as Mr O had suggested. The fact that it was a white elephant had left Dublin City Council with few options. This news was tinged with sadness however: Mr O had passed away six months earlier. What a thrill it would have been for the old man to see his dreams realised!

In one day, a month before, two major stories had competed for front-page news: the former chairman of a big bank had fled the country in the company of a young German woman, hours before warrants for his arrest were issued. Both the Fraud Squad and the Criminal Assets Bureau were seeking his extradition from Northern

Cyprus. The former head of risk at the same bank was returning from abroad to give evidence to a government tribunal of inquiry. It was rumoured that this man, who was said to have made a fortune out of the credit collapse, would be offered a very senior position by the Irish government as it sought to restructure the Irish banking industry.

Side by side with this news was the story that a major newspaper group had made three hundred people redundant. Eddie was finally out of a job.

* * *

As she entered the visitors' room he yearned for two things: the warm touch of her hands, her cheek; and to see Des, who he knew was out in her car but was not allowed in. As a special concession at Easter the governor had allowed him into his office to look out to the car park. He had wanted to call the dog's name, but then thought how unfair that would be. He could work out why they were separated; God knows how poor Des would react.

— You look so well, she said as she sat down.

— I'm fine. God, I'd like to eat you. When I get out you'll be on my menu 24/7, he said.

— Maybe sooner than you think, she said. — I have some news.

He looked at her like a small boy, albeit one with a beard, looking at his favorite teacher.

She said, — The Polish au pair says she wants to change her evidence.

— Wow! Are you serious?

— She now admits she never saw you strike the blow.

— That's amazing!

— I know, she said. — It is. She's returning to Ireland next week.

He had sworn not to get carried away by hope, to wait until what he wished for actually happened. As they chatted on she took his hand and squeezed it. After some minutes she asked,

— Otherwise, how's it coming?

— Good. I, ah, I'm nearly finished, actually.

— *Finished?*

The solitary guard looked around the corner, one eyebrow cocked, finger to his lips.

— Yeah, I mean, the first chapter is nearly finished, I think, he said. — There's a lot of work to be done, of course, but I think I'm getting the hang of it.

— Oh, you're something else, she said and leaned over and hugged him. — When can I read it?

— I'm nervous.

— Don't do this to me!

— Maybe I could first read it to you? I mean, I've had to change things, like all the names, for obvious reasons.

— Who am I? she asked.

— Well, you'll be Gwen, when I get that far, and I'll be Lee, I think I will, at any rate.

— *Gwen?*

— Yes, Gwen, he said.

— I'll get used to it, I suppose, she said. — And who is… *she?*

— She's Medb-Marie. You know, I thought I'd model her on Queen Maeve, the ancient queen of Connacht.

— A war queen.

— Exactly.

— I always knew you were an author, she said. — And him?

— He's Albert. Albert Barr.

There was the sound of the door opening and a man in a pinstripe appeared. Lee recognised him immediately and got up and went over to meet him. After a few minutes he came back, his face radiant.

— That was my senior counsel, he said.

— I know, she said. — What did he want?

—Albert Barr opened his eyes for the first time this morning.

— Oh, that's incredible.

— He spoke, apparently.

— What did he say?

— He asked for his wife, Lee said.

They sat together in bemused and happy silence for some moments. She crossed her legs and closed her eyes.

— I'm ready, she said.

He cleared his throat.

— *Sometimes on those Saturday mornings Albert wondered if he was ever going to be free. To soar beyond his worries and be truly happy, to wake up one Saturday morning and not have to think about the net-net, the bottom line…*

Through the top of the open window floated in the whistles of the trains, coming and going to the distant corners of Ireland.

OXFORD CITY AND COUNTY
MUSEUM
INTRODUCTION
LIBRARIES